Saguaro, Snowflakes, and Murder

An absolutely charming cactus and cowboys cozy mystery

Jenna Hendricks

Books by Jenna Hendricks (Clean & Wholesome Romance)

<u>Triple J Ranch</u> –

Book 0 - Finding Love in Montana (Join my newsletter to get this book for free)

Book 1 - Second Chance Ranch

Book 2 – Cowboy Ranch

Book 3 – Runaway Cowgirl Bride

Book 4 – Faith of a Cowboy

Book 5 – Cowboy Blessings

Book 6 – The Cowboy's Game

<u>Big Sky Christmas</u> –

Book 1 – Her Montana Christmas Cowboy

Book 2 – Her Christmas Rodeo Cowboy

Book 3 – Her Mistletoe Cowboy

Book 4 – Her Sleigh Ride Christmas Cowboy

<u>Crooked Arrow Ranch</u> –

Book 0 - Wounded Hearts Ranch (join my newsletter to get this free)

Book 1 – A Broken Heart Mended

Book 2 – Hope's Healing Love

Book 3 - Love's Healing Balm

Book 4 – A Crooked Arrow Christmas

Book 5 – Tripping Over Christmas

<u>Saguaro Bookshop Mysteries</u> –

Book 1 – Saguaro, Snowflakes, and Murder

<u>Standalone Novels</u> –

Christmas Crazy in July

Rebel Hearts Anthology

See these titles and more: https://JennaHendricks.com

Newsletter Sign-up

Do you love clean & wholesome contemporary cowboy romance? Want more? Then check out Finding Love in Montana today!

By signing up for my newsletter, you'll not only receive this book, but a couple more free stories as well!

If you want to make sure you hear about the latest and greatest, sign up for my newsletter at: Subscribe to Jenna Hendricks newsletter. I will only send out a few e-mails a month. I'll do cover reveals, snippets of new books, and giveaways or promos in the newsletter, some of which will only be available to newsletter subscribers. (https://jennahendricks.com/newsletter/)

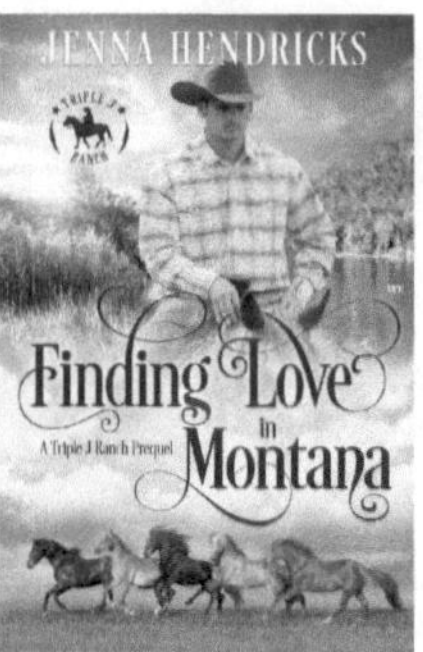

Contents

Acknowledgements

I want to thank everyone who helped me with the creation and writing of this new series. It was an absolute labor of love for me as Cozy Mystery has been my favorite genre to listen to on audiobook for quite some time. The author community is very supportive, and it was them who gave me the courage to write in the Cozy Mystery genre. For years they've encouraged me to do it, and finally, I did. So, thank you to all of the Indie Authors who told me I could do this.

I especially want to thank all of the subscribers to my newsletter. We've talked about not letting fear get in the way for a while now, and I decided to conquer my fear of writing a mystery and just do it. I'm so glad I did!

The beta readers really helped me to fix some issues I had with this book, and the story is much better because of them. A few were too shy to let me name them, but others said I could, so I'm going to: Laura B. (and Jamie her cat), my cousin Dawnya who has read everything I've ever written, even the stuff not published. Ginny, an old family friend who I lost contact with, discovered my books and then reached out to me because she enjoyed them. Thank you all for your suggestions and support, it means the world to me!

Prologue

"I don't understand why I'm the one who inherited everything. Why didn't it go to you, or someone else in the family?" Not that Great-Aunt Jo had many other family members. I knew that we didn't have much in the way of family. Most of my life it was just us, but there were a few distant relatives that Great-Aunt Jo might have kept in touch with.

Who am I? I'm Maisy Bransky and today was the funeral for my Great-Aunt Jo, a woman I totally adored and will miss for the rest of my days.

Before my mom, Annabelle Bransky, could respond, I took a bite of the cake she had just placed on my plate, closed my eyes, and moaned. "I had forgotten how wonderful this prickly pear cake is. We should have made it ourselves back in Florida." The sweet-tart taste settled on my tongue, and I knew that one piece wouldn't be enough. The secret ingredient was the lemon in the cake and the frosting, in addition to the prickly pear cactus.

Mom placed her fingers on my left hand, since it wasn't trying to dive back into the best bundt cake ever created. "I know, sweetheart. I miss Aunt Jo, too. Now that she's gone, I regret not visiting more. We should have come back more often."

"And we should have planned to spend this Christmas with her." I know that wasn't what killed my Great-Aunt Jo, she died of a heart attack. But it could have been possible her heart would have stayed strong enough to see her through one more Christmas and we could have had one more special holiday with her in Westcott, Arizona - the place that was forever known for its cactus and cowboys.

Mom's eyes turned down as she realized what she had chosen over family. She wasn't alone in her feelings. Mom had signed up to go on a Christmas cruise with a group of her friends and her new boyfriend. I had planned to stay in Florida with my lame ex-boyfriend. In my defense, I hadn't known he was lame until my Great-Aunt Jo Barton had died. That was when all of the previous signs had finally clicked.

It didn't hurt that I caught him canoodling with his barely legal assistant, either. The lout couldn't even wait twenty-four hours after I told him about Great-Aunt Jo dying. I left his house, and *she* must have been lying in wait for me to leave.

Ten minutes later I came back to get my scarf I'd left at his house and what did I find, but them making out in front of his window for everyone to see.

The very next day I packed up all of my things and set up movers before coming to Arizona for the funeral. It was a good thing I had some very helpful friends back in Florida. With ten pairs of helping hands, I had completed the packing in just one day.

Now I'm staying in Westcott, Arizona and living in my great-aunt's house and taking over her bookshop. The Saguaro Bookshop was a place I loved to spend hours upon hours reading and just soaking in the book ambiance every summer when I visited.

I took another bite and sighed. The prickly pear bundt cake had been my great-aunt's creation. Everyone always wanted the recipe, but only mom and I had it. Every time I had this back home, I thought of Great-Aunt Jo. Maybe that was why I had stopped making it a few years back. I always felt guilty for not coming to visit her.

"I know, Aunt Jo always makes...made... the best bundt cake. And the reason she gave you everything is because she knows I would have sold it." Mom arched a perfectly manicured brow.

My mother had never taken to life in the desert. She hated the dry skin and dust in just about everything, especially after storms. She had once confided that if she inherited anything from her Aunt Jo, she'd sell it.

Me? I loved the desert. The Saguaro cactus is my favorite plant on Earth. And the cowboy ways of Westcott always had me smiling, and missing the place every time I went back to Florida.

I raised my fork with a bite of pink and yellow cake hanging precariously from the tines. "Yup. Her bookstore is the best. In all of my travels I've never found another quite like it. I won't be selling." I looked out the back window of the kitchen onto the desert landscape backyard as a tear rolled down my cheek.

Mom reached over and wiped the tear from my face. "I know, sweetie. It will get easier." She sniffed. "I miss her, too. We should have come last Christmas when she invited us."

"Shoulda, woulda, coulda. And this Christmas you're going to be on a cruise. Guess I'll be here all alone, like Aunt Jo always was." Hindsight was something I hadn't really thought too much about until recently.

Chapter 1

When I moved here, I had expected to celebrate Christmas, and frankly every holiday, alone. However, all of Great-Aunt Jo's friends had already made the rounds and promised to look out for me, and it wasn't even Thanksgiving yet. Not that I needed any babysitters, but it would be nice to spend time with Great-Aunt Jo's friends and learn more about her and how she celebrated Christmas when my mom and I weren't around.

Verna Henderson, one of Jo's best friends, already invited me over to celebrate what sounded like a huge Thanksgiving dinner. Another one of Great-Aunt Jo's friends, Ada Hopkins, was hosting the get-together this year. It seemed they took turns.

I couldn't remember the last time I celebrated Thanksgiving with a large traditional meal. Usually, I went out to eat with a few friends and my mom. If this invitation was any indication of how things went here, I'd be celebrating a ton of holidays in style.

Speak of the devil...

One of my great-aunt's friends, Verna Henderson, was walking up the steps to the bookshop now. This one was the president of the local Cactus Club, and she looked the part, down to the cactus t-shirt she wore underneath her light green and white checked flannel jacket. She paired her Saguaro cactus shirt with a pair of dark blue jeans and brown cowgirl boots. Most everyone around here wore boots. It was almost as though it was a prerequisite for being a resident.

I smiled as I remembered one summer when I asked Great-Aunt Jo why everyone wore boots. She told me, "boots protect your feet from the local snakes and scorpions."

"Snakes and scorpions? How so?" I remember wondering what a boot could do against a snake that could slither up your leg if it wanted to.

"Most rattlesnakes will coil up before attacking, they usually don't get up higher than above the ankle. A good pair of boots will stop the bite of the snake from penetrating and getting to your skin. Same with the sting of a scorpion." She shrugged. "Plus, they are easier to stomp on snakes, scorpions, and any creepy-crawly thing."

After that, I wore boots all the time, even with my shorts.

I stepped to the door and opened it before I waved and smiled. "Hi, Verna. Nice to see you. But you know I'm not open yet, right?" The funeral had only been ten days ago, and I wasn't quite ready to open. I had placed some orders for books and checked the inventory. Just before she passed, Great-Aunt Jo had already placed a large order for Christmas that should arrive any day. I just added a few books I thought would be nice. As well as a couple of knick-knacks I hoped would sell.

Verna swatted her hand in front of her face. "I know, I know. I just wanted to come and check in on you, sweetie. I promised Jo that if anything ever happened to her, I'd be sure to look in on her favorite niece."

I walked outside and hugged the lady who had to be in her eighties, if not older. I had to lean down quite a bit since Verna was barely five feet tall. But before I could respond to her offer of kindness, I heard a thunk on the window of my shop. "What? Who?" I stood up to my full height of five feet, six inches and turned around and caught sight of an old guy, the same one who had disrupted the funeral service. My hands fisted at my side, and I pursed my lips before I could utter something unladylike.

Verna wasn't the least bit worried about saying anything rude. In fact, I felt my face heat up as she railed at the old guy. "Homer Kimball. If your momma was still here, she'd tan your hide. What has gotten into your fool's head?" The woman also said a few choice words that I'd only heard come out of a biker's mouth before, but I wasn't about to correct her, not when she was on a roll. The fact that Verna had treated him like a young man, escaped his notice as he ignored her completely.

Homer raised his fist. "Jo got exactly what she deserved!" He threw another clump of dirt and missed the window entirely. Instead, he hit me.

"Ah! What is your problem, old man?" Normally, I wouldn't be so disrespectful of my elders, but that crazy old coot had gone too far. I looked down at the front of my tan t-shirt with a picture of the Saguaro cactus that sat out front of my Great-Aunt Jo's bookstore and sighed. Great-Aunt Jo had sent me this t-shirt not a month before she died. It was the last gift I had from her.

Verna tsked and yelled out a few more obscenities toward Homer. The crazy old man cackled like one of those cartoon characters and then ran off yelling, "She got what she deserved, and so did you! She got what she deserved, and so did you!"

The last thing I heard was his grating voice and attempt at a laugh before he turned the corner.

Verna put a hand on my shoulder and turned me back around. "Come on, honey. Let's get you cleaned up." She led me back inside the bookstore.

Once upon a time, Great-Aunt Jo had lived in the tiny apartment above the bookstore. Now, it served more as a breakroom and over-stock room for the store. Thankfully, Jo had ordered a decent number of the t-shirts. The new bookshop logo was a circle with a picture of the four-armed Saguaro cactus growing in front of the bookshop right in the middle of the circle. The name of the shop, Saguaro Bookshop, was in a beautiful font around the inner circle.

Fortunately, I had already located her overstock of them and put them aside, praying they would be good sellers for Christmas.

While I was cleaning up, I purposely thought about the Saguaro cactus out front. It was a much nicer thought than the other one that had flitted through my mind. At first, I had dreamed of Homer falling into the Saguaro and getting pointy needles all over his body. Then, guilt overtook me, and I shook the thought from my head. However, it did make me think about a picture Jo had sent me a few Christmases ago. She had begun putting Christmas lights all around the Saguaro, making it look like a Christmas cactus tree.

With Christmas just over a month away, I needed to decorate the shop. Great-Aunt Jo loved Christmas so much. A tear trailed down my cheek as I remembered the years when I was a kid and mom would send me here to spend most of the holiday with Great-Aunt Jo. When my dad left us, he really left us. Mom worked two jobs just to make ends meet. When I was too young to stay home alone, Jo would send a plane ticket and I'd come here to visit with her. Christmas was always fun, and the tree had more than enough presents for me.

Although, most years mom couldn't come.

When I was old enough to stay home alone during the day, I only came for part of the school break. I wanted to spend Christmas with my mom. We didn't decorate much, but we did have a tree and she'd have a couple of presents for me. Plus, Great-Aunt Jo always sent us a box with a bunch of gifts.

As an adult, I worked all the time since Christmas wasn't really my thing, still wasn't, but it was Jo's.

This first year without her I was going to do it up just like she would. Make it a memorial to her wonderful memory. If nothing else, I'd have the memories. And maybe I could see the holiday through Jo's eyes and understand why she loved it so much.

As I was washing the tears from my face, I heard a loud crash downstairs. I threw the towel down and ran downstairs as quickly as my Skechers allowed. I still hadn't picked up the requisite cowgirl boots, but it was on my list. If I was going to run a shop in Westcott, Arizona, I'd have to look the part.

"Verna? Are you alright?" I called out when I turned the corner from the back stairs and walked inside the shop. "What?" My hand covered my mouth and my eyes widened.

Aunt Jo's best friend turned to look at me. Her mouth opened and closed like a fish before tears ran down her cheeks.

"Are you alright? What happened?" I called out as I ran to her side. She was standing near a table in the front of the store that at one point had held a collection of glass cactus ornaments and figurines. All types and sizes of the variety one could find in the local desert had been represented on the table. Most had been hand blown by a local artisan and were kinda pricey. It was just the sort of thing visitors bought and took home to give as gifts as well as to add to their own glass ornament collections.

The loss of money was nothing compared with the look of utter horror and pain on Verna's face. I looked her up and down, but didn't see any blood. She was far enough from the display that she should have been fine. But her tears...

Then it dawned on me.

The front window.

There was more than broken glass from a table full of glass ornaments. A chill weaved its way in from the gaping hole in the front window and surrounded my heart.

Not only was the front window broken, but a rock lay on the ground next to the table that held the remnants of the cactus ornaments and figurines. It looked like an explosion uprooted the cactus and spilled all over the floor.

Slowly, I walked toward the thing that had ruined the bookshop, crunching glass beneath my tennis shoes. I bent over and started to reach for it.

"Stop! Don't touch it." Verna called out in her deep, raspy voice. The woman had smoked almost her entire life, and it was very evident in her harsh, crackly voice.

I had seen plenty of mystery movies to know this, but for some reason I hadn't been thinking about fingerprints. I was too shocked to think at all. "Right. Thanks." I stood back up and pulled my cell phone from my back pocket. "Did you see who did this?"

I turned around and looked at Verna. The fear and pain had left her face to be replaced with anger and something that had me backing up a bit. "I'm going to kill Homer Kimball for this." She looked out the window when we both heard the sirens blaring.

My phone was still in my hand, I hadn't called the cops. Verna had been too shaken up to call so I wondered who had called them. Probably a witness to the attack on my Great-Aunt Jo's beloved store. She wasn't even cold in her grave and her store was already under attack from the man who had been her nemesis.

Was he now my nemesis as well?

Chapter 2

"Is anyone hurt?" A deep, raspy masculine voice called out as I continued to stare at the gaping hole in my store.

Something in the back of my mind was trying to tell me to move, but I couldn't. All I could think was that Homer had gone certifiably nuts. "Please tell me you've already caught him, and he's being taken to a padded cell?"

"If not, I'm going to hunt him down like the vermin he is." Verna crossed her arms and narrowed her gaze at the man in my store.

I hadn't really looked at him yet, but as I saw the look in Verna's eyes change from anger to hatred, I knew something was up. My head turned of its own accord, and I noticed the man. The badge on his chest said he was the sheriff.

He wasn't an impressive man, more like someone from one of those comedy shows. He wore his brown and green uniform, as I expected. But, with a second look I'd say the uniform wore him. It was too large and hung off of his large frame. That's not to say he was tall, because he was shorter than my five feet six inches. But what he lacked in height, he more than made up for in girth.

Normally I had deep respect for the law. However, this man did not instill a sense of respect. Nope, he made me think that he was more along the lines of the donut shop type of cop. Of course, the fact that he had a coffee stain on his shirt pocket and more than a few crumbs of what must be donuts hanging around the line of buttons on his shirt, probably had something to do with my opinion.

I hoped I was wrong.

"Verna Henderson, I should have known." The sheriff sniffed and hiked up his pants by the belt. "What kind of nonsense are you into today?"

She put a hand to her chest and blinked. "Me? You think I did this?"

The sheriff turned his head around the shop. He didn't even give me a second look. "I don't see anyone else here named Verna, do you?"

I couldn't help it; I rolled my eyes. Heaven help me, but we had someone worse than a Barney Fife. "Ah, Sheriff?" I waved my hand to catch his attention.

Slowly, oh so slowly, he turned his gaze from Verna to me. When his eyes finally stopped on me, he tried to stand a bit taller. While he had been taller than Verna, I now towered over him. All I could think of was "wait until I started wearing boots". I'd be at least another two inches taller than he was.

I had to bite my lower lip to keep from giggling. Men who were older and shorter typically had the Napoleon syndrome down pat, and this one seemed as though he'd mastered it long ago. His chin rose, and he tried looking down at me through his bulbous nose, but it only made him look shorter. "And just who might you be? Verna's accomplice? You do know this here store is closed, right?" He put his hands on his hips and tried to give me a stern look, but it came off kinda lopsided.

"We haven't been introduced yet, I'm Maisy Bransky, the great-niece of Jo Barton, and the new owner of this shop." I put my hand out to be neighborly, but he ignored it. On second thought, I was glad he had and put my arm down by my side. I didn't need his sticky donut remnants all over my hand.

"Is this the culprit?" He pointed at Verna.

I furrowed my brow. "Huh?"

"Are you slow, or something?" He shook his head. In a slower voice he tried again. "Is this the woman who broke your window?"

I wanted to ask if he was slow, but bit my tongue. "No. Verna is a friend. The person who threw a rock through the window and destroyed an entire display of glass cactus..."

His sharp intake of breath stopped me mid-sentence.

"The display of hand-blown glass ornaments and cactus statues are all gone?" He moved so quickly toward the table that I barely saw him move. A sound like a choking squirrel escaped his lips.

Verna looked at me and started to laugh, then slapped a hand over her mouth.

"No, no, no." His hands flew in the air. Then he turned around and glared at Verna. "This is all your fault, isn't it." He pointed at her. "You know every year I buy a new cactus ornament for my Delilah. She looks forward to it every Christmas morning."

I shook my head. "Look, I don't know what your deal is with Verna, but she had nothing to do with this. It was Homer Kimball."

"How dare you!" Another voice interrupted the story I was trying to convey to the Sheriff.

My head whipped toward the open door as a very handsome and tall man walked in. His black hair was tousled just right to look like he hadn't done anything with it, but had probably spent an hour on getting it to set just right. Along with about a hundred dollars in hair products. He obviously spent more time on his looks than I did.

Subconsciously, I patted my messy ponytail and wished I had put forth some effort in getting ready that morning. I wasn't supposed to have any customers since the store wasn't scheduled to open again for a few days. After today's fiasco, I'll be lucky to open by Black Friday. "I'm sorry, but we aren't open yet."

He drew up short when he looked at me. The anger that had been present on his face changed and he smiled. When he did, his eyes were bright, and his white teeth shone in the sunlight blaring through the broken window. "I'm not here to shop, I'm actually looking for my grandfather, Homer."

A memory from my childhood struck me at the wrong moment and I felt my cheeks burn. I knew this handsome man. Or rather, I had known him when we were children. "Jason?"

He tilted his head. "Maisy-girl? Is it really you?" He took two steps toward me and acted as though he was going to hug me, then stopped and put a hand out.

I took his and instead of shaking my hand, he brought it up to his lips and lightly kissed the back of it. Like something out of a romance novel. His lips were silky soft on my skin. I felt tingles all the way down to my toes. As a young girl I had dreamt of him kissing me.

I felt the heat run up my neck and into my cheeks before I could stop the blushing. "Jason, wow. How long has it been?"

He stood up tall and I realized that he had to be over six feet tall. "Too long." Then his smile faded, and he cleared his throat. "I was very sorry to hear about your Aunt Jo. She's going to be missed by everyone."

My throat clogged and I had to clear it before I started crying again. I'd done enough crying, and I certainly didn't want to cry in front of Jason. "Thank you."

He ran a hand through the back of his hair. "Um, what was it you were saying about my grandpops?"

That's right. I had forgotten that Homer was Jason's Grandfather. The old man I'd seen today and at the funeral was so different from the confident, and lucid, man I'd known as a kid. He and Jo had always been at odds, but he'd never done anything so malicious before. At least, not that I knew of. Had their age-old rivalry turned violent before Aunt Jo's death?

"Jason," the sheriff interrupted, "I'm sure little Maisy here has it wrong. She's been gone a long time and probably has your grandfather confused with someone else."

I put a hand on my hip and jutted it out. "First off, I'm not "Little Maisy" any longer." I pursed my lips and used the brow arch that my Great-Aunt Jo was famous for using when she wanted to let everyone know she was very displeased.

The sheriff pulled up his belt and opened his mouth, but I cut in before he could say anything, "And second, I'm not mistaken. Homer has been causing a lot of problems since I arrived." I turned my attention to Jason. "Did you know he showed up at Jo's memorial service and caused a ruckus?"

Jason's eyebrows shot high above his hairline. "Surely not. It must have been someone else."

Verna scoffed. "Please, Jason. You know as well as I do that your grandfather lost his marbles long ago. That's why you had to come home and take over the family ranch."

A look of something I couldn't make out crossed Jason's face too quickly for me to understand. Then he put on a very condescending smile and tilted his head. "Now, Miss Verna, that isn't very nice."

"Neither is yelling out at a funeral that Jo Barton got exactly what she deserved." Verna narrowed her eyes and glared at Jason.

"Now, now. It wasn't all that bad." The sheriff stepped in between Jason and Verna.

I raised my hand to get everyone's attention. "Ah, yes it was, and worse. He yelled at everyone and called my Great-Aunt Jo a thief, and a few other choice words that I choose not to repeat." I had to clear my throat to unclog the emotion building up.

Once I had myself back under control, I ran a calming hand down the front of my new Saguaro Bookshop t-shirt. "Earlier today, he came by and threw mud at my shop, then at me. Yelling again. I tell you Sheriff, that man needs to be put in a padded cell. Then he came back and threw the rock through my window." I pointed down at the offending rock.

Jason's mouth hung open. "Are you serious? He did all that?" He sighed and ran a hand down his face.

"Yes, he did. I'm sorry to be the one to tell you, but I think your grandfather needs help. The kind where he shouldn't be alone any-more." I had other thoughts on the crazy old man, but decided to play nice with my old childhood friend. "However, I do need him to pay for the damage he's done today."

When a choking sound came from Verna, I turned to see her shaking her head. "Maisy, dear, Homer has lost his family's fortune. He was about to lose the ranch when Jason came home and bought it from the bank."

I turned to see Jason hanging his head.

I sighed.

Was I supposed to ask Jason to pay for the damage? It was probably going to cost more than five thousand dollars. That was money I knew I didn't have. And since I didn't have access to Jo's bank accounts yet, I had no idea if she did. The lawyer said I'd get access to Jo's bank accounts in a few days; he was working with the bank and the local judge to get the will pushed through. At the very least, I'd have access to the business accounts since the business already transferred into my name.

I made a mental note to go to the bank first thing the next day to see where I was. Jo had always been good with money, so I was confident that the business account would be in the black.

The last thing I wanted to do was make Jason feel bad about his crazy old Grandfather. But the loss...could I cover it? Would the store's insurance cover it? I hadn't contacted them yet about the change in ownership, so I had no clue.

Jason lifted his head and pasted on a fake smile. It was very evident by the tight lines around his mouth that it wasn't a real one. "If my grandfather really did this, I'll cover the damages." He sighed. "I'm sorry, grandpops is having a tough time right now."

It wasn't as though I hadn't seen elderly people go through this before, my grandfather passed away a few years ago after suffering from Dementia. It wasn't easy to watch. And if I wasn't mistaken, Homer had Dementia, too. Now I was feeling bad for calling him a crazy old coot. The man was sick, not crazy. I sighed.

"How about I check with the insurance and see what can be done?" I figured the insurance would cover the loss and Jason could cover the deductible. That seemed fair. Hopefully, it wasn't a large deductible.

Jason shook his head. "No, please don't mess with the insurance. With the place changing hands right now, I don't even know if Jo's insurance is active. Have you checked?"

My shoulders sagged and I shook my head. "No. I hadn't gotten around to that part yet. There is still so much I have to do before I can open the store."

"And now you have to fix the window and replace all of this?" He pointed to the floor where thousands of dollars in glass figurines and ornaments lay scattered in a million pieces across the faux wood laminate floor.

"I still don't think it was Homer." The sheriff gruffed, but no one listened to him.

"Thank you, Jason. I appreciate your help." I took out my cell phone and began taking photos before I attempted to clean it up. Once I was done, I noticed the sheriff was still there. "Did you need something, Sheriff?"

Both of the man's hands were on his belt and he shimmied it up his waist. He cleared his throat. "If you want to file a report, come on down to the station with those photos you just took, and I can get one of the deputies to help you." Then he turned and left my store without waiting for me to respond.

I wasn't going to file a report. If Jason paid for the damage, then that was fine with me.

Jason's eyes widened and he looked at me.

I knew what his eyes were asking, so I answered his unspoken request. "Don't worry, I'm not going to file charges against your grandfather." I bit my lower lip and rubbed my cheek. "But, um, can you talk to him? Ask him to stop throwing things at me and the store? And maybe even get him to stop yelling out that Aunt Jo got what she deserved?" That last part hurt the most.

My aunt was one of the nicest people around. She always gave generously to local charities. I remembered from when I used to come visit every summer and Christmas that she was always helping out the local families. She had a wonderful tradition that I wanted to keep going.

Aunt Jo would keep an empty chair next to the table. She always made room for anyone who needed a meal, especially a holiday meal. We always had extra people come for Christmas dinner. Sometimes it was someone who was all alone, and sometimes it was a family who couldn't afford to make a big turkey or ham dinner. I couldn't even remember all of the different people who had shared Christmas Day with us over the years. And every kid always had something under the tree at Jo's house for them.

He nodded. "Of course, I'll speak with my grandfather. He shouldn't be doing any of that. Especially now. I'm really sorry for his behavior."

I put a hand on Jason's shoulder and felt a bit of a spark when I realized that cowboys really were in great shape. His shoulder was as hard as a rock, only it looked much nicer than the one with shards of glass on it that was sitting on my bookstore floor.

Chapter 3

Word really did spread quickly in a small town. Before I had even finished cleaning up the glass from the broken window, Jade Stinson and Ada Hopkins showed up offering to help. They were the other two parts of my Great-Aunt Jo's Fearsome Foursome. When I was a kid, the four of them would play cards for hours and hours.

Ada was my favorite. She always carried peppermint candies in her purse and would sneak me some when Jo wasn't looking.

"I can't believe that Homer has gotten so bad as to do all this." Jade pointed to the damage and shook her head. "I remember when he kept his anger to just filing lawsuits against Jo."

"Lawsuits?" I knew that Homer and Jo never got along, but I didn't realize he had sued my great-aunt many times if the plural use of the word was any indication. "What for?"

Ada sighed and handed me a piece of peppermint candy. "Here, dear." She put the candy in my hand and took the broom from me.

I blinked and wondered what had happened. One moment I was cleaning up the glass, and the next moment I was eating candy like I did when I was a kid while the ladies cleaned my shop. Before I could say anything, they had it all tidied up.

"Do we have any boards I can use to cover up the window until I can get the glass replaced?" I wasn't even sure who to call to do that. At least I knew who to contact about replacing the glass ornaments and figurines. Those were locally sourced from a Native American woman Jo had been buying from for years.

"I can call Tony, he'll come over here and help us with the window." Ada pulled her cell phone out and dialed her husband. She was the only one who still had her husband.

Jade's husband had passed away at least ten years earlier. And Verna's husband only passed two years ago. I remembered each time Jo had called me to let me know when the funerals were scheduled. Jade's husband died while I was in college, and I couldn't get away. But two years ago, I was too wrapped up in my own life to consider coming back here for the funeral of a man I barely remembered from my childhood.

I should have come back, and I knew it.

Hindsight was more than 20/20...

It was strange how the death of a loved one made one regret past decisions. Decisions that one had never regretted before. Coming back for Mr. Stinson's funeral wouldn't have been for him, it would have been for Jo. He was her best friend's husband. The same with Mr. Henderson. Jade and Verna may not have needed me, but Jo did. I remembered how much she called me back then, and how sad she was that I couldn't come.

But she never made me feel bad for not coming to visit, no matter how many times she asked, and I said no. *Lord, if Aunt Jo is near you, please tell her I'm sorry. I should have come to visit more, a lot more. I wish I would have.*

I think I thought that Jo would be around forever. You never know when a loved one is going to die from anything. We don't always have a heads up, like with Aunt Jo. Her heart attack surprised everyone. Even though she was getting older and taking medicine for her blood pressure, no one thought she'd die. But that was the way of life, wasn't it? She could have just as easily died from a car accident, instead of a heart attack in her sleep.

The only things in life that are certain are death and taxes. I shivered realizing that this year my taxes were going to be difficult. I had no clue how it would work with inheriting a business and a house. Hopefully, Aunt Jo's taxman will be able to handle my taxes come April.

"Okay, I don't know about you all, but I'm famished. How about I take us all out for a late lunch, my treat." It was the least I could do since they had all helped me clean up.

Tony was already done with boarding up the front window. He must have had three sheets of plywood in his garage. I'd have to remember to pick up some to replace these, and let Jason know the cost for those as well. However, I'd go ahead and cover the cost of this meal without expecting to be paid back.

All four of them smiled and called out at the same time, "Cactus Joe's?"

I couldn't help it, a giggle escaped. Every time I visited, we would all go there for Sunday suppers, when someone hadn't put a roast on. If I had to guess, I'd say we had our Sunday Suppers at Cactus Joe's at least twice a month when I was in town. "Of course, I wouldn't suggest any other place. Do you still do Sunday supper there?"

For the first time in what felt like hours, Verna smiled. "We have a standing reservation there for every Sunday after church."

"That's right, none of us bother with putting on a roast anymore." Jade Stinson, the shortest of the gang, blinked back tears. She wasn't even five feet tall, but she always seemed to have the largest heart. Not that she cried a lot, but she was always the soft spoken one who refused to even kill a spider.

"Do you remember that summer when I was about twelve?" I asked out of nowhere. Memories that I hadn't cared to think of in years had been coming back in droves since I returned.

"I remember every visit, sweetheart." Jade put a hand over her heart and her eyes misted over with unshed tears. "Jo was never happier than when you were here. She'd be so happy that you're going to keep her store running."

My throat clogged and I felt my nose twinge. I'd become the crier of the group if I wasn't careful. "Remember when that Gila Monster followed you inside your house?" The memory cleared up my tears and put a smile on my face.

I hadn't been present when it happened, but I'd heard the story so many times that summer, and for the next few visits, that I'd swear I was present. The memory was so vivid.

Verna, Ada, and Tony all laughed with me.

"Lordy! That little monster became her sidekick." Verna sniffed. "You know, I think it's still alive. I swear I see a Gila Monster hiding out around your house every now and then."

Jade looked around and in a low voice said, "It's his grandbaby that keeps coming around. Jack died a long time ago, but he had his little wife and they had kids, and their kids had kids. Now, I keep getting a little pet that loves my home, just like Jack did."

"Seriously? Aren't they poisonous?" I didn't know a lot about Gila Monsters, but I had read somewhere that their venom was very dangerous.

Jade waved her concerns off. "I don't actually pet them, or anything. I just talk to them when they come around and leave them some food once in a while. Did you know that they are great at keeping bugs and other small rodents away?"

"Huh." I wasn't sure if Jade was pulling my leg, or if she was being serious. I might have to ask Verna about the woman's mind. Keeping a dangerous and poisonous animal around didn't seem smart. What if it bit her? Then a horrible idea hit me.

I stopped in my tracks and sucked in a breath. "No!" I covered my mouth and shook my head.

"What's the matter, Maisy?" Ada asked.

Verna put an arm around my shoulder. "Don't worry, Jade knows what she's doing. If anyone is going to get along with a Gila Monster, it's Jade Stinson." Verna smiled at her friend and patted my back.

"No, that's not it. What if Aunt Jo was bit by a Gila Monster? Would that cause her to have an early heart attack?" As far as I knew, poison would kill an elderly person much easier, and quicker, than a healthy young person, like me. Wouldn't it?

Verna pulled me closer. "Don't worry, dear. I did ask that same question. I even asked the sheriff to look into Jo's death. But he said the coroner ruled it natural causes."

I relaxed into her hug and almost cried. "So, there was no reason for the heart attack? Just her age?"

It was awfully quiet, so I looked up and caught the looks going around all four of them. "What? What don't I know?"

Tony, who was usually pretty quiet, put up a hand. "Now, don't go getting Maisy all riled up. We all know that Jo had some health issues. It was her time, that is all."

Verna pursed her lips and her nostrils flared. "I tried to get a full autopsy, but the Sheriff was having none of it. He said that Jo was an old woman, and we should all be happy she went out in her sleep."

Jade scoffed. "She wasn't that old. She was only a few months older than me when she passed. And I know that I'm going to be around for many years to come. Your aunt should still be here, too."

That was exactly what I thought. "Does that mean you think foul play was involved?"

They all shook their heads.

"Sadly, or maybe it's a good thing. I don't rightly know, but I'm sure that Jo died of natural causes. She was on medication and had been complaining about her heart lately. It seems she was having palpitations. In fact, she had been scheduled to see her doctor only a few days after she passed away." Ada wiped a tear from her eyes. "I'm sure there wasn't any foul play involved. It's just hard to accept, that's all."

I completely understood her emotions. Mine had been all over the place, like a roller coaster at Magic Mountain. Up one minute, then all of a sudden, I was down and had lost my lunch. Then not two seconds later I was up again. It made no sense to me.

"Come on, now. Let's think about happier times." Tony took his wife's hand and put it through the crook of his arm and led us all to the restaurant. They were such a cute couple.

As we all walked to Cactus Joe's, my emotions calmed down and I pulled out my phone. After looking up Gila Monster bites, I felt better. If Aunt Jo had been bitten by a Gila Monster, it would have hurt like the dickens, and she would have called for emergency services, or knowing her, driven herself to the local clinic. And I know none of that happened.

My nose was still stuck on the screen of my phone, and I didn't realize that we had already arrived. I almost tripped over the curb in front of the cutest western diner in the world. Cactus Joe's was painted a pale green with brown trim. There were all sorts of cacti painted on the walls outside. There was also a nice variety of live cacti planted in the ground around the sides of the building. And out front was the largest neon Saguaro I'd ever seen, but it wasn't nearly as pretty as Aunt Jo's real Saguaro. Hers had four arms and Joe's only had two neon green arms. Next to the sparkly cactus was the sign – Cactus Joe's.

Lunch was better than I remembered. The Cactus Chili was five alarm hot and exactly what I needed after the day we had just had. The corn bread was unbelievable with honey butter. "Oh, I missed this place."

Ada patted my hand. "And we've all missed you, too. I'm so glad you moved here."

"Me too." And I meant it.

When the bell above the door sounded, all eyes turned to see who was walking through the door. I couldn't help but smile, it was my old crush. And he was alone. Maybe we could get him to join us for dessert.

Jason Kimball sauntered over to our table with a little smirk just for me. When he stopped in front of us, he tipped his hat. The man had "Sexy Cowboy" down pat. He wore Ariat boot cut jeans that fit his hips and thighs as though they were cut just for his body. And if I wasn't mistaken, under those boot-cut jeans, he was also sporting Ariat boots. The rattlesnake pattern matched the belt he wore and the green in the shirt seemed to accentuate the belt, boots, and the strap in his hat.

His warm, brown eyes sparkled when he smiled at me, and I felt just like I did as a young girl whenever he smiled my way. In all these years, I still hadn't met anyone who had a better smile than Jason Kimball.

"Hi, there. Care to join us?" I should have asked the group before speaking, but all I could think of was how handsome he was, and how many years it had been since I'd seen the man. Well, he'd been just a boy the last time I was here, and now he was a man. The kind of man that I knew I'd be dreaming about later that night.

I'd always preferred cowboys to men in suits.

"Why thank you, I'd love to." Jason took his hat off and held it in front of him. He looked at the rest of my lunch companions. "That is, if you all don't mind?"

Verna pursed her lips and moved over. "Please, do join us. Although, we've already had our lunch. We were just about to order dessert."

"Sounds perfect. I love to start a late lunch with dessert." He winked at me, and my stomach fluttered all over town.

Before Jason had a chance to scootch in, the waitress came over with a smile a mile wide, and it was all for Jason. I watched him as he smiled and winked at her. Was he dating our waitress? She was a pretty blonde woman in her early twenties. I didn't notice a ring on her finger, so she'd probably be a good candidate for Jason.

Although, they didn't seem to be very close. When Jason's hand lightly touched hers, she fluttered her eyelashes and a pretty shade of pink crawled up her cheeks to land in the perfect spot, accentuating her high cheekbones.

Great, now I was jealous of a girl barely out of high school. Jason had better not be anything at all like Jeff, my skeezy ex. I didn't think he was, but the way he smiled at the waitress had me wondering.

Then I woke up and realized that after what I went through with Jeff, I most likely wouldn't be trusting a man any time soon, no matter how handsome, or nice, he was.

I sighed and turned back to the last few bites of my chili. It was really good. I'd have to try making this at home. There was nothing better than a few different soups, stews, and chili's just chillin' in the freezer during the winter. I'd be able to pull out exactly what I needed on a long winter's day and heat it up. Saltines and chili were one of those quintessential winter meals. I hoped I'd have time to cook up a few batches and prepare the freezer for my go-to meals before I opened the store.

Next week was Thanksgiving and my plan was to open the store on Wednesday. Then take Thanksgiving off and open up for Black Friday for all of the sales that Jo had planned. Thankfully, she was a planner. She had outlined everything. And I do mean everything.

As I mentally checked off what was already planned out by Jo, I noticed that Jason had finished placing his order, and finished flirting. He was now trying to get my attention. "Oh, sorry." I chuckled. "I was off thinking about this next week and all of the things I still needed to do."

"No worries, I just wanted to ask if you were able to secure that hole in the front of your shop." Jason looked directly into my eyes, and he slowly began to smile.

The man knew how to flirt, I'd give him that. And he was handsome, I doubted I could find anyone who'd disagree with me on that count. So, the real question was, did he want to just flirt? Or did he hope to start something up with me?

The last time I saw him we had been thirteen and dealing with some crazy hormones. I think Spin the Bottle was all the craze back then and if memory served, Jason was my first kiss. I saved that bottle after kissing him at least a dozen times. Of course, I kissed the other boys, too, but the majority of my kisses had gone to Jason. Somehow, the bottle always landed on him when I spun it. And his spin had always seemed to land on me.

And he had walked me home that day, and every day for the rest of that summer.

Chapter 4

I could feel the heat bursting up my neck and all through my face as I thought about how many times we had kissed that summer. I must have cried myself to sleep every night for a month when I got home to Florida.

Then I met Max. Ah, young love.

I blinked and came back to the present. "Sorry, I don't think I'm really present much today."

"I asked if you were able to get that window boarded up without any issues." Jason's warm smile landed right on me and sent me back to those hot summer days we spent together.

"Yes, thanks to Tony, my store is secure. I was planning on calling the local handyman after lunch to see if he could replace my window or direct me to the proper person who could do it this week." I wouldn't be able to open up without having the window in place. Well, I could, but it would seem very strange to have a boarded-up window while trying to re-open Great-Aunt Jo's bookstore.

And I still needed to decorate the store for Christmas. Not to mention reorganize so that all of the holiday books would be out on display. And I still needed to order more blown glass cactus. Maybe going to lunch wasn't the best thing to have done today?

"How about I call the local glass shop for you? We only have one supplier of window glass and I'd bet he was the one who also updated your aunt's logo on the front. He probably still has all of the measurements and could get it done this week." He leaned forward with his forearms on the table and held a cup of coffee between his two hands.

I sighed with relief. "Really? You'd do that for me?"

Jason sat back straight in his seat. "Of course. It's the least I can do to help. And why don't I come over and help you with anything else you need once I've put in the order for the glass."

"That would be wonderful. I have several boxes upstairs I could use help carrying down. Then I have to decorate the entire store before we open up again." I listed out the other things in my mental to-do list, not expecting him to help with everything, but hoping he'd find a few things he wanted to help with. Give us more time together. To get caught up. Yup, that was all I was interested in. Too much going on to think about anything more than that.

Jason chuckled and nodded before setting his mug down. The waitress brought over his dessert before giving us ours even though we had ordered first, but that was to be expected after the way he flirted with her.

When she put my plate holding a generous slice of Cactus Cream Pie in front of me, she didn't look at me and almost dumped it in my lap. For just a second, I thought she might have done it on purpose, but she didn't even flinch. I figured she wasn't paying me the least bit of attention. Guess I'd have to watch my P's and Q's when Jason was around. I highly doubted this would be the last time a waitress almost dumped something on me because she was too enamored with him.

But really, who could blame her? If I was interested in him, which I am not, then I would probably tune out most of the world around me, too. He was handsome, like cowboy-model handsome. I could easily picture him up on one of those giant roadside billboards selling jeans or boots.

I hadn't had cactus cream pie since the last time I was in Wescott, Arizona. This tiny little western town was the only place I'd ever seen this particular dessert. It was a cross between a Coconut Cream Pie and a Key Lime Pie, but with the cactus flavor I loved so much. I grinned after taking just one bite.

The food here was so much better than back in Florida. Well, the desserts were anyways. I still missed my Conch fritters and Conch chowder, but maybe I could find a way to make them here myself. Then I'd have the best of both worlds.

It wasn't two hours later, and I was all alone in my bookstore finishing up the decorations. Jason had come back with me and helped me bring down boxes. Man, was that boy strong. Or should I have thought *boy, was that man strong*? I shook my head. I still thought of him as the boy I once knew - and crushed on.

However, his help meant that I could get all of the decorations put up tonight before going home. Tomorrow, I'd focus on the business side of things and get to reorganizing the shelves and tables in preparation for my grand re-opening next week. I even had some ideas about social media marketing and of course, the old standard – tacking flyers all over town. Folks here still enjoyed a good flier in the front of stores or on light poles. There was even a Community Events board just outside of Fry's and the Ace Hardware store.

Jason had brought down all of the Christmas decoration boxes, but he only helped me to put up the indoor Christmas lights. The look on his face when I asked him to help me decorate outside was priceless. One would think that I'd asked him to hug a cactus.

I laughed almost as much over the memory as I did when his eyes widened, and he sucked in a deep breath. When he said, "I don't think that's in my wheelhouse." I broke out laughing.

"Jason," I said, "You don't have to decorate the cactus, I can do that. Just help put up the lights on the outside of the bookstore." It wasn't as though I couldn't do it myself. I just needed a good ladder and then I'd be able to use the hooks that were already up on the eaves.

I didn't even bother mentioning the bull on top of the building. He'd probably have an aneurism if I asked him to put a Santa hat on top of the bull up on the second story roof.

Instead, he looked at his watch. "Oh, I didn't realize how late it was getting. I need to get back and make sure Grandpops is doing alright."

I couldn't exactly argue with that. Homer did seem to be in a bad way earlier, so I let Jason off the hook and wished him a goodnight.

Now, the smile was off my face, and I stood outside staring at the large Saguaro cactus that my Great-Aunt Jo loved so much, she'd gone and had her store and the cactus listed on a national registry. Thanks to the cactus, her store would never be torn down to make way for newer stores like so many other small towns all over the country. Not that there was a threat of taking down anything on this block.

It was known as Western Row, but the actual street name was Cactus Lane. All of the shops had to have some sort of western theme. They could sell whatever they wanted, but the shops had to maintain the historical look from one hundred years ago. They all had the southwestern colors of tan, brick, and wood. Some also had cactus green doors. While one shop had a turquoise door and the eaves above their shop were painted to match the door. It was a bit kitschy, but it worked. It was a pottery studio with glass windows, like mine, and the Sonoran arched window and doorways.

I always wondered how doors worked in an arched entryway. When I was in Junior High School, I learned that those types of doors were always custom made and cost an arm and a leg. But they sure were cool.

A bright color racing across the alleyway caught my attention and I turned to see Jade Stinson racing down the lane faster than anyone her age should.

"Jade! Hey, Jade. What's the hurry?" For just a moment I thought I saw someone following her, but then the shadow turned out to be nothing more than one of the Gila Monsters she loved so much. It was keeping a good three-feet distance behind her, but it was hot on her tail. "Do you need help?"

Jade waved. "Not now, gotta run." Then she turned a corner, with the little brown and orange monster slithering behind her.

I swear, every time I saw one of those I thought about the serpent in the Bible. The one from Genesis before the fall of Adam and Eve. It had feet on it, until God punished it for tempting Eve to eat the fruit from the knowledge of good and evil tree. I could only imagine it slithering around the ground just like a Gila Monster, using its front legs to help it move faster while the tail did the slithering along the ground.

Although, it could just be that the forked tongue that hissed out of the Gila Monster's mouth freaked me out just as much as a snake's tongue.

"Huh, I wonder where she's off to in such a hurry?" I pulled out my phone to see if there was a message from anyone, or an alert, but nothing showed up in my notifications.

Jade seemed fine, she was just in a hurry. Probably late to a meeting of monster lovers, or some such crazy event.

I turned back around and eyed the nine-foot-tall cactus in the front of my shop. Every year Jo put Christmas lights on it and a Santa hat on top of each of the arms. The thing was so tall, I doubted she did it without help from a cherry picker, or a lift of some sort.

I turned my head from side to side and imagined how I might use a ladder to help me get the lights on this thing. Great-Aunt Jo did it every year, so if she could do it, so could I.

Then inspiration hit!

I ran inside and up the stairs to the storage rooms. I rummaged around until I found what I was looking for – a long pole with a grabber on the end and a small hook. Most people used these to put Christmas lights on the eaves of their homes, not to help them drape lights around a giant four-armed cactus. But that was exactly what Great-Aunt Jo had used it for.

She probably also used it to put up the lights around her bookshop, but at the moment all I could think of was the cactus that Jo loved so much, it had become a part of the family.

In fact, last Christmas Jo sent out Christmas cards with her and her cactus. The way the photographer shot it, it seemed as though she had an arm around it, all snug and tight like one would a loved one. She even signed it, Love Jo and SG. She had named her Saguaro cactus SG, short for Siggy.

Even though I was smiling at the memory, my nose twitched, and I had to blink away tears. I knew that one day I'd no longer start to cry whenever I thought of my Aunt Jo, but I doubted it would be any time soon.

I brought the long pole, rolled up lights marked "Siggy", and Santa hats outside with me. I put my earbuds in and played Manheim

Steamroller's Christmas album to help me get into the mood. Their pop sounds always put me in the Christmas spirit.

I took the string of lights and the pole and began running the lights around the cactus, starting at the top. It was easy to walk around the green beast as I set the lights onto parts of the cactus that stuck out in just the right places. I first went around the top center stump, then went up and down each of the two arms on top. After those looked good, I ran the long string of lights around the center stump that led down to the bottom two arms.

Partway through the cactus I realized that Jo must have had these lights custom made to fit this cactus. I'd never seen a string of lights so long before. In fact, the top of the light string didn't have a male or female plug, it just had a colored light at the end. That was how I knew to put it on top.

Before I knew it, I was at the bottom of the cactus and had the male end in just the right place to plug in. The cactus had been planted in a dirt patch that was also covered in small rocks. In the back of the cactus was a small electrical receptacle with two plugs and covers. When I plugged in the string, the lights came on. Not a single bulb was out.

Honestly, that had been my biggest concern. If one bulb was out, would the entire string fail? Or still work? Aunt Jo had spent the extra money to get the high-quality lights, which made me think that as long as the filament in the bulb was in working order, the bulb would work.

I hoped.

The only way I'd know for sure was if one bulb was out and the rest of the string worked, or not.

I stood back admiring my handywork. "Nicely done, Maisy." I had mentally patted myself on my back and grinned. Then I turned around and looked at the roofline.

One of the boxes was marked, "roof lights." I arched my brow and shook my head. This was going to require a bit more effort and a ladder. Before I even began something that might kill me, I took out my phone and did a search for "putting lights on my roof." About a gazillion responses showed up, per usual. I chose the first one with a YouTube video and began to watch as they used a tool similar to the one I used for putting the lights on ol' Siggy.

It only took two hours and five bandages on my fingers, but I got it done. The eaves up on the second story had lights attached to the plastic clips that were left on. I was even able to reach out of one window up in the attic and using the light pole, I put some lights on the horns of the iconic bull on the roof.

And I ended with attaching lights to the outside of the first story facia boards. The store looked really good, if I did say so myself. All that was left was some window decorations, and those could wait for another day.

I didn't understand how my eighty-year-old great aunt was able to do this year after year all by herself without a trip to the ER. But if she could do this, then I could, too.

Now to go home and do it all over again there.

Chapter 5

Turns out doing the house was so much simpler than the store. Great-Aunt Jo cheated; she left the light hangers up on the inside of her eaves last year. All I had to do was attach the lights to the plastic hangers.

I had been feeling really great doing something I've never done before, that was until I noticed that the second story of the house also had light hangers under the eaves. My shoulders sagged and I shook my head. "Jo, how in the world did you get lights on the second story of the house?"

Since it was already dark and I was hungry, I put everything away and decided I'd ask Verna, or one of Jo's other besties, how she did her outside lights.

Dinner was a simple homemade chicken burrito I'd created for myself when I was in college. Well, what I had back in college I'd named my Poor College Student burrito. And it didn't have chicken in it unless I had some leftover chicken from the cafeteria.

Basically, I used canned corn, canned refried beans, shredded cheese, lettuce, and salsa. I mixed corn, beans, and cheese on a tortilla. Then I put it in my mini microwave for forty seconds. Once it was ready, I topped it off with lettuce and salsa. Since it had all of the major food groups, I felt that I was eating healthily when I didn't have time to head over to the campus cafeteria. Or I'd run out of money on my meal card. Those frou-frou coffees weren't cheap. And I had a habit of drinking them almost daily.

Since graduating and earning real money, I've been adding chicken on a regular basis. In fact, I only made them when I was in a hurry, or just didn't have any idea what I wanted to make for dinner. Which was exactly how I felt after decorating the store and getting some of the lights up outside of Jo's house. Well, I supposed it was my house n ow.

How long before I called it my house?

It still felt weird to wake up in my old room at Great-Aunt Jo's house. Would I ever get used to living here? And would I ever move into Jo's room? I hadn't cleaned her room out yet, it was exactly the same as it was when I first arrived. Well, I did change the sheets and make the bed. I figured the sheets she'd died in should be burned, so I put them in a burn pit out at one of the ranches, not the Flyin' K Ranch. Jo had plenty of friends who didn't even bat an eye when I asked who was going to burn their trash next.

The idea of washing and then using the sheets my favorite aunt died in curdled my stomach. I also burned her comforter and pillows. So for now, her bed had no pillows and no comforter, just clean sheets and a blanket from the linen closet.

The sun had already begun its ascent in the November Arizona sky so I figured it had to be close to eight in the morning. Normally, I was up by six back in Florida. But here, the sun rose a little later and I tended to let the sun wake me, instead of an alarm clock.

However, I did still have a lot of work to get done before I could open up the store. One of the things on my list to do today was head to the bank and see about the business accounts. I still had enough savings to float the store any money it needed, but that wouldn't last more than a month, two at most. And I needed to see about replacing all of the broken figurines.

Before going to bed I found an old accounting file from a few years back and it seemed Aunt Jo always sold out of those figurines at Christmas. In fact, the year I looked at she'd sold about four times what was lost no thanks to Homer Kimball.

So, with the thought of possibly throttling the old man, I jumped out of bed and headed downstairs to make coffee. Aunt Jo loved her tea, but she also had a hankering for coffee. I'd found a bag of strong beans and made them my first morning there and discovered that I loved the local beans. I chuckled when I first looked at the image on the bag, it was a Saguaro cactus, of course, and a pirate skull and crossbones on top. Pirates and Cactus was the brand, but the brew was what caused me to laugh outright, Walk The Christmas Plank.

It had to be the most flavorful Christmas blend I'd ever had. And it was now my favorite cup of Joe. As I savored the hot coffee, I was able to identify hints of chicory, citrus, cinnamon, but there was something else I couldn't put my finger on - I liked it very much.

Turns out the local coffee shop made it themselves. The owner, Gavin O'Reilly, was a reformed Irish pirate. I wasn't exactly sure what an Irish pirate was, but he seemed to be a very jolly old man who loved anything to do with pirate lore and coffee. His shop, Seven Savory Seas, also had its own bakery. It was my new favorite place to go for a breakfast bagel and coffee before I went to my shop and began working.

Once I was all ready for another long day at the shop, I walked outside and locked the door. What I saw when I turned around halted me before I could walk off the porch and it had my mouth falling open.

Someone had decorated the street. The light posts all had wreaths with red bows, large ornaments adorned each wreath, and the best part was the snowman holding up the Stop sign at the corner of Desert Drive and Saguaro Heights Lane.

We lived on Saguaro Heights, only three houses from Desert Drive. If my memory from childhood served, there would be giant candy canes on the other side of Desert Drive holding that Stop sign. And in an instant, I was twelve years old again and anxiously waiting for Christmas Day to arrive.

I sighed deeply and inhaled the scents of cinnamon, orange, and Christmas spice. If we were in a regular city, this street would have been renamed – Candy Cane Lane. I could already see neighbors outside setting up their lights and front lawn decorations. By Thanksgiving weekend this street would be lit up like a Great American Family Christmas movie. I couldn't wait.

A young man across the street turned and smiled at me. Then he waved a good morning.

"Hi!" I waved and wracked my brain trying to remember his name. I'd seen him around but didn't think he lived across the street from me. Then it dawned on me and I instantly felt like a fool. The past two Christmas seasons Jo had raved about a neighbor kid who helped her decorate her house, as well as most of those on her street. It was his business. And how he paid for college classes one at a time.

"Joey!" I called out and he set down Santa's head before jogging over to see me.

"Maisy, I'm sorry I haven't been in to see you yet, but it looks like you already got a good start on Jo's Christmas display." He winced. "I mean yours. Sorry."

I felt tears form in the back of my eyes, but sniffed and did my best to hold them back. "Don't be. I still think of this as her house, too. I'm the one who should be sorry. I know she's hired you the past couple of years to decorate the outside of her house. I'd love to keep the tradition going, if you have time?" I wasn't sure if he was interested in helping me. I'd gladly pay him whatever he wanted.

"Really?" Joey's eyes popped open wide and he smiled from ear to ear. Then he looked down at his feet. "I could come by the store later today to discuss details if you like."

I had a few items on my agenda that would take me out of the shop during the day, but I nodded anyway. "Yes, that would be great. Just call first. I won't be in the store the entire day."

His head popped up and his eyes shone with excitement. "Will Cassidy be there helping you?"

Cassidy Beaumont was Aunt Jo's part-time shop assistant. She attended the local community college and worked at the store eight to ten hours a week when classes were in session. "Not today. But she will be back helping me next week, on Wednesday." I noticed how the light left his eyes when I said she wasn't going to be around for a few more days. I knew a crush when I saw one and Joey was totally crushing on Cassidy. The only question was, did she feel the same way?

Before I could think any more about the possible couple, a grating voice interrupted our conversation. "Miss Bransky, I need you to come with me."

I did my best to keep my emotions in check. Now was not the time for the local Sheriff to finally get around to taking my complaints about Homer seriously. Then a nasty thought came to mind. "Please tell me that crazy old man didn't set my store on fire, or something just as heinous?" The last thing I needed was anything messing up this Christmas and my plans to honor my Great-Aunt Jo.

Sheriff Anderson sniffed and using both of his hands, pulled his pants up a little bit higher. Probably to ensure no one on the Christmas committee could see how horribly his uniform fit him. At least it meant he was losing weight, which was a good thing. Probably. "No, he didn't."

I furrowed my brow. "Then why do you need to talk to me?"

"Because Homer Kimball is dead." The Sheriff couldn't even ease into the bad news. Nor did he ask me again. Instead, he opened the back door of his Sheriff's SUV and motioned for me to get in.

Chapter 6

I'd never been inside the Westcott Sheriff's office before. At least, not that I could remember. The Sheriff had driven me to his office and sitting in the back seat, I couldn't help but feel that he thought I was a suspect. I didn't see how I could have done it, I was home all night. "How'd he die?" I had asked, but the Sheriff didn't say a word.

The entire ride to the station he was quiet. If that was how he started out his interrogations, I could see why people would eventually talk. Even though I knew better than to say anything if he thought I was a suspect, I wanted to tell him every single thing I did yesterday. If for no other reason than to get him to let me go.

Spending a few hours in the company of Sheriff Oscar Anderson wasn't exactly my idea of time well spent.

At the moment, we were in his office and I sat in a hard, wooden chair across from Oscar Anderson. He sat on the other side of his big, oak desk just staring at me.

The room needed a good coat of paint, maybe even two. The walls were so dingy, I'd bet Siggy that this room hadn't been painted since the Sheriff took office. However, the partially packed moving boxes piqued my interest in the man. Maybe he was going to have the room painted?

Sheriff Anderson cleared his throat, and I gave him my attention.

"Do I need a lawyer?" I didn't know of a criminal attorney in the area, but I was sure that Aunt Jo's probate lawyer would know who to contact if I did need legal help.

The sheriff tilted his head to one side, and he squinted at me, as though he was trying to see something on my face but just couldn't without the aid of his glasses. Then he leaned forward and in a low voice asked, "Do you think you need one?"

On the one hand, it felt like he was trying intimidation tactics he'd seen on a movie, but on the other, it seemed like the man didn't really know what he was doing.

"What's going on here? Why did you bring me here?" As an avid reader, I'd read my share of mystery and thriller novels and knew that the Sheriff had to let me know why he'd brought me in. Just stating someone died wasn't enough. Plus, he'd not asked me any questions yet, so I had no clue what he wanted from me.

The man intertwined his fingers together like he was going to pray, then turned his hands inside out and cracked his knuckles. The sound was akin to nails scratching down a chalkboard. I couldn't help it, but I cringed.

"It seems someone got tired of the antics poor, old Homer had been getting up to lately." Sheriff Anderson arched a brow, but it was weak. Instead of a high arch like Aunt Jo used to do, his bushy brows looked more like a worm undulating through the earth.

I know it was silly, but I had to do it.

My left brow arched so high; I was sure it couldn't be seen under my bangs. I'd just had a haircut, so my bangs were short. But I arched it as high as my non-Botox forehead would allow. With pirate coffee still on my mind, since I'd be missing my morning cup from Seven Savory Seas, I narrowed my eyes and mentally said, "*On guard you blasted landlubber.*" It helped that my brow was arched so high, it was practically a sharp weapon.

The sheriff knew what I was up to. He cleared his throat and rubbed his bushy brow. "Yes, well. I need to know where you were last night at about eight P.M."

I lowered my weapon when I realized he'd waved the white flag. And that I had a good alibi. "I was home decorating the outside of my aunt's house. You can ask most of the neighbors. You know how Saguaro Lane Heights, AKA Candy Cane Lane, gets this time of year."

While I didn't see anyone else outside last night while I was working on the decorations, I knew that people were watching me behind their curtains and faux wood blinds. No way would anyone miss what I was doing. And there was absolutely no way anyone would skip out on watching me try to decorate. They had some sort of association that governed the decorations on my street at Christmas. The details were something out of a Christmas movie.

Which was why my aunt's friends didn't live on her street. They were all close by, but they said they were smart by not living on a street that made a month of Christmas celebrations the most important thing in the world.

Which was probably why Joey Mancuso seemed to be doing a nice little side hustle.

The sheriff didn't live on my street, but he did live close by. That much I did know. Mainly because his wife had me and my mom over for tea the day after Aunt Jo's funeral. I was grateful that the Sheriff wasn't home when we were there.

Then mom left to go back home to Florida, leaving me to begin settling into my new life.

He turned his gaze away from me and his lips began to twitch. I couldn't hear what he was mumbling, but I thought I heard the word "retirement". "Fine, but I'll be checking with your neighbors. And if there is any way you weren't in your front yard during the window of opportunity, then I'll be coming back with a warrant."

"Does that mean I'm free to go?" I rubbed my hands together in my lap and tried to keep from sounding like a teenager waiting to hear if she could go to the Depeche Mode concert that was coming to town.

He nodded, then put a finger in the air and pointed it at me. "But you aren't to leave town. Got it?"

I blew out the breath of air I had been holding and returned his nod. "Yes."

"Good, now get out of here." The sheriff made a shooing motion like one would do when they were trying to get a kid to get going.

I got up and moved quickly to his office door, but before I exited, I turned back around. "Sheriff, where did you find Homer's body?" The man hadn't given me any details, and I wondered why he had targeted me for this crime. Most likely it was because I was new to town.

He looked up from the piles of paper on his desk and I could have sworn the man was about to shed a tear. His eyes were puffy, red, and he couldn't seem to focus on me. "I'm sorry, but I can't share details of an ongoing investigation."

I bit my lip, trying to hold back my anger. "Do you suspect foul play?" He must if he thought I could have done something to the poor old man, but the Sheriff didn't really call me a suspect. Something wasn't adding up here.

Sheriff Anderson shook his head. "I can't talk about it." He turned his face back down to his papers and huffed out a sigh.

I took that to mean he was done talking to me. And before he changed his mind, I hightailed it out of there.

Even though the Sheriff had wasted a good hour of my time, I still headed over to the Seven Savory Seas for my morning coffee and pastry. This was one day that I not only needed it, but also felt I deserved it.

I hadn't even put both feet inside the door of the coffee shop when Gavin O'Reilly, the owner of the Seven Savory Seas greeted me. "Ahoy! Good to see that the old scallywag didn't lock you up, lass."

"How?" Living in a small town had its drawbacks, like with the gossip mill. Back home in Florida no one would have known that the Sheriff had brought me in for questioning unless I'd gone home and said something. If anyone had seen me taken to the police station in an official vehicle, they would have just assumed that someone had broken into my house, or worse, but no one would have assumed that I would have done anything wrong.

"Come in, come in, before you let any of those pesky flies inside." Gavin waved me in.

I shook my head and decided not to ask, then pushed the door open wide, and stepped through. A few faces I recognized nodded or smiled at me, but for the most part they ignored me as I walked up to the counter.

Now Gavin knew how to decorate a building. He'd also painted in the past decade, probably much sooner. His theme, of course, was pirate chic. In the far corner was a playhouse shaped like a pirate ship, with a mast and pirate colors as well. Kids could step inside the ship and sit on small chairs or stand at the wheel and pretend they were pirate captains ordering about the crew. I knew that up in the crow's nest, a tiny kitten had laid claim. Gavin had rescued the tiny guy right around Great-Aunt Jo's funeral, so I couldn't remember the name, but I had a feeling it was pirate themed.

One kid was standing before the wheel. His black pirate eye patch stood out in dark contrast to his light blond hair. He had a black and white striped shirt on and torn blue jeans. He looked just like a little pirate captain. I couldn't help but smile. And above him the kitten had a little paw out trying to bat his hat off.

Coming here was totally the right thing to do.

"Argh, matey!" The boy raised a hand and pointed to another little kid. "It be time ye walk the plank. No landlubbers allowed here."

I chuckled and looked at Gavin whose eyes had misted over. "A boy after me own heart." He put a hand over his chest and stood taller.

"Is he your boy?" The kid looked a bit too young to be his, but men over the age of fifty could still father children, couldn't they? If I wasn't mistaken, Gavin was in his early seventies, and I didn't think he had any kids.

"That there be my great-nephew, Simon." He pointed to the pirate boy. "My sister had seven kids and Simon is the youngest of her grandkids. He's only eight, but I think he's already on his way to being just like his Seadog." He pounded his fist against his chest.

"Your family call you Seadog?" I knew that meant old pirate, but why would his family call him that?

"Only the young ones. They love pirate lore and names." Before he could continue, I decided to change the topic. I was in a hurry, after all.

"So, do you still have my favorite breakfast treats?" All I could think of was getting back to the quiet of my shop and having my morning treat before starting a busy day of work.

"How about a Christmas Pirate with a lassy bread?" Gavin had turned his full attention back on me.

I looked past him at the menu board on the wall but didn't see anything like what he'd just suggested. "What's that?"

He grinned from ear to ear. "I'm trying out something new. With all of the out of towners coming in I thought it might grab their attention."

"Okay, but what is it?" I hated it when I had to repeat my questions. But Gavin made the best coffee so it wasn't worth crossing swords with him.

His one eye narrowed on me, and he turned around. When he had the espresso machine whirring and steaming, he decided to enlighten me. "A Christmas Pirate is a peppermint mocha made using my proprietary blend of Christmas Coffee, Walk the Christmas Plank. And the lassy bread is just toast with butter and guacamole. I can make it spicy, if you like." He grinned, knowing that my version of spicy was very different from his.

The last time I tried something he called "spicy", it took me an hour of guzzling milk, tea, and even chewing on ice chips before my mouth no longer hurt from the heat. Floridians aren't accustomed to high heat food. "Ah, no thank you. I'll take it mild." I did love a good piece of avocado toast.

He passed me a to-go cup of his latest concoction and I took a sip. "Whoa, that's really good. His Christmas coffee paired very well with the peppermint and mocha flavors. I might have to make some Christmas scones to go with the Christmas Pirate next week.

"So, what did the Sheriff want? Did he finally figure out that Homer was only trying to hornswoggle Jo out of her holdings?" Gavin was close in age to my Aunt Jo and her friends. I was pretty sure he had a crush on one of them, but couldn't tell if it was Verna or Jade. He always smiled and chatted with the both of them. But if I was to choose right now, I would have to say it was Jade. She's so sweet and friendly. And Verna? Well, she has her charms, but most men don't find an opinionated woman who's just about ready to turn eighty exciting or sexy.

The fact that he knew something about the battle between Jo and Homer had me thinking about what sort of questions I needed to ask Gavin. "Say, what exactly was going on with Homer and Aunt Jo?"

"Hmm, let me see." Gavin scratched his eye under the patch. I knew there was an eye there because when he wasn't working, he wasn't wearing an eye patch. I loved that he was totally in on his costume during working hours. It made him even more likable. "Yes, Homer thought that most of the properties your aunt owned had been swindled from his own family."

"Wait, what? Great-Aunt Jo swindled his family? No way." I knew my aunt owned a lot of property in town. Her family were one of the original settlers here. But since I don't have all of the inheritance yet, I'm not really sure how many properties she owned here. Not that I was going to tell anyone that I inherited the entirety of her holdings. All I was willing to admit to at the moment was that I got her house and bookshop.

Jo's attorney was in the process of putting together a list for me, with addresses and everything. I did know that the only stipulation in her will was that I not sell any of the properties unless I was in dire circumstances. But since her bookshop and house were free and clear, and the shop made a pretty penny, I didn't think I'd ever need to worry about selling off property. However, I did not know the exact situation with the other properties, only that they were all currently rented out and the estate would be receiving rent money shortly.

The main thing holding everything up was the judge signing off on the will. Since Jo had listed me as her heir, it should be quick and easy. But with the holiday, and the fact that the judge was out of town at the moment, I was just waiting to see what was what.

I shook my head as Gavin rubbed at the scruff on his chin he called a beard. The man was bald but still grew hair on his face. I hoped I didn't have such issues when I got older. Like no hair on my head, but still needing to shave my legs.

"That's the thing, for years Homer was moaning and groaning about the bad deal his grandfather made with Jo's grandfather. Then all of a sudden, he had this piece of paper that made him think Jo swindled the Kimball's out of their land. But she said her grandfather bought the land fair and square that the Kimball's once owned."

When two slices of toasted wheat bread popped up, Gavin reached for them. He buttered them both and leaned down and from a mini fridge under the counter he pulled out a small package of guacamole. Once he wrapped it all up and put it in a small brown bag, he handed it to me.

"Thanks. But if he had paperwork backing up his claim, why didn't a judge, or even my aunt, do something about it?" I'd not heard about this before. I mean, I knew that they had issues with each other, but Jo had always said the man was confused about some dealings over a hundred years earlier.

"That's just it, your aunt had paperwork showing the sale and the fact that the tax roles showed her as the legal owner, only backed up her claim. No one believed that Homer's paperwork was legitimate. So, Homer got more and more aggressive with his hatred. Earlier this summer, he painted some not so nice things on the side of the book-store. Thankfully, it was easy to cover up with paint." Gavin seemed to know a lot about what had been going on lately, which had me wondering how good of friends he was with my aunt.

I narrowed my eyes.

He handed me a bill.

I sighed and took out a twenty. "Keep the change." I didn't always have enough cash to tip him, so when I did, I usually added a lot more to cover the days when I hadn't stopped at the ATM first.

Before I headed out to my store I had one more question. "So, if Homer had a problem with Jo, then that would mean he'd most likely start attacking me and my character next, right?"

Gavin's eyes widened. "Which would make you the person with the most reason to kill him." He leaned on the counter. "How'd you do it?"

I was spluttering when he winked.

"Just joking. I know you didn't do it. The entire town knows you were trying to decorate the front of Jo's house last night. The town's Facebook page has pictures and time stamps of you working on it." Gavin stood up straight and chuckled. "Aye, be off with ya now, lass."

His pirate speech was back and he turned his head to greet a newcomer to the store.

The man who walked in almost stole my breath away. The handsome creature was so tall, his head looked as though it might touch the top of the doorway, but the measurement markings on the side of the door pegged him at six feet, two inches. His warm brown skin, black hair, and brown eyes had me guessing he was a Native American. His clothes were plain jeans and a jewel-toned Henley. Nothing screamed tourist or visitor. In fact, his worn-in snakeskin boots made me think that he lived in the area.

Not that I was looking for a new boyfriend, but a little local eye candy might be nice.

When I smiled a greeting, he tipped his hat and returned my smile.

All of a sudden, I felt weak in the knees. If I was anything like most of the heroines in the romance novels I would be swooning soon. But I was a real human, and no way was I going to swoon right into this stranger's arms. No matter how much I wanted to feel what looked like some serious muscle on his forearms.

"Ma'am." And that was it. I no longer thought of him as the hero of my imaginative romance novel. Since when did I become a ma'am? What happened to the days when men called me miss?

I was barely in my thirties, for cactus sake!

Chapter 7

I t didn't take long to put the handsome man out of my thoughts, the moment I opened the door to my bookshop reality hit. The table in front of the store that had held the cactus figurines and ornaments was still vacant of anything to sell. The only things on it were metal and wood display holders. At least they didn't break when the brick came through the window.

Before I could finish my avocado toast, my cell rang and the day began in earnest. A shipment of books Jo had ordered arrived, which had me busy adding them to the inventory system and then shelving them. The window repair man showed up not long after the shipment, and then I received a call from the Native American woman who made most of the glass ornaments and figurines. She did have some stock ready, but she couldn't deliver it until next week as she was out of town. But, if I wanted, I could drive out to her house and her nephew would load my car.

Since her place was an hour away, I made arrangements to drive out early the next day.

After lunch I headed over to the bank to see what they could tell me about all of Jo's accounts. The only thing they could share was that I was solvent. However, the business accounts needed a few signatures from me and the attorney. We took care of that, and I discovered that not only was the store insurance all paid up through the new year, but I would not have any trouble replacing the lost stock. Jo had left me more than solvent.

At least one thing went right that day. After the signatures were dry, the bank manager allowed me to withdraw some petty cash and they requested new debit and credit cards for my use on the business accounts.

"Miss Bransky, due to Judge Charles' vacation, I don't think I'll be able to give you access to the personal accounts of Jo Barton until after Christmas." The bank manager pushed his glasses up his nose before clearing his throat. "However, we could arrange a short-term personal loan should you need funds before then."

"Thank you, Mister Cane, but I'll be fine." The one thing that both my mother and my aunt stressed the entire time I was growing up was to keep at least three months' savings in the bank. Since I had been saving up to buy a house back in Florida, I actually had more than that in my savings account. I hated touching it if I didn't need to, but that was what it was for. And since I no longer had a need for a down payment on a house in Florida, I'd keep that in mind should cash flow become an issue.

Thankfully, I wouldn't have to worry about money for a few months. So even if the Judge took his own sweet time signing the documents to give me access to Jo's personal accounts, I'd be just fine. As would the store. With Christmas just around the corner, the store would be swimming in cash. I hoped. Scratch that, I prayed I would sell a lot over the coming weeks.

The sun had set a long time before I realized that my stomach had been growling. When I checked my cell for the time, I shook my head. It was almost eight at night. I had been on my knees in front of a bookshelf making room for another shipment that was scheduled to arrive before the official opening next week. I debated finishing up or leaving it for the next day when my stomach turned and growled its displeasure at my thoughts of continuing to work.

"Okay, okay. I get it." I rubbed my belly then stood up, leaving the books where they were. No one was going to be in the store the next day, at least not in the morning, so leaving a mess would be fine.

After grabbing my purse and jacket, I went around the shop to ensure everything was locked tight and the lights were out. Then I made my way to the front door and froze as I noticed a shadow of a person looking through the door.

The front of the store was mostly arched glass windows with a thick stucco in between the windows and door. The front door was a massive oak door that had been custom built to fit the arched opening. While the broken window had been replaced earlier that day, the logo and store name had not yet been put on. That would take a couple of days.

The shadow appeared in front of the window that had just been replaced. For a moment, I thought that Homer was back to break it again. Then I remembered what had happened and sighed. It was probably someone coming by to see what Homer had done. The rumor mill had gone crazy that day.

Part of the reason I still hadn't eaten was because of so many people stopping in to check on me.

While it was after eight at night, this was Westcott, Arizona, not Los Angeles, California. I could go out front and see who was looking through my windows without having to worry.

Although, someone had been murdered only twenty-four hours earlier...

"Can I help you?" I had my phone in my hand ready to dial for help should the person out front turn out to be a murderous stranger.

The man in front of the window turned to me and I gasped. "Jason? Is that you?"

"Maisy, you're still here?" His brows furrowed and he ran a hand through his mussed-up hair. Yesterday, his hair was mussed in a fashionable way. Tonight? It looked as though he'd been through the ringer. But of course, his grandfather had been murdered.

And the murderer was still on the loose. He was probably sick with worry, and maybe a little bit of fear.

"Come inside. It's cold out here." I looked him up and down. "Where's your jacket?" All he had on were his blue jeans and a long-sleeved button-down shirt. It was nice, but not nearly warm enough for this cold weather. It had to be in the low sixties, maybe even upper fifties.

As if Jason had just realized he was cold, he shivered and ran a hand down his arm. "I...I think...I don't know."

Once we were inside, I closed the front door. Then I turned on the front of house lights. "Here, take a seat." I led him to the little reading nook that had a comfortable overstuffed chair for those who wanted to sit in the store while reading. "Would you like a cup of hot tea? Or coffee? I can run upstairs and make you one quickly." I stood by him, shoulders stiff, and bit my nail.

He shook his head. "Did you see my grandfather the night he was murdered?"

Jason must have been in shock. And I couldn't blame him. I felt something similar when I got the call about Great-Aunt Jo dying. I knelt down next to him and put my warm hand on his cold one. "I'm so sorry for your loss. Is there anything I can do for you?"

His eyes turned to me and for just a moment, I wasn't sure what I saw, fear? "Who killed my grandfather? The Sheriff said you were seen by your entire street so it couldn't be you. If not you, then who?"

The sound of his words had me falling back on my backside. It sounded as though he thought I had done it until he learned I had an airtight alibi. "Jason, I did not wish your grandfather anything bad. Yes, I was upset with him, but when I realized how sick he was, my anger turned to sympathy for a man who needed medical help." I paused for a moment to catch my breath. "I let my anger go at the feet of Jesus and never took it back."

"So, Jesus did this? He let someone kill my grandfather to help you get even?" Jason stood up and ran a hand through his hair again. His eyes were wide and if he had been a complete stranger, I would have worried for my life. Instead, I knew what was happening with him – the shock and pain of losing his grandfather was sending him over the edge. While I didn't fear him, I did think he needed some help.

I stood up and pulled my phone from my back pocket. When I dialed 911 the operator said she'd send a paramedic to come and check on him. And if I felt for my safety I should go outside.

She must have been from the city. The sidewalks closed up shop before eight here in Westcott, unless there was a rodeo in town. Which there wasn't. No one would be out on the street here in the middle of Western Row. I didn't even think shopkeepers lived above their stores here anymore.

"Jason, stay here. I'm going to get you a cup of hot coffee." I ran upstairs and sent a prayer to Jesus to ask him to thank Jo for putting in an instant coffee maker. The last time I'd been here she didn't have one. Now, she had a very nice and large K-cup machine that could make those instant pods or a full pot of coffee. I opted for a cup of black coffee.

When I came back downstairs, Jason was exactly where I left him. "Here, drink this. It should help you feel better." I'd read somewhere that hot coffee after a big shock could help calm nerves. I wasn't sure if it was clickbait, fake news, or real. But it was worth trying.

He took a sip and held the hot mug in his hands. After he took two more sips, the unnatural glaze in his eyes dimmed just a bit and he began looking almost normal.

"Jason, I didn't ask Jesus to hurt your granddad. I asked Him to take my anger away, and to help your grandfather get the help he needed. It was someone evil who killed your grandfather. I've heard rumors that Jo wasn't the only one he had upset. The sheriff has his work cut out for him." That was an understatement. And I worried that Sherriff Anderson wouldn't be up for the challenge.

"Yes, I do." A loud booming voice said before I turned to stare directly into the face of the handsome man I'd seen at Seven Savory Seas earlier that day.

"Excuse me, but we're closed. I'll be opening up on Wednesday. Please come back then." I wasn't sure what a man was doing coming into my store this late at night, no stores on this street stayed open past eight at night. And I was positive that the closed sign was up on the door.

He reached for something in his jacket pocket, and I eyed him warily. I had to remind myself that it was a safe town, except for the murder the night before. Then I heard the sirens for the paramedic and felt a bit of the trepidation that had brought my shoulders up tight to ease. My arms relaxed at my sides, but not two seconds later my hand shot up to cover the scream I was about to emit when I saw what was in this stranger's hand.

Chapter 8

"Ma'am, I'm Sheriff Sam Madrid. We got a call that you had someone in your store who needed some help. That's me." He held out a wallet with his badge and ID. The man wasn't wearing a Sheriff's uniform, but he did seem to have the right credentials.

Except for one problem...

"Ah, we have a sheriff." I had only seen this man once, that was earlier in the day at the coffee shop. So, I wasn't exactly sure who he was, since small towns didn't have two sheriffs.

He smiled and put his wallet away. "I see the grapevine hasn't heard yet. Sheriff Oscar Anderson is retiring at the end of the year, and I'm his replacement."

My eyebrows shot so high, I knew he could no longer see them under the jungle that was my bangs after a long day of work. "You're early. The end of the year isn't for a few more weeks."

Sheriff Madrid's chuckle was deep and sexy. I couldn't help but hope that he would be nice to work with.

When his bombshell settled in my brain, I thought about my early morning meeting with the other sheriff and those boxes I saw in Sheriff Anderson's office made more sense. But he still needed to realize I wasn't older than him, so calling me Ma'am was just plain rude. "I'm Maisy Bransky, and this," I gestured to Jason, "is Jason Kimball. His grandfather was murdered last night, and he isn't taking it so well."

Sheriff Madrid took in a slow breath, then let it out, and nodded. He rested one hand on his service revolver that was holstered on his right hip. A gun I hadn't seen on him earlier in the day. He must have added it when he got the call to come to my shop just now.

The other he used to rub his chin. I hadn't noticed it before, but there was some stubble there making me think that he'd been up very early that morning. When I first saw him less than twelve hours earlier, he didn't have any stubble.

Plus, he was wearing the same dusty boots, jeans, and button up shirt. Sheriff Anderson probably was running him ragged. I prayed this meant that Sheriff Anderson was no longer on the case and this man in front of me would be able to find the actual killer, instead of trying to pin the murder rap on me.

"Jason, I'm sorry to hear about your grandfather. He was always nice to me when I was a kid." A distant look crossed the sheriff's face, as though he was thinking of times long gone. "I remember once I snuck into his barn and was about to head out to the pasture on a dare to see how close I could get to his bull." Sheriff Madrid looked to his right and shook his head. But before he did, I noticed a perfectly adorable dimple on his right cheek. I bet the women all over town would be agog over the new sheriff by lunch tomorrow.

One edge of Jason's mouth turned up in an almost smile and his eyes softened. "I remember that summer. I think I was the one who put you up to it."

Sheriff Madrid snorted. "You know, I think you might be right. But your grandfather caught me just after I entered the fenced-in area where the bull was kept. I'll never forget how he grabbed me by my scruff and yanked me back into the next field." The man ran a hand down his face.

"I know, it was a good thing he was there," Jason added.

"That bull of his charged and ran right into the fence we were standing next to. It scared me so badly that I never wanted to get near a bull again." Sheriff Madrid chuckled. "It's probably why I didn't go into ranching like a lot of families in my tribe did."

"Yeah, I think I remember when you became a tribal police officer. I even told grandpa it was all because of him. He laughed it off, but I know he was proud of you."

I'd stood by listening to the men as they traveled down memory lane, but I had questions. Ones I wanted to ask before the paramedics entered and took over. If I wasn't mistaken, they had just pulled up and were exiting their vehicle.

"So, you two go way back? Childhood friends?" I wracked my brain trying to think of any of the Native American kids I knew back when I spent summers here with Great-Aunt Jo, but I couldn't.

"Maisy, you know Sam. He hung out with us once in a while during the summer." It was as though Jason had never had a breakdown. He stood up, dusted off his pants, and walked over to where I stood next to Sam – er…Sheriff Madrid.

I looked between the two men and when the sheriff gave me a real smile, I finally saw the kid he had once been. The boy I knew was short, scruffy, and always getting into trouble. In fact, he had led me down some not too nice paths back in the day. "Sammy? Really?"

It took seeing his full face when he smiled, and that dimple, to remember him.

"Little Maisy. It's good to see you again. I heard you were back in town." He put his hand out and I shook it.

Just then, the door opened and the bell above the door dinged letting me know we had visitors.

Two men dressed in the typical blue paramedic uniform stopped in front of us. The taller man looked at me and asked, "who needed medical help?"

The other man looked at Sam then over to Jason. His brows furrowed in confusion, and he set the box down he had carried in.

I winced. "Sorry, Jason here was having a panic attack, I think." I pointed to the man and mouthed "sorry" before he could say anything.

"I'm fine now. Just having trouble processing some horrid news, that's all." The light that had been shining in Jason's eyes only moments before had faded.

"Since we're here, we should take your vitals, at least," the tall man said.

"Wait." The second guy took a step closer to Jason and looked him in the face. "Jason Kimball? Man, I'm so sorry about your grandfather. I was on the scene last night" He shook his head but didn't say anything else.

Jason's nostrils flared. "Please tell me you know who did that to my grandpops." The poor guy had his emotions all over the place tonight.

It was different for me, Jo wasn't murdered, she died peacefully in her sleep. But Homer? I still didn't know the details, maybe I could get the new sheriff to share a bit of how Homer died.

"Nah, sorry, man." The paramedic whose name badge said, "Carl", shook his head. "We weren't called out to the scene until after it happened. And your grandfather had already passed on to the great beyond."

I never understood why people would use different words to express where a person went after they died. If the Bible was true, and I believed it was, then people went to one of two places, heaven or hell. Then I thought about Homer and winced. While I didn't know for sure, I doubted Homer went up. Most likely, he went downstairs. I would never label that the "Great Beyond." More like the "Pit of Despair."

But, none of us will know who went where until we meet our Maker at those pearly gates, or St. Peter, depending on how it actually works.

Jason fell back onto the chair that was behind him. "What is this world coming to? I don't get it. Westcott is such a safe town; how could this happen to an old man?"

I had to bite my tongue to keep from saying what I thought about Homer. That man had enemies up the wazoo. Didn't matter that Westcott was a safe town, anyone could flip a switch and become a murderer. Well, almost anyone. I didn't think I could ever kill someone on purpose.

"How do we know Homer was murdered? When the sheriff questioned me earlier, he didn't say how Homer died. Just that he had died under suspicious circumstances. Could it have been an accident?" If the man was shot, that wouldn't be an accident, unless it was a hunting accident. And if that had been the case, he wouldn't have been in town.

Shoot, I didn't even know where in town the body was found. Man, what was I thinking when the sheriff questioned me? I should have pressed him for some details. Or asked someone else on my way out of the station.

To be fair, it was my first murder to be around. Plus, Jo had just died leaving me her business and it was crazy with Black Friday just around the corner followed up by the entire Christmas season. None of this was something I was prepared to handle.

It was a good thing that Jo always talked about her business, and I grew up spending a lot of time here.

My business background didn't hurt matters, either. But a Contracts Administrator was very different from a bookshop owner.

One side of Sheriff Madrid's mouth quirked up, almost like he was about to smile, then caught himself and stopped. "We know it was murder because the man was poisoned. And it happened just one block from here."

That was a bombshell if ever I heard one. It was no wonder the other sheriff thought I might have done it.

I put one hand to my forehead and using the other one, I felt for the wall behind me. The air rushed out of my lungs quickly and I slowly shook my head. "Last night, about eight o'clock he was poisoned just around the corner? But how? What kind of poison?"

"That's as much as I'm at liberty to say right now." Sheriff Madrid's smile had completely vanished, and he looked at me as though he thought I might have something to do with it after all.

"I had an airtight alibi. So don't go looking at me like that." I'd already looked at the town's Facebook page and saw the video of me trying to hang those lights. To say I wasn't very coordinated would have been an understatement. In my defense, there were rocks under the ladder. If it hadn't been so wobbly, I wouldn't have fallen.

Thankfully, it was only once, and not from a high step.

Although, if it weren't for the murder happening at the same time as my video mishap, I would have been very unhappy with my neighbors for posting that video, and then taking turns telling jokes about what they saw.

Even adults can be mean.

The two paramedics got to work on Jason, and I stepped closer to Sheriff Madrid. But before I could try to wheedle out any more information, that bell above my door dinged again, and I could hear three very distinct voices calling out my name.

Chapter 9

"Maisy, Maisy, are you alright?" The deep, husky voice of Verna Henderson overrode any of the whispering by the local paramedics as they asked Jason some personal health questions.

I raised an arm so they could see where I was.

The way the store was laid out made it difficult to see the reading nook past the shelves of romance and local Indie Author books. Jo had said that romance books are what put the store in the black, but the Indie author books are what make her store stand out from those big box ones.

You wouldn't find any self-published books in the grocery store. And my own experience showed that the big chain bookstores rarely had Indie Published books on their shelves. But here, at Saguaro Bookshop, one might find the latest cozy mystery by Jenna Hendricks, or a science fiction novel by Martin Craigson, or the hugely popular urban fantasy series by Michael Masterson that never seems to stay on the shelves very long. At least, according to Jo, the last time we talked about books.

The Indie Author shelves have grown over the past few years and those books were starting to become the bigger sellers here at the Saguaro Bookshop. I kinda liked that anyone who had a good story, and the ability to write it out in a novel, could sell their own work. The big publishers will never go away, but now that independent authors had this ability, readers had so much more to choose from. Which gave me a great idea, one that Jo hadn't gotten around to yet – online book sales.

I had found myself binging on Inspirational Cowboy Romance the last time I was here, and I never stopped reading that genre. It wasn't the only one I read, but I did read a lot of it.

So, when Verna came around the shelves holding up a Cowboy Romance book, I wasn't shocked. Cowboy romances were hugely popular - especially here in Arizona. The dog-eared pages told me it wasn't one of mine, she must have brought it with her.

"Maisy, is everything alright?" Jade Stinson, the quintessential grandma of the group, asked.

"I'm fine. Jason is...well..." I quirked my lips to the side. I really didn't want to tell everyone what had happened to the poor man. They didn't need to know. "He's having a tough time with the death of his grandfather."

There, that should be enough to appease someone, right? A man's medical issues aren't anyone else's business.

Verna pursed her lips while Jade put a hand over her heart. And Ada? Well, she walked over to where the paramedics stood and butted right in.

And for just one second, I had forgotten that I was in a small town.

Of course, Jason's medical business wasn't his alone. The entire town needed to know that he'd had a panic attack, or something like that. And these women would be the ones to help out the town and spread the gossip... er, I mean news.

I worked very hard to keep from rolling my eyes. The one thing I never missed while being away was the nosey busy-bodies and their incessant need to know everything going on with everyone.

"Oh, you poor thing." Ada Hopkins put a hand to her chest and tsk'd. "How about I bring you a pot of my famous two-alarm chili with honey cornbread. I can take you home too, if these boys will release you now." She took a few steps closer to Jason.

Huh, that wasn't what I was expecting.

Verna crossed her arms over her chest and only watched. She stayed quiet, but didn't seem to have much sympathy for Jason. I knew Verna didn't like Homer, but I thought she was fine with Jason.

When Jason looked down at the ground in front of him, I realized he was embarrassed. Most men didn't like to be seen as weak. I didn't think he was weak for what had happened, but he might see it that way.

When Aunt Jo died, I cried for days. Shoot, I still cried. While Jason didn't cry, he did seem to be having a very tough time of it.

So, I did the only thing I could, I changed the focus of everyone. "Sam, how do you know it was poison that killed Homer? And how was it delivered?"

The three women who had just entered my shop turned shocked expressions on me and the new sheriff.

"What? Homer was poisoned?" Jade put a hand to her mouth and shook her head. "How was that possible?"

"I heard he was found right outside of this very shop." Ada pursed her lips and put her hands on her hips. "Now, little Sammy, you aren't suggesting that Maisy had anything to do with Homer's death, are you? If you've done your homework, you'll know that she was at her house for several hours that night. It's all on Facebook."

Verna, who was normally very vocal, stayed quiet and watched everyone with an eagle eye. Sheriff Madrid noticed how quiet she was.

"Ladies, you know I can't discuss an ongoing investigation. And please, it's Sheriff Madrid now. I haven't been little Sammy for more than fifteen years now." He arched a brow and stared at Ada.

"Fine, Sheriff..." Ada slowly drew out his name, "Madrid. Maisy doesn't sell any food here, and she certainly wouldn't have murdered him. So why are you here?"

Sam smiled and opened his arms wide. "Ladies, why don't you head back to where you came from, and Maisy can join you when she locks up. This is a personal matter."

"But, Jason?" Jade began to argue with Sam, then she threw her hands in the air.

Ada looked back at Jason who had raised his head at some point during the conversation and was watching with keen interest. He couldn't seem to keep his brown eyes off of me. "Jason, if you need anything, please call me."

Surely, he didn't think I had anything to do with what happened to his grandfather, did he? I thought we already discussed it.

He nodded. "I will Miss Ada. Thank you."

I walked the ladies to the door. "Where were you and what drew you here at this time of night?"

After Verna walked outside, she turned around. "We were at Cactus Joe's discussing our book of the week." She held up the dog-eared copy of Second Chance Ranch by Jenna Hendricks and I grinned.

"Do you ladies have your own book club?" I had thought of starting one in the bookshop, but wanted to wait until after Christmas. I also wanted to see about the possibility of adding a small coffee shop inside the store so I could sell coffee and treats to not only those shopping in the store, but also to anyone who wanted to attend a book club. There was just something about sipping hot coffee, eating a tasty pastry, and talking about romance novels that always appealed to me.

Verna grinned. "We do. And your Aunt Jo used to join us."

Jade held up a hand adorned with a variety of turquoise rings. The woman loved turquoise. And she also loved Christmas. So, her red shirt with a picture of a small Organ Pipe cactus with a dozen appendages wearing little Santa hats on all of its extremities wasn't a surprise. Even though it wasn't Thanksgiving yet, Jade had already decorated her house and was wearing Christmas clothing. I kinda liked that about her. She had her own thing going and it suited her nicely.

"You can pick the next book, if you like?" Jade wiggled her brows. "I hear you have a thing for cowboy romances, just like we do."

Why was I not surprised that Aunt Jo had told her friends about the books I always bought from her. I chuckled. "How about you let me get through Christmas and New Year's and then we can talk about book club."

"Deal!" All three said in unison.

I was just about to turn around and head back inside when I heard the bell above my door ding. I turned to see the sheriff coming outside.

"Verna, can I have a moment of your time?" While Sam's voice was polite, the hard edge I'd seen earlier was back in his eyes.

"What's going on?" I asked.

He turned to me. "Maisy, why don't you go back inside and sit with Jason while the paramedics pack up. He's going to be just fine."

I knew a brush-off when I heard one, but I wasn't too keen on the sheriff questioning Verna. Surely, he didn't suspect her, did he?

I looked at my aunt's best friend, and she smiled. "Go on, sweetie. I'll be fine. And it looked like Jason could use a friend."

Jason did need a friend, but so did Verna. I was torn between the two.

Ada patted my arm. "I'll stay with Verna. No need to worry."

When Jade took two steps closer to Verna, I had to admit that she was better off than Jason was. I knew he had other family members, but none of them lived in town. The poor man probably didn't have anyone to help him through this horrible event.

"Okay, but let me know what's going on, will ya?" I eyed Sam, but he ignored me.

Jade reassured me she would keep me in the loop. And with that, I turned and walked back inside of my shop.

Chapter 10

By the next afternoon I still hadn't heard from Verna, Ada, or Jade. I was getting a bit worried about Verna. I was able to get some work done in the shop today, but not a lot. I was too worried about everyone. Not only was Verna at the top of my mind, but so was Jason.

However, once three o'clock chimed on the clock, I was done – mentally. I had been sitting there at the counter just staring at my laptop screen, not doing anything. The numbers were blurring on the screen, so I shut my laptop and picked up my phone. When I dialed Verna, it went straight to voicemail – not a good sign.

Finally, I reached Ada. She told me that the new sheriff took Verna in for questioning last night, but he let her go after an hour of interrogation. Okay, so maybe Ada didn't use the term *interrogated*, but an hour of questioning had to feel like he was grilling her.

"Ada, have you seen Verna today?" I was still worried about the poor woman. While she was fairly spry, she was still a Septuagenarian and something like this could cause health issues.

"Not since last night when I walked her home. But don't worry, dear. Verna is made of sterner stuff than most. She's probably sticking close to her cactus today." Ada hung up after promising to let me know when she heard from Verna.

None of it made sense to me. I racked my brain to try and see how Verna could be involved. How was it that Verna needed to be questioned for so long? What made Sam think she could have possibly had anything to do with Homer's murder? "That's it." I jumped up and snapped my fingers. After unplugging my laptop and putting it away in the upstairs office, I grabbed my purse and jacket and headed out the back door.

The alleyway out back provided a shorter walk to Verna's house, and I needed a walk instead of a drive. It wasn't that she lived too far away, it was maybe a fifteen-minute walk from the back door.

But the moment I stepped outside, I almost regretted it. A thumping sound came from the trash bins. "Hello? Anyone there?" If I was back home in downtown Hollywood – no, not the one in Lala land. I'm talking about Hollywood in Florida. Where the weather is always a breezy seventy-degrees, and the sun is shining. Except when there is a hurricane, then the weather isn't so fine. But if I was back home, I'd think there were a couple of homeless people hanging out behind the large, green dumpster. But here? In teeny tiny Westcott? Not very likely.

"If anyone is back there, I won't hurt you." More likely, they were just hiding out, afraid I might call the cops on them. I wouldn't, unless they were doing something they shouldn't be, like drugs. I had a zero-drug tolerance policy.

I heard a whimper, and prayed it wasn't someone back there nursing an injury. "Do you need help?"

A few swishing sounds and then I understood what was back there.

Out came the cutest, and dirtiest, little French bulldog I'd ever seen. I knelt down and held out my hand. "Aren't you just the cutest little thing, ever. Come here, I won't hurt you. I promise."

The little dog slowly came near me. I looked under her belly, which looked as though she hadn't eaten in a while, and bit back a tear. This little dog was seriously injured. She had gashes all over her little body, no wonder she was whimpering. I pulled out my phone and looked for the nearest animal hospital. Living in a western town had a few advantages. One being all of the animals. Which meant that we had multiple offices to choose from. I found the one closest to me and called them.

"Hi, I just found an injured Frenchie behind my shop on Cactus Lane. She doesn't have a collar, but she needs help. Can I bring her to you?" I didn't care how much it cost, I wasn't going to let this poor little thing stay on the streets and develop infections all over her body.

"Of course, we are open until nine every night, so feel free to come in before then," The woman on the other side of the call said.

"Thanks, I'll be right there. I'm only about a five-minute walk away." And I was. Too bad it was the opposite direction from Verna's house. But this little doggy needed my attention and help. I hung up my phone and put it in my purse. Then leaned down to try and pick up the dog.

She whimpered and backed up.

"I'm sorry, but I need to get you to the hospital. It might hurt when I pick you up, but I will be as careful as I can." I bent back down, and she squirmed away again. When I stood up, I pulled my keys out of my purse and opened the back door. "Wait here, I have an idea." I was already talking to the little doggy as though she was a human. I'd seen plenty of dog-owners doing this and wondered if their pets understood. Now I knew why, it didn't matter if she understood me,

I was the one who needed the words spoken. And maybe, just maybe the dog did understand English.

Five minutes later, I had the little dog wrapped in an old throw blanket I'd seen upstairs and we were on our way. At first, the dog eyed me, but after a few steps, she nuzzled up next to my chest and relaxed. "That's a good girl. Hang tight, we're almost there."

I walked in and the place was almost empty. I was a bit worried that an empty animal hospital might mean they weren't very good, but the smile on the receptionist not only put me at ease, but also little Frenchie. She licked the underside of my chin and I giggled.

"Oh, isn't she just adorable? Are you the one who just called about an injured dog?" The lady stepped around the desk and came over to us. She put her hand out for the dog to sniff. It only took a second and her little pink tongue was out and licking the hand in front of her.

"Yes, that's us. I found her behind my shop. I'll pay for her care if you can fix her up." I may not have had access to Jo's money, yet, but I did have my own and I could take care of the cutest little dog in the world. Even if it meant I was eating hot dogs and mac 'n cheese for the next month.

"What's her name?" The woman had walked back behind the counter. I noticed her name plate said, "Lucy Mason."

"Ah, good question. I just found her and don't know." I bit my lip as I looked around the reception area. Off to one side was a fenced-in playground for dogs. It wasn't large but it did have a few of those cement steps I'd seen at a dog park, and two different sized cylinders for dogs to run through. I knew I wouldn't be scooching through them, but the dog could.

Then, a book caught my eye. Books usually did catch my attention no matter where I went. This one was old with brown leather binding. It looked worn, like someone had read it a lot. A slow smile crossed my face, and I knew what I wanted to name the little scamp. "How about Ollie?" When I was a kid, I read Oliver Twist and loved the name. I remember asking my mom if she could have a boy and name him Oliver. Then when I got a bit older, I wanted a dog named Ollie. Neither ever happened...until now.

"Ollie? Isn't that a boy's name?" Lucy tilted her head and looked at little Ollie. Then she nodded. "You know, I think it suits her. Ollie it is." She took Ollie from me and handed her to another technician who came forward with a smile.

"I'll take her into exam room three. When you're done with the paperwork, you can join us." The woman in light pink scrubs walked away talking in baby talk to Ollie. It was really cute.

"Okay, what's this about paperwork?" I hated paperwork.

"I can help you. But beware, if little Ollie has a microchip, we might be contacting her owner." Lucy took a clipboard with a stack of papers and leaned over the counter.

The last thing I wanted to think about was someone owning Ollie and letting her get the way I found her. Anyone who didn't properly care for a dog didn't deserve the dog. Same for cats. Or any animal, really.

I could have sworn that the paperwork had me signing over my first-born child, or something similar. And it took forever, but in reality, I only promised to pay for the services rendered if an owner wasn't found.

When we finally got out of there, I realized why so many people didn't have pets, they were expensive. I knew enough to know that one didn't normally buy the fancy dog food from the vet's office. But since it was already getting late and poor little Ollie had to be tired and hungry, I went ahead and bought a small bag of dry prescription dog food along with a dozen cans of moist food.

While I waited for them to finish cleaning and fixing up Ollie, I went back to the store and drove my car back to the animal hospital. We were also going to have to stop in at the local pet store to pick up a few important things like toys and a doggie bed. When Ollie's injuries healed, I wanted to start dressing her in cute sweaters, too. But just for the cold months.

"Okay, Ollie. How do you feel about living with me?" The animal hospital said she didn't have a microchip. They went ahead and put one in for me and loaded up my information. I wasn't about to lose my cute little baby, now that I had her. Lucy told me she was a Blue French Bull Dog. They were typically rare and expensive. But Ollie wasn't blue, she was gray. Apparently, everyone said the same thing.

Ollie yipped and nodded her head once, which I took to mean she wanted to live with me. Look at me, I've been a dog owner for barely an hour, and I already understood dog language.

I grinned at Ollie and then headed to the local pet store, which as it turned out, is also the local feed store. Since Westcott was a Western town with lots of horses and a variety of cattle, and it hosted many rodeos during the year, we had a very large feed store. When I pulled into the parking lot, it reminded me of an old-timey general store. The front was covered in actual wood siding, not the fake stuff. I couldn't believe they had hitching posts all along the front, as though cowboys rode their horses to the store, instead of driving their one-ton trucks into town to shop.

"Alright, Ollie, let's go in and see what kind of stuff you'll need for your new home." Several hundred dollars later, and two shopping carts full of stuff, we were ready for Ollie's new beginning.

And mine, too.

I was even able to get a cute little dog-bone shaped name tag made while we waited. It was engraved with Ollie's name and my cell number, in case she was ever lost. I also picked up a nice little dog collar with rhinestone cactus all around. The matching leash had the cactus print, but no rhinestones. I felt having rhinestones on the leash itself was overkill. Plus, it was an extra forty dollars. I wasn't going to be in the poorhouse, but I did need to be careful.

The store had so many cute outfits, toys, and necessary items for dogs and their loving owners, that if I wasn't careful, I would be in the poorhouse.

The one thing I did not buy, that we still needed, was a dog bed. I remembered seeing a couple in the local Costco. And since I was going to need two of them, one for home and one for the store, I figured we'd head over there the next day. The ones in the feed store started out at one hundred dollars each. I hoped I could get two for less than the price of one.

If anyone thought I was going to leave little Ollie at home all day long, they had another thing coming. I knew shop cats were a big thing in bookstores, but I'd heard that shop dogs were becoming more popular. And since we lived in a town that had a thing for animals of all sorts, I figured no one would mind in the least bit if Ollie joined me at work. She could make a good watchdog, too.

Everyone knew that dogs were the best judge of characters. If Ollie didn't like someone, I figured she'd tell me.

"Okay, Ollie. I think tonight I'll just make you a little bed using some blankets. And tomorrow you can help me to choose the bed you like best."

Using her nose, she moved my arm so she could get into my lap.

"Interesting. Did you want to drive, too?" I looked down at the little gray dog in my lap and grinned when she put a paw on my steering wheel. "Okay, girl. Let's head home."

Chapter 11

No one ever talks about how dogs wake their owners up in the middle of the night to go outside and do their business. I wished that someone would have said something to me about that. I'd have to see about getting a doggie door so Ollie could take herself out at night.

Thankfully, I did have a fenced-in backyard. So, she should be safe enough for just a potty break.

As long as coyotes weren't apt to come this far into town. Not that I was far from the wilds of the Arizona high desert, but my aunt's house was more central to the small town, which meant that I was only a few blocks from the shop. On a nice day it was a good walk. Which meant that a coyote would have to travel pretty far to get into my yard and attack little Ollie.

Hmm, maybe I should ask the vet about that next time I see them. Or a neighbor?

Jade had a family of Gila Monsters who liked to hang out at her house. While she was several blocks from my place, she was closer to the desert than I was. The bite from a Gila Monster could kill a small dog.

But her need to go outside several times last night meant I was going to need extra strong coffee if I was going to finish putting the final touches on the store before opening day next week. Today was Friday, and I only had a few days left to prepare for the grand re-opening on Wednesday.

Which reminded me.

I pulled out my cell phone and ran through my local contacts. I grinned when I saw the name I was looking for. "Cassidy? Hi, this is Maisy. How'd you like to get some extra hours this weekend?"

"Maisy, yes. That would be great. Thank you." The enthusiastic acceptance of extra hours told me I'd done the right thing.

Since I had so many other people I needed to speak to now, having Cassidy help me to get the store ready for the big sale on Wednesday was the best thing I could have done. And with that to-do item done, I took my dog and we headed to Seven Savory Seas for breakfast.

I wasn't sure if dogs were allowed in there, but better to ask for forgiveness then permission. At least, that was what my mom usually said. But not until after I was all grown and out of her house. I grinned thinking about my mom. I'd have to call her later and tell her all about her new grandbaby. Because make no bones about it, Ollie was my new little baby.

And I wasn't the only one to call her that.

I opened up the door to my favorite local coffee shop and when Ollie pranced inside, most of the store grinned.

"Maisy, when did you get a dog?" Gavin asked as he dried his hands on a kitchen towel.

"Last night. I rescued her from the dumpster behind my shop. Isn't she adorable?" I couldn't help the smile that crossed my face. Even though I was tired from being woken up so much, just like a new mother with a human baby, I was excited to show my little baby off to everyone.

"Come on in, we have a special menu just for dogs." Gavin pointed to a small chalkboard off to the side of the register.

"Doggy ice cream? Really?" I chuckled. While it wasn't hot out this time of year, we did have some seriously hot summers. The ice cream might be a nice treat down the road.

"Maisy, good morning." Jason's deep voice called out from behind me, sending little shivers up my spine.

I turned around and ran a hand down the front of my green and black sweater. Underneath, I had one of the bookshop tees on, but it was cold, and my arms needed the extra warmth from the cardigan. It also had nice pockets that held a couple dog treats. Yup, I was going to be that kind of dog-mom – treats in my pockets for whenever my little girl needed one, or two.

"Jason, how are you doing today?" I almost felt guilty that I hadn't really thought much about him, or the death of his grandfather, since finding Ollie. She had taken up all of my thoughts since yesterday afternoon.

"Better, thank you." He rubbed his chin and looked down. "I wanted to apologize for the other day. I'm not normally so..." he shrugged. "I was having a very bad day. Thank you for being so kind and helpful."

I put a hand on his arm. "Don't even think about it. I'm here if you want to talk. Losing Aunt Jo did a number on me, too. I know it's different, but I do understand."

He nodded. "Thank you. I might take you up on your offer." He looked down at Ollie who was sniffing his pant leg. "Who is this little beauty?"

When he knelt down, Jason began scratching between Ollie's ears. Then he moved a finger under her bedazzled collar and scratched there.

She was one shameful puppy. I decided then and there that I was going to have to teach her some manners. Who ever heard of a dog shaking her leg when a man scratched her head. Even her tongue was out to the side lolling.

"Who's a little cutie?" Jason said as he rubbed her back.

Ollie licked his face and we both laughed.

Gavin walked over and offered his hand to the puppy. Ollie sniffed it and licked it. Then from behind his waist he brought out his other hand and handed her a bone shaped biscuit. "It's peanut butter and pumpkin. The dogs around here love this flavor. The first one is free, then you gotta pay." He stood up and with his eye that wasn't covered with a pirate patch, he winked.

"Ah hah! I know what you are up to. You're just like a drug dealer, getting my baby hooked on your biscuits and then going to charge me an arm and a leg to keep her happy, right?" I may have been over exaggerating, as I had seen the price for his dog biscuits, they were only one dollar each. The pirate barista must love dogs.

"Blimey, you caught me." He slapped his hand over his heart. "I do love to get the local dogs hooked on my biscuits so that their owners always bring them by."

I chuckled. "I don't need anything extra to get me to stop in every morning. In fact, we came in for my regular order. Guess I'm going to have to change that order to include a doggy bone everyday now."

"One Walk The Plank latte and a breakfast sandwich. Coming right up." Gavin turned and headed back behind the counter where he washed his hands before he put my sandwich into the mini oven on the counter and then turned to begin making my drink. One of these days I was going to have to try one of his year-round drinks so that I could figure out what I liked before Christmas was over. However, I just loved the Christmas coffee so much, I could never bring myself to order something different.

Maybe after Christmas I'd try the Jolly Roger Mocha.

Plus, having one thing the same everyday was soothing. Moving here the way I did still had me spinning. In just a few days, I lost my aunt, dumped my boyfriend, quit my job, and moved across the country. I doubted anyone in my shoes could have done what I did and not had some ill side effects. I was sure there were those out there who would have already made the transition without any problems. Maybe if I was younger and had more family it wouldn't have hit me so hard.

Not that I'm old, mind you. But I was just about to celebrate my thirty-second birthday. Maybe that was what had me clinging to the familiar? I was no longer in my twenties, and still unmarried. Some might call me a Spinster. If I hadn't wasted so many years with he-who-shall-not-be-named, I'd probably be married with at least one kid by now. A kid who would have met Aunt Jo. One more regret to stack on the massive pile of regrets.

Hindsight keeps kicking me in my new Wranglers.

"So, you open the store this Wednesday?" Jason's question brought me out of my morose thoughts.

I turned to look at him and noticed he was looking closely at my face. And smiling. I pulled a few strands of my reddish hair and began flipping the ends through my fingers. It was a bad habit I'd picked up in high school and hadn't been able to break. I only did it when I was nervous. And for some strange reason, Jason had my stomach full of butterflies.

I had sworn off men when I discovered what my ex was up to. And really, I didn't have time right now to deal with any romance, but Jason? I sighed. "Yeah, I had to call in reinforcements to help me."

Jason blinked. "Reinforcements?"

I tilted my head to the side and smiled. "The mur...I mean with everything going on," I almost said something that I knew would make Jason uncomfortable. So, I kept it vague. "I needed a couple more hands to help me get the store into shape so I called up Cassidy Beaumont and offered her hours this weekend. Did you know that she worked part-time for Jo?"

He nodded. "Please tell me you've been able to clean up the mess my..." he cleared his throat. "My grandfather made?" The light that had been in his eyes fled at the mention of his grandfather.

I waved my hand in front of me. "That was done the same day. And as I'm sure you noticed the other day, the new window is in. All is fine. It's just that I'm making some changes to the layout of the store, and I need it all done before we open on Wednesday."

Jason rubbed his chin. "I wasn't exactly paying attention to your store when I was in there. Sorry."

"No worries." I went on to explain some of the changes I'd planned, and he nodded as though he was following me, but I noticed the glazed expression in his eyes and wrapped it up quickly. Just in time, too, since Gavin had just brought me my breakfast and coffee. "Well, I better be going. Lots to do and all."

I bit my lower lip and hesitated for a moment.

"Yes? Was there something else?" Jason bent down to pet Ollie again, and this time she licked his face just like a brazen little hussy.

"Ollie! That's rude. Don't lick other people's faces." I could feel my cheeks warming as I pulled on her leash. "Jason, I'm so sorry. I just got her last night, and it seems she needs some serious training."

He chuckled. "Don't worry about it. A dog licking my face is so much better than a cow doing it...or a bull."

"A bull? You got your face licked by a bull and lived to talk about it?" Even though I didn't know too much about bulls, I knew enough to know that you did not want your face anywhere near one.

Jason laughed and I couldn't help but smile at the sound. "Well, to be honest, it was a baby bull. He was only a few days old and I had to check something out on him. My face was right next to his and he bent his head to taste me."

I shivered. "Eww. I hope he decided that humans didn't taste good. And therefore, would never try to eat one. Especially after growing up."

"No need to worry that I've got a zombie bull, Killer would much rather gore you with his horns than eat you." Jason chuckled.

I blinked. Guess I'd be staying away from Jason's ranch. No way did I want to get anywhere near a bull that would gore me. "Right, well...see ya later." I waved to Jason and Gavin before taking Ollie and my treats off to the bookshop.

"So, Ollie, what do you think about Jason now?" I looked down as my little Frenchie yipped and then hop-stepped. "Traitor."

Chapter 12

I was beginning to think Ollie didn't like me much. An hour after I finished off my coffee, Sheriff Sam Madrid stopped by. The moment he entered my shop, Ollie only had eyes for him.

She was a bit too boy crazy if you asked me.

"Ollie, what a little cutie." Sam leaned down and scratched under her chin. "Are you going to protect your momma?"

Ollie licked his hand and nodded her head as though she totally understood what he was asking her. When she turned and looked at me, for just one moment, I thought she just might understand him.

"Sheriff, what can I do for you?" I didn't feel comfortable calling him Sam when he was dressed in his official Sheriff's uniform. The tan and green really looked good on him. So much better than the other Sheriff.

He stood up and straightened his tie. "I've officially been given the case since Sheriff Anderson is about to retire."

I nodded. It made sense the new guy would get the case. Part of me was glad, but another wasn't sure if I trusted him. Just because I knew him one summer as a kid didn't mean that I knew and felt confident in the man he'd become, no matter how handsome he was.

Sam cleared his throat. "I need to go over your statement from the night of the murder."

My head jerked back. "Really? Didn't you see the video on Facebook? I had no idea that Homer had been murdered until Sheriff Anderson picked me up and told me about it."

Sheriff Madrid held his hands up in front of him. "I am not here to accuse you of anything. I just need to hear from you what happened earlier in the day. When he was here at your shop." He arched his brow. "I heard you and the victim had an altercation."

I snorted. Very unladylike, I know, but it couldn't be helped.

Sheriff Madrid's eyes widened just a bit and his lips turned up in a half-smile.

My right hand went up and I shook my head. "Yes, but it wasn't so much of an altercation as it was Homer acting out like a spoiled brat."

The smile left the sheriff's face, and he pulled his notepad out from his breast pocket. "Tell me more."

I told him about how Homer threw dirt at the store, and me. Then he came back later and threw a brick through the front window. "I still haven't replaced all of the broken figurines, but I'm working on it."

"I understand a police report wasn't filed after the event?"

I nodded and didn't really feel the need to go over why I chose not to report Homer, even though the other sheriff had been by and seen the damage. Jason was going to pay for it all. In fact, the glazier billed Jason directly for the window, bypassing me. I couldn't complain about that. There was still the issue of finding enough replacements for the hand-blown glass figurines, but I was on the case.

Sam turned his head and looked at the window. "Nice job by the glazier. I can't even tell that it's been replaced."

His comment halted my inner musings. "Wait, you've been here in my store before?" I had heard that Sam had just moved back to town. It must have been a while since he'd been in the shop.

"I moved from the reservation to town recently. However, my old house was only about a twenty-minute drive into town. And everyone shops here." He nodded toward the stacks of books. "If Jo didn't have what someone wanted, she ordered it for them." He shrugged. "People in these here parts like to support one another. We don't need overnight shipping from a large corporation."

I'd heard that before. Small towns might buy some stuff online, but they did like their local shops. Which was good for me. "What sort of books do you like to read?" While I wanted to ensure we had stock for the genre that the new sheriff liked, learning what his favorite authors were would tell me a lot about the man.

He grinned. "Let's get back to the topic at hand. How did Verna react when she said Homer had destroyed your window and glass displays?"

I sighed. "It wasn't Verna."

The sheriff took a beat before asking, "and how do you know this? Was she with you when Homer was killed?"

"No, but there is no way Verna would have killed him. She might have been angry with him, but she's no killer." Of that I was certain.

Sam put his notepad back in his pocket. "Do you know how Homer was killed?"

I started to open my mouth, but my mind went blank. "Ah, no. No one has told me the details yet."

"Poison. The man was poisoned." The sheriff's statement sent my nerves into overdrive.

If Homer was poisoned, then did I really have an alibi for the murder? "Was it a quick acting poison?"

According to all of the mystery books I'd ever read, poison was a favorite murder weapon for women. Which meant that I could still very much be a suspect.

"Yes. The coroner confirms that the time you were home putting up your lights was about the time that someone must have given the poison to Homer. It was found in his stomach along with the remnants of a tuna salad sandwich."

I scrunched my nose. "Death by tuna salad sandwich? Sounds fishy to me."

The deep chuckle from the handsome sheriff had me thinking back over my words. "Oh, no pun intended."

Ollie yipped and I leaned down to pick her up. She licked my neck.

"Do you like tuna salad sandwiches, Ollie?" I wasn't really sure what to say. Sam had shared details about the case I'd not heard of yet. Which had me wondering, where could he have gotten the sandwich. Only one place I knew of that sold a tuna salad sandwich. Gavin was odd, but a killer?"

"I take it you know that the only place in town that is currently selling these sandwiches?" The sheriff opened his notepad once more. "Have you seen Homer and Gavin ever get into any sort of disagreement?"

"I haven't been here long enough to know who gets along with who. But I can say that Homer has upset a lot of people lately. Did you know what he was saying about my aunt?" Even though telling the sheriff about Homer and Jo's arguments, and legal battles, might make me look more like a possible killer, I also knew that he didn't think it was me. Most likely, he'd already checked my alibi and was able to rule out any possibilities of me poisoning the sandwich.

When the sheriff's shoulders slumped, I knew he had already heard. "Yes, and I've read the court filings that Homer had filed this past summer."

"Well, Jade told me that Homer has been upsetting a lot of people lately." I paused and thought about how best to say what I wanted to. Sometimes, I didn't think about my words and they came out all wrong. This was one time when thinking first was the only way to go.

"I noticed some things about Homer that might explain his behavior." I bit my lower lip. "You might want to speak with his doctor."

"What did you notice?" The tone the sheriff used was all business. His friendly demeanor was replaced with an emotionless, almost robotic voice.

"Well," I winced, "he had been cackling like a crazy old man." I held up a hand. "I know, he was old. Which got me thinking that he might have Alzheimer's or Dementia. He was acting...like someone from a movie. Totally over the top and mean."

"Thank you for your insights." He wrote a few things down in his notebook, then changed direction. "What about the fight with Verna?"

"Fight? What fight?" That day Verna had been inside the store and Homer outside when he attacked my window. And when Homer threw the dirt, I was there the entire time. She and he never got close enough to each other to touch.

Sheriff Sam raised a brow and stared me straight in the eyes. "There were multiple witnesses on the street who heard Verna yelling at Homer. Do you want to tell me your version of the events?"

Shoot. Thinking back to the day, I knew that Verna would look more likely. Especially since Homer was poisoned. With Verna's green thumb, she'd have no problems finding poisonous flora. Although Jade would be the one to see regarding venomous fauna.

"Um." I scratched the tip of my nose. When I was nervous, it usually itched. And sometimes, depending on how nervous I was, I sneezed. A lot. I felt a sneezing fit coming on so I turned back to the counter to see if I could find some tissue. Just in case.

"Well? Are you going to answer me? Or do I need to take you down to the station for a more formal statement?" When I turned back around the sheriff had his hand on his gun belt. He wasn't holding the gun, but his fingers were close enough to send a very strong message.

"Hold your horses, I'm gonna tell you about it. I just..." right then the sneezing fits started. "Achoo!" I lost count after sneeze number nine. Thankfully, I had a handful of tissues and was able to keep from sneezing all over the store.

When I finally stopped, I noticed that the sheriff had backed up a few steps, but he did have a worried look on his face. "Should I call for a paramedic? Are you alright?"

I put a hand up. "I'm fine." My voice didn't sound like me at all. Since my sinuses were now all congested, I sounded as though I was plugging my nose while trying to talk. I blew my nose a few more times before I felt as though I could talk without sounding too horrible. "Sorry, allergies." While it wasn't exactly the truth, it wasn't really a lie, either. I did seem to have an allergic reaction when it came to my nerves.

He nodded. "Alright, if you're sure. How about you finish telling me about the altercation between Verna and Homer?"

I sighed, realizing that I needed to choose my battles and this was one I wasn't about to win. Once I had told him everything I remembered, he closed his notepad. "Thank you for telling me. What you said basically corroborates what the witnesses outside said."

When he left, I felt like I had just turned Verna in. But as I thought more about it, I realized that I didn't know these women. My aunt was close friends with them most of her life, and I had known them somewhat back in the day. But now? I barely knew them from Adam. My gut may be saying Verna is innocent, but my mind wasn't quite in agreement.

I tried to think about what Verna did after leaving my store that day, but I couldn't remember if she told me. I went home and started working on decorating my house, but Verna? Was that the night she went over to Jade's? I wasn't sure what she had done that night.

"There's nothing else to do." I looked down when Ollie chuffed. "Do you agree with me? I need to just call Verna and ask her, right?"

Ollie hunkered down under a display case and whimpered when I mentioned Verna.

"Hey now, it's alright. No one here is going to hurt you." I bent down and put my hand out for her to sniff. While I hadn't bonded yet with Ollie, I hoped she did see me as a safe person. Once she took a big sniff, she licked my fingers and then scootched out from under the shelves. "There's my big girl." I leaned down and picked her up. I scratched behind her ears and held her tight to my chest.

Ollie looked up at me with her big black eyes and before I could move, she had stuck her tongue right through my open mouth.

"Blagh." I wiped my mouth and chuckled. "Hey now, I'm not that sort of girl. No kissing without at least several dates and one nice dinner." I lifted my chin and used the arm holding her to me to move her down enough that she wouldn't be able to French kiss me again.

I was about to put Ollie back on the ground and pull my phone out to call Verna when I heard the bell above the door ding. I was very glad for that piece of old school tech. It wasn't like it was going to run out of batteries and stop working at the most inopportune time.

"Verna? Where have you been?" I set Ollie back on the ground and put my hands on my hips.

Chapter 13

"Maisy, what did the fuzz want? Is he trying to pin this on me?" Verna looked back over her shoulder and moved away from the front of the store. It was as though she was trying to hide her whereabouts.

"Verna, are you alright? I've been worried about you." I stepped toward her, but Ollie began growling and stood next to my feet.

"Ollie, it's alright. This is Verna, she's a friend." I leaned down and picked up the small dog and tried to get her to sniff Verna, but she bared her teeth instead. "That's enough of that." I looked up and grimaced. "I'm sorry. I just rescued Ollie last night from the dumpster and she's probably still a bit gun-shy."

Verna stood taller and looked down her nose at Ollie. "Don't worry, dear. Dogs generally don't like me. Probably because I smell like cactus all of the time."

A small giggle escaped my mouth and it turned into a chuckle. "You smell like cactus?"

She crossed her arms over her chest and nodded. "Yes, since I spend most of my time in a cactus garden, I usually have something from the cactus on me. A lot of the time, there's an errant needle, or two, and that probably turns dogs off. And cats too. The needles prick when a dog sniffs."

I could understand why the scent of sand and cactus might not appeal to animals. So I chalked up Ollie's dislike of Verna to that and moved on.

"Is that where you've been all day-your cactus garden?" I knew that Verna had her own garden, but there were several plots around town that she managed and worked hard on keeping in good shape, especially during the hot and dry summers.

"Not mine, but yes, I was gardening all day. It soothes my mind. Speaking of, what was the fuzz doing here?" Verna narrowed her eyes just a bit, but it was enough to signal to me that she might not trust me at this point in time.

"Sheriff Madrid..." I eyed her warily. I wasn't accustomed to jargon like *the fuzz*. It reminded me more of a Laurel & Hardy act than a real cop. "He just wanted to go over my statement from the day of the murder, when Homer had been in here." I turned to look at the mostly empty table that should be stuffed full of beautiful green and clear cactus figurines.

"What did you say?" Did Verna's lower lip quiver? Or was it my imagination?

"Nothing that he didn't already know." I tilted my head and took in my aunt's best friend. "Is there something you need to tell me?"

She shook her head. "No, that fool man got himself into trouble on many fronts. I'm just surprised it took so long for anyone to take him out."

The response was a bit cold, but the look in Verna's eyes told me she really didn't feel that coldly about Homer's death. The lack of shine in her eyes told me she wasn't crying over his death, but the way her mouth turned down and her eyes seemed vacant had me a bit worried. I put a hand on her shoulder. "Are you alright?"

She moved out of my reach and sniffed. "I'm fine. Just allergies." Verna paused for a moment and then looked out the front window. "You know, I've known Homer and Jo since I was a little girl. We all met on the playground as little tikes. I think I was only four or five when I first met Jo. And it wasn't too much longer before I met Homer. We all grew up together." She shook her head.

"Two people you've known for almost seventy years die within just a few weeks of each other. That can't be easy, no matter how you felt about Homer." While I knew that Verna and Homer were no longer friends, they had known each other their entire lives. Or at least as long as they could remember. Something like this had to be difficult. It probably made her wonder how long before she died.

A person's mortality could bring them down, but so could something else. I bit my lower lip and wondered if she knew something about Homer's death. "Verna, do you know something about Homer you haven't told anyone else about?"

She pursed her lips and the lines around her eyes deepened and tightened.

I held my hand up in surrender. "Verna, I don't believe for one second that you did. But I do get the feeling that you're keeping something back. If you know something, you should tell the sheriff."

"Hmph. Like that young man knows how to investigate anything." She turned to look at me and her former vacant eyes now held anger, and maybe even a little bit of fire. "He actually thought I had something to do with Homer's death. Said I might have gotten a bit angry at the poor fool with the way he was acting up."

"A lot of people were angry with Homer, but not many would commit murder." I paused and thought about it. I really didn't have any suspects. Although, I wasn't investigating the case so I shouldn't have any suspects. "Do you know of anyone who might have it in them to do this? Poison is usually a woman's tool for murder."

"But it was in a tuna salad sandwich which suggests Gavin might have done it." Verna shook her head. "But I don't see that man killing a fly. He's a big old softy, not a killer."

"Could it be someone who works for him? Who made the sandwich that Homer ate? I think that's what the sheriff needs to be asking." And I would be asking the sheriff the next time I saw him. But for now, I needed to get moving. I looked around for Ollie but couldn't find her. "Ollie!" I called out.

"Who's Ollie?" Verna asked.

"My dog." I didn't bother looking near Verna, Ollie made it clear she didn't like the cactus lady. And it was too soon for me to know her favorite places. But since she had been on the streets for a while, if her dirty fur was any indication, she was probably looking for food. I had made a big deal of showing her the break room upstairs where I kept her doggy dishes with food and water. "She's probably upstairs eating."

"Hm, that dog needs a lot of food. She's too skinny. Where did you get her from?" Verna started looking around the bookcases and she even leaned over and looked under a few tables.

"I found her injured and starving out back. I think someone dumped her off, or she ran away. Either way, no one has put out a missing dog report for her, and she didn't have tags or an ID chip. So she's mine now." I knew it was still possible someone would come forward claiming her, but unless they could prove it, she was mine. I hurried upstairs to see if she was up there and sighed. She had fallen asleep on the pile of blankets I'd put down for her. I still needed to head to the big box store to get her two doggy beds.

"Ollie, sweety, we gotta go now." I hoped she wouldn't be upset about me waking her up. I needn't have worried. The little girl jumped up and her backside moved from side to side and her eyes were bright with excitement. I chuckled. "Do you like car rides?" The dog barked. "Who's a good girl?" She sat right at my feet and looked directly at me, just waiting to see what we were going to do.

I scratched the top of her head and her eyes closed halfway and her tongue lolled out the side and I could tell she was very happy. But so was I. "Come on, girl. We're gonna go bye-bye."

When we got back downstairs, Verna had already left. "Well, shoot. I was hoping you'd have a chance to get to know Verna better and like her. She really is a nice lady." I walked behind the counter and picked up the leash. I knew better than to let Ollie outside of the store without a leash. She'd lived on the streets long enough that I worried I might lose her, and I didn't want that. Once I had her trained, and she knew how to get home and back to the store, I might try letting her run around outside without a leash. Maybe.

I looked around and couldn't find my dog again. The little scamp seemed to enjoy exploring the store. "Ollie. Where are you girl?" I pulled a treat out of my coat pocket and held it up. "I have a treat for you." I stood still in the middle of the store, but she didn't come running.

I looked around, and when I heard scratching, I headed in the direction of the sound.

Chapter 14

Behind the check-out counter was a small room with a door that locked. Jo used to use it to keep some of the books that people ordered from her, until they came to pick them up. In it was a small desk, chair, lamp, and a few shelves. The room couldn't have been bigger than six feet by six feet. Larger than a broom closet, but smaller than a bedroom.

Since we weren't open yet, I'd been keeping the door open. I put the boxes of books and trinkets I'd ordered in there when I wasn't in the middle of putting them out on the sales floor. Before I opened up, they would go back upstairs. I knew that cats liked to play in empty boxes, but I didn't think that was a dog thing.

In addition to the books and other items I sold, I had several boxes that needed to be cut down before taking them to the recycling bin in the back alley. That was where I'd found Ollie originally, near the recycling bin. Maybe she felt comfortable near cardboard? "Ollie?"

I heard more scratching; this time it was louder and more insistent. When I stepped inside, I couldn't see the dog, but I could hear her.

She was in here, somewhere. When I didn't see her anywhere, I got down on my hands and knees and looked under the desk, it was the only place left, besides behind a shelf. "Ollie? What are you doing back there?"

In the space under the desk, Ollie had scooched to the back, next to the old brick wall. At one time, this had been a brick building. Part of the brick inside had been covered with sheets of drywall. But this wall had been left alone.

The dog was scratching at what appeared to be a loose brick, if the cement shavings next to the dog were any indication. "What do you have there?"

Ollied turned her head and grinned at me. That was the only way I could describe her look. Her eyes were wide, her tongue hung out the side of her mouth and she was panting. A light chuff came from her, and she moved away so I could get back there better.

It took a moment, but I was able to dislodge the old brick. However, I couldn't see what was in the void behind the brick. I pulled my phone out of my jacket pocket and turned on the flashlight.

I inhaled when I saw what was inside, then had a coughing fit that lasted a few minutes. I backed out of the space and got up, then took off my coat, as I could feel perspiration dripping down my face and even down my back. "Eww."

Thankful that I'd worn a simple, long sleeve cotton henley, I wiped my brow with my sleeve and looked around for a proper flashlight - and picked up a bottle of water. After downing a few long gulps, I got back down on the floor with the flashlight and scooted back to the opening.

Another brick was loose, so I pulled that one out, as well. Behind the two bricks was a secret storage area. It was small, only big enough to hold a few books. And there were two books inside. One was wrapped in what I guessed was an acid free clear plastic bag – the kind used to store rare or valuable books.

And underneath that one, was an old leather-bound journal. I knew that because the word *Journal* was stenciled on the cover. The edges were frayed, and parts of the cover showed signs of wear and tear. But it didn't appear to be so old it might be valuable, only well loved.

I pulled myself out of the small space from under the desk, after putting the bricks back in place and cleaning up the cement dust.

From behind, Ollie barked, and I popped up too soon and hit the back of my head on the underside of the desk drawer. "Ouch." I rubbed the back of my head and lowered it a smidge before scooting back more.

When I stood up, everything wobbled, including myself. Thankful that I didn't fall, I sat down in the desk chair and rubbed the back of my head again.

Ollie was near my feet, wiggling her tail and grinning at me. I looked at her and she barked.

"Okay, yes. You did very well, Ollie. Thank you for finding that hiding place." I reached for my jacket and pulled out a small dog biscuit. Ollied put her front paws on my leg and panted.

"You are such a little beggar, aren't you?" I patted her head, then motioned for her to get down with my empty hand.

She ignored me. Her eyes were focused on the treat in my other hand.

Sensing that the only way to get her to learn was to use the biscuit, I motioned with it for her to get down. "Down." I commanded in my most forceful voice I could muster for the cutest little dog in the world.

She obeyed. "Good girl." I gave her the treat and she laid down on the ground with the bone between her front paws as she bit off large bites and chewed it down, quickly.

While Ollie was busy licking her chops, because let's get real, she finished the bone so quickly I didn't even have time to get up and start moving. I finally stood up and picked up the books. I was hesitant to open the plastic bag, so I put that book on the top of my desk. Then I took the journal and opened it to the first page.

The writing had me smiling. It was Great-Aunt Jo's writing; I'd know it anywhere. People today didn't have the sort of penmanship woman of Jo's generation did. Her sloping handwriting was reminiscent of what one might expect from a handwritten invitation back in the eighteen hundreds.

"This is the journal of Jo Barton. Please return to the Saguaro Bookstore if you find it."

She didn't even demand that the person looking at it not read it. I would have written that down if I kept a paper journal. I wasn't big at journaling, but I did have an app on my phone that I used once in a while. Sometimes technology was helpful.

However, if Jo had used an app, I wouldn't have this slice of her memories to keep around. Maybe I should think about printing my journals out once they were big enough to fill a book.

I shelved that idea for a later date. At this point in time, I needed to decide if I should read Jo's journal, or store it for safekeeping without reading it, yet.

I wasn't the sort to read biographies, or memoirs, but I knew that a lot of people did enjoy reading them if the content was engaging, or exciting. Presidents always published a book when they left office. I'd purchased a few of them, but the only one I actually read was President Regan's. He was a bit before my time, but his autobiography had been required reading in my high school civic course. Probably because he was the most loved President of the past hundred years.

Normally, I wouldn't read someone else's journal, unless they'd been dead a long time, and I knew that it would contain something exciting. But this was my Great-Aunt Jo's journal. Even if it wasn't exciting, it might help me feel closer to the woman I missed so much. "What the heck, why not." I opened the journal and skimmed a few pages before I realized it was more of a journal than a diary.

Jo wrote down important family events, store happenings, and even some property sales. My great-aunt was a real estate mogul. I wondered how many of these properties were still a part of her portfolio. And was I now the owner of all of this?

When Jo's will had been read, I wasn't really listening. Once the attorney told me that I had inherited most of her estate, I went numb. Inheriting the bookstore wasn't surprising, and even the house could have been expected, but everything? When it was all over, my mother told me I needed to read the details in the will. She had noticed that I'd tuned out.

My mom reiterated a few important things, like what she received, and the fact that I couldn't sell anything right away. The other big item was that Jo wanted me to live in her house and keep running the bookshop. She'd understand if I discovered after a couple of years that it wasn't for me, but she wanted me to try. Mom and I both agreed that it was the right thing to do.

I even wanted it.

But I'd never gotten around to reading the will in order to discover exactly what I owned. Getting the bookshop back up and running had taken all of my energy. I figured I'd find out soon enough, when the judge approved the will and everything changed over to my name.

Plus, things like Family Trust, and Corporate Holdings, had my mind swirling. There was time for me to sort it all out later. Like after the new year.

When Ollie patted my leg with one of her paws, I looked up and realized that the sun was setting already. "Yikes. Sorry, I was really engrossed in what Jo had written down. Did you know that she had met quite a few celebrities? She even had some major authors, like Stephen King and John Grisham, sign books here in her store."

Ollie tilted her head to the side and her eyes narrowed just enough to signal that she didn't believe me. "Of course, it was very early in their careers. Before they became household names."

The dog's head nodded in understanding, then she began licking her chops.

"Are you hungry?" I needn't have asked. This dog had no issues eating whenever I put any food down for her.

She barked once, then turned and headed out of the tiny office.

I put the two books back in the hole under the desk, deciding that there had to be something very important in them to hide them. I could pull them back out later and read more. I noticed the book in the plastic bag was another journal, but on the cover, it was embossed in gold that had almost completely flaked off – Yavapai County Property Records 1850 – 1899.

"What was Jo doing with official county property records from the years when this region was settled?" That was a mystery for another day.

Once we had locked up the store and set the alarm, I headed out to the car. Ollie and I had plans for more shopping and dinner. I'd heard that some of the fast-food burger joints made puppy patties that were good for dogs. I'd bet my little Ollie would love a burger. I knew I would.

But before we could get into the car, Jason walked up. "Jason, how are you doing?"

He looked between me and Ollie. "I was just coming to visit you. Are you and this precious puppy heading out already?"

"Yes, we need to go to Costco for a doggy bed and then I was thinking about hitting up the burger joint in the parking lot for dinner. Wanna join us?" Since Jason lost his grandfather, he'd been all alone in town. Well, he had help on his ranch, but those guys were employees, not family. Or even friends as far as I could tell. In fact, I'd not seen Jason with anyone else in the past week.

"Are you sure I wouldn't be an inconvenience?" While he looked like he was doing fine, he did seem a bit unsure of himself. Which was odd considering how he'd always come off as someone who was confident in himself.

"Of course, you're welcome to join us. In fact, I insist. And dinner will be my treat."

"Alright, how about I drive? Your small car might not fit us all and a trip to Costco." He chuckled. And he was right. I was going to need to get a bigger car. The small subcompact I drove across the country was great on gas mileage, but not so great with carrying a lot of stuff.

"Sounds good to me." I looked to Ollie who chuffed her agreement, too.

Chapter 15

"Wow, it's been forever since I spent Christmas here in Westcott. Is it all still the same? Big tree in the center of town, all of the businesses going crazy with decorations, and sales?" I was sitting in the passenger seat of Jason's Ford F150 on our way to the local Costco, but when I say local, I mean like a thirty-minute drive to get there on the open road. Our little town of Westcott is too small for a Costco or Sam's Club of its own.

Jason chuckled. "You know, I've only been back for just over a year."

"Really? I knew you moved away, but for some reason I thought you had come back a few years ago. Did you just buy the ranch from your grandfather last year?" I turned a little in my seat to see him better.

He nodded. "Yeah." Jason cleared his throat. "Grandpops needed help on the ranch, and it was always planned that I'd take over one day. It just happened earlier than I expected." He ran a hand down his face and sighed.

"I'm sorry. I shouldn't have brought up your grandfather." I bit my lip. "But how have you enjoyed the ranch? You said you always expected to come back, were you glad to do it now?" What I wanted to ask was if he left a girlfriend behind, or had plans to bring her out here any time soon. But, that wasn't exactly the right thing to ask at this point. I didn't want him getting the wrong idea.

While I did find Jason very attractive, I needed to stay focused on my business and getting it all figured out. Then I needed to get through the Christmas season rush and the new year. Maybe by Spring I could think about dating.

"You know, I really do love it in Westcott. I was tired of life in a big city. You know I lived in New York, right?" He turned his head and waited for my reply.

I nodded, then frowned when I watched him take his right hand off the steering wheel and put it on the arm rest between us. His left hand moved to the top of the steering wheel and it was all he used to guide the giant truck. The road to Costco wasn't difficult, but it was only a two-lane highway once we were out of town. The road was one of those narrow winding kinds that always had crosses at the side of the road because of traffic accidents. If I were driving, I would have kept both of my hands on the steering wheel. It would be at least another ten minutes of winding roads before we were on a straight path to Sun City West, and a safer road.

"I had heard something about that. I've always wanted to live in the Big Apple, but only for like a year or two. Guess that won't be happening any time soon." I nervously chuckled as I kept my eyes peeled for any oncoming traffic that could pose a problem.

"It's not all it's cracked up to be, but living there for a year would probably be nice. A good way to see the best parts and walk away with fond memories."

His statement made it sound like something bad happened in New York. "How long were you there?"

"Just over five years - about three years too long." He chuckled and shook his head. "It's really not that bad, I just had...well...I was going to get married, and she cheated on me with one of my friends. Or should I say ex-friend."

"Yeah, I hear ya on that. Today it seems cheating is a normal part of life in big cities. Although, I bet it happens everywhere." My ex had cheated on me, and we lived in a beach community in Florida. Certainly not the same as New York, but bigger than Westcott.

Jason sighed and rubbed his right hand down his jeans-clad leg. "Yeah, I guess it's the same everywhere. But in small towns, it's really difficult to hide the fact that someone is cheating. Everyone here knows your business."

I couldn't help it, but I laughed. Like really loudly. At least I didn't snort laugh. That would have been embarrassing. "Too true." I was thinking about the post on Facebook the other night showcasing my ability to put up Christmas lights. Or was it my inability? Either way, the entire town knew what I was doing that night. Although, it turned out to be a blessing in disguise. Since no one could think I had a chance to kill poor Homer.

Every time I mentioned his grandfather, or the night he was murdered, Jason tensed up, which made me feel that it was going to take Jason a while to get over this loss.

I needed to change the topic, so I thought of next week. "So, what will you do for Thanksgiving? Living on a ranch, do you hunt and shoot your own turkey?" I had heard stories of people shooting wild turkeys, and some even shot wild boar, but I wasn't too sure about that. At least, not in Westcott, Arizona. The wild boar here seemed like they'd be rather tough, and not tender and juicy.

He chuckled. "Wild turkeys have a distinctive flavor. Some might call it gamey. But I have shot my fair share of wild turkeys here in Arizona."

"Does that mean you've got plans to hunt for your Thanksgiving turkey? Will your ranch hands celebrate the day with you?" I wasn't sure how it worked on a ranch. I knew that no matter the day, animals needed to be fed and cared for, but other ranch duties could wait a day.

It took him a minute, but he finally answered my question. "My ranch hands all have the day off since they have family in the area that they'll stay with. I don't think I'll be messing with a big dinner. I was thinking about ordering a nice juicy steak from the tavern and just watching football with all of the guys in the tavern."

I knew that the local tavern made some seriously good meals, I'd already decided that I was going to frequent them on Fridays for their fish-Friday menu. They had a wonderful Beer-battered Cod with fries. And they were only a block away from the bookstore, so it would be easy to order for pick-up – especially when I was manning the store all alone. "I love their steak, but for Thanksgiving? Why don't you join us for Thanksgiving dinner? There is going to be so much food that day. Not to mention all of the people who will be at Ada and Tony's house."

"Thanks, but I don't want to impose. The tavern will be just fine." Jason's voice sounded so bland.

I didn't get the impression he wanted me to pressure him into coming, but I also didn't think he was excited about Thanksgiving dinner at the bar. That was something he could do all weekend, and still catch football games. The nurturer in me took over. "Please, do join us. I think you'll have a good time. And if I remember correctly, Jade makes the best sausage stuffing I've ever had. You can't pass that up." I grinned when I noticed him licking his lips.

"You know, Miss Jade's sausage stuffing is legendary. If you're sure they won't mind me coming without an invite, I'd like that." A small smile turned up in the corner of his lips.

I grinned and knew that I'd made the right choice in inviting him to have Thanksgiving dinner with us all. And Aunt Jo would have been proud. She always said that no one should have to eat alone on a holiday. Her empty chair philosophy was known all over town.

After that, it was a quick trip to Costco. Where I did find two dog beds that Ollie loved. I also picked up a few cases of paper goods and food that would last me a very long time. When we were done, I offered to buy Jason a hot dog and soda as my way of thanking him.

Yes, I am a big spender...

Ollie got a hot dog, without the bun or soda, and she was very content and slept for most of the way back to Westcott.

I did have one more question for Jason that I knew was going to be tough, so I waited until I had unloaded all of my stuff and he was about to leave. "Um," I bit the inside of my bottom lip wondering how to ask this question. "When will the, ah, funeral be?" I scratched the back of my head as I looked down at my feet.

"The rest of the family won't be in town until the weekend after Thanksgiving, so we are going to hold it then. I'll put the word out soon with the details. I know a lot of people will want to come, even though my grandpops had ruffled some feathers lately." Jason was standing next to his truck and had one hand on the driver's side door.

"One of the nice things about a small town is how they all rally around each other in times of need. It doesn't matter what Homer did before, everyone is going to be there for you. And that includes me." I put a hand on his arm. "If you ever want to talk, just let me know. I'll be here for you." And I meant it, too. Having a friend to talk to really helps the grieving process.

Even though Verna, Jade, and Ada were Jo's friends, they had been very helpful to me over the past couple of weeks. My mom and I still spoke several times a week and I even kept in touch with my bestie back in Florida, Tina Mason. At first, we spoke daily on the phone. Now it's down to two to three times a week.

I had no clue who Jason had to talk with about all of this. And the fact that not one person from his family would be in town for at least another week, spoke volumes about their lack of closeness.

Church on Sunday was interesting. Homer's death was all anyone could talk about before and after services. But what caught my attention was someone I hadn't noticed before at church.

"Lucy, hi there. I didn't know you attended church here." I waved to the Veterinarian Technician who helped me with Ollie last week. The woman was short, probably barely five feet three or four inches. She had short brown hair with vibrant blue eyes that always sparkled. This was one happy woman. But really, who could blame her? She got to work with animals all day long.

"Maisy, how ya doing? How's little Ollie?" Lucy put out a hand and I shook it.

"Ollie is wonderful, but I think she's a bit boy crazy." I laughed and Lucy joined me.

"Let me guess, she loves to give her attention to the men in your life?" Lucy hit the nail right on the head.

I put my thumbs through the belt hoops on my new jeans I picked up only the day before, along with my new cowgirl boots. I had debated between the red boots and the brown ones, then decided I could wear the brown boots with just about everything. So I went with them. And today I was glad I did. Wearing jeans, an emerald green blouse, and my brown boots were perfect for church. Most everyone else was in either denim jeans or denim skirts and boots.

"That she does. At first, I wondered if she even liked me, but I think she does. Even though she gets very excited when men give her attention." I was thinking about how she reacted to both Jason and Sam. Ollie had good taste.

Lucy chuckled. "Well, maybe she'll help you pick out the right cowboy."

I held up my hands and waved. "No, I can't. Nope. Not right now. There's too much going on to even think about dating."

Her eyes wandered around the group standing around outside. When her gaze landed on someone behind me, she smiled and waved. I turned around to see who she was waving over and had to blink away the light shining off of Sheriff Madrid's shiny badge. He must have been on duty because he was decked out in his sheriff's green and tan uniform. But for today, it was nicely pressed and his boots were shined up like he was about to submit to an inspection.

"Sheriff, nice to see you." I smiled when he stopped next to us.

"Lucy, Maisy, good to see you both." He took his brown cowboy hat off and held it in his hands.

I wasn't sure if I just hadn't been paying attention to who attended this church these days, or if new people were trying it out today, but I knew I hadn't seen Sam Madrid at this church before.

"Sam, I'm so glad you came. I told you we had a good preacher, didn't I?" Lucy beamed up at the sheriff and it dawned on me – they had a thing going. Or at least Lucy was trying to get something going with the sheriff.

Part of me was happy for them, and a teeny tiny part was sad for me. Not that I had room for a boyfriend or anything, and there was Jason. But, I guess I had thought I might want to get to know Sam better before I set my sights on Jason, or anyone else for that matter.

This new development was better. It had to be. But seeing Lucy next to Sam, I wasn't sure they made a good couple. He was so tall, about a foot taller than her. Although, they wouldn't be the first couple to have such a height difference. Besides, I wasn't much taller than Lucy, maybe two inches.

They had been chatting and I wasn't really listening, so when Sam called my name, I had to ask him to repeat his question.

"I wanted to know if you wanted to join me and Lucy for lunch at Cactus Joe's today?" Sam smiled and looked like he really did want me to join them.

I sucked in my lips before I could say yes. "I already have lunch plans. In fact, every Sunday I'm having lunch with my Aunt's friends over at Cactus Joe's. They have a standing order and reservation for the back corner booth." I shrugged. "So, I guess I'll see you both there if you sit near us."

While Lucy's eyes were still bright, she did seem like she wanted me to go with them. Maybe this was really new for them and they wanted a third wheel, or a wingman, to help them along. I wondered for a moment if I shouldn't invite them to join us, but decided against it. They needed to spend this time together to see if they could make it work. They were adults and didn't need my help, or anyone else's.

The sheriff put his hat back on and tipped his hat in my direction. "See ya around, Maisy." He put his elbow out and Lucy took it. But before they walked away, she looked back over her shoulder and grinned at me.

Verna walked up next to me. "Ready to head out?"

"Yup, I'm starved and looking forward to pot roast and all the fixings." While I wouldn't eat so much every Sunday, I had been crazy busy this weekend with getting the last minute stuff done that needed it. I had two days left after today to put the finishing touches on Aunt Jo's store before opening up on Wednesday. And I needed the energy.

When we arrived, Sam and Lucy had been seated near enough to our booth that I intentionally chose a seat with my back to them. Had I not done that, I'd be focused on their date and not on my friends. This time each week was for us to all get to know one another better and share Aunt Jo stories. That was what I wanted more than anything, to learn more about my wonderful great-aunt.

"You know, it feels like Jo is here with us." I put a hand to my heart and felt tears prick behind my eyes. When would I stop tearing up every time I thought about her?

Ada put her hand on mine that was still on the table. "Dear, I know she would be so proud of what you've done so far. I know we all are. And we are here for you, think of us as your aunties."

"And uncle," Tony Hopkins chimed in with a grin.

I felt my genuine smile from ear to ear. "Thank you all so much. I don't know how I'd get through this without you. I just wish I'd have come back home more to visit than I did." My smile faded and my guilt began to creep back in.

"Now don't you go doing that. Jo wouldn't want you to feel guilty." How Verna knew exactly what I was feeling, I'd never know. But that woman had some seriously great instincts.

Jade smiled at me from across the table. "Jo never once said anything negative about you. She was so proud of the young woman you've become. And we have been here for her, so you see, she was never really alone. Just like you're never going to be alone, either. You are part of our family."

Sometimes, found-family bonds were stronger than blood-family bonds. And that was when Jason entered my thoughts. I hadn't said anything about him coming to Thanksgiving dinner yet, so I decided now was the time to inform them. "I hope you have enough food on Thursday for one more person." I grinned, showing my teeth and hoping that no one would be upset.

Ada looked up from her plate. "Who did you want to invite?"

I bit my lip. "I hope it's alright, but I kinda already invited Jason." I hunched over and prepared for someone, most likely Verna, to shoot down my idea.

"I think that's a right nice thing. He doesn't have any family out here." Ada smiled and nodded her head.

"I think it's a great idea. I'd like to get to know Jason better myself." Tony chimed in.

When Jade piped up, I sat up straighter. "You know, I heard his family isn't coming to town until after Thanksgiving. Like a week after." She shook her head.

Verna harrumphed. "Well, the Kimballs haven't been my favorite family in quite some time, but if Jo were here, she'd say the empty chair was saved just for Jason.'"

I knew right then and there that this was my kind of family.

Chapter 16

M onday flew by in a blur.

Tuesday was my last day before I opened the store and by lunchtime, I felt that I had it all in hand. I prayed. The last of the replacement glass-blown figurines had arrived that morning and I had moved a few around so that they weren't all on the same table.

I stood back and looked at the assortment of cactus, western themed items such as boots and horses, and grinned. "There, that should do it." The original table still held a large assortment, but on a few other tables and bookshelves I had placed in strategic locations, some of the duplicates. One piece was a black blown glass cowboy hat with a real leather band around it. I loved that it also held a small red feather in the band. This piece I had placed next to the Harry Potter bookends.

While I didn't have a sorting hat, I thought the cowboy hat was a nice local addition. I hoped shoppers would agree.

"Ollie?" I called out as I took one last look around the shop. While I'd been preparing the shop, I let Ollie have the run of the place.

But come Wednesday morning, she'd have to be kept upstairs in the makeshift break room. Not only for her safety, but for the safety of the shoppers. Until Ollie was used to being a sedate shop dog, she'd have to stay upstairs while we had lots of people in the store.

I only hoped I'd find the time to take her out for potty breaks before she was in urgent need of them.

A knock sounded on the front door. After all of the people coming in last week, I had decided it was necessary to keep the front door locked while I was working. Too many interruptions would have put me behind schedule. Even with Cassidy here all day Saturday and Monday night to help.

I patted my leg and Ollie joined me at the door. I could see who it was the moment I walked toward the door, and I grinned. Ollied did a little wiggle dance as we opened the front door. "Jason, how nice to see you. Come on in."

"Maisy," he bent down and smiled at my dog. "Ollie, hey there little cutie. Are you a working dog?"

I'd heard the term before, a "working dog" was one on a ranch that helped the ranchers to move cattle. But I'd never heard a "shop dog" called that before. "She's actually a shop dog. I don't think real working dogs would appreciate being put in the same context as a dog like Ollie." I chuckled. "And I don't think Ollie would be able to keep up with your shepherds."

Jason stood up smiling. "We have several breeds of dogs who help. Australian Shepherds are really great at herding. But I've also found the Boxer/Pitbull mixes are quite good, too. Once they get some of their energy out."

"I bet the Boxer-Pits are territorial, too." While I'd never had a dog, I knew plenty of people who did. And I remembered quite fondly one Boxer/Pitbull, that was a brindle with white paws. He was very territorial and quite protective of his family.

"That they are. But, I'm not here to talk about dogs." Jason said.

Ollie chuffed.

"Sorry, Ollie. I'm always happy to talk about you." Jason bent back down and scratched under her chin. He had that dog wrapped around his little finger.

I folded my hands in front of my stomach. "Then to what do I owe the pleasure of your company?"

Jason stood up, removed his black Stetson and held it in his hands. The confident swagger was all gone and the boy of my youth stood in front of me, not quite able to look me in the eye. "I...well...I was wondering if I could take you out to dinner?"

Ollie barked.

I grinned.

"Ollie, you'd be welcome to join us, too. I was thinking about that steak dinner that we spoke about the other day. You know, the one at the Barrel Tavern? I was hoping you'd join me tonight for dinner there." His eyes darted up for a quick peek, before moving back down to the floor.

I almost jumped up and down, but then I stopped the emotions from taking over. "Jason, that is a wonderful offer. But tomorrow is the first day I'm open, and it is going to be an extremely busy day. I had planned to head home and microwave some leftovers and head to bed early. I need a good night's rest."

He looked up at me and tilted his head. "Okay, how about after this long weekend?"

I bit my lip and winced. "As a date?"

Pink tinged his cheeks and a lock of hair flipped down and covered one of his eyes. He really was a handsome man.

"Yes, I'd like to take you out on a date." He looked me in the eyes and a tiny smile emerged.

I felt myself returning his smile. "I'd like that, but I think it's too soon."

The space between his eyes crinkled, and his smile vanished. "Too soon?"

"Just last month I ended a serious relationship with a cheater. I need some time to get over what happened. And besides, I don't think you're in a place right now to start anything new, either." It almost killed my heart to admit this, as I really did want to see if we would make a good couple.

"I'm sorry, I didn't know about your ex." He said.

"Yeah, I found out the day I got the call about Jo dying. Right after I told him, his not very legal, legal assistant came over to his house. I had left, and I swear she had been waiting somewhere on the street for me to leave. Anyway," I waved a hand in the air and took a deep breath. "When I went back to get something I'd left at his house, I saw them through the front room window. They were all over each other."

My nostrils flared. "I still remember the feeling of my heart breaking and then the exclamation of the woman out walking her dog and a young child. She had put a hand over the kid's eyes and gave me a sad smile. While I didn't know her, I'd seen her in the neighborhood before. They walked quickly, practically running, past me and the spectacle." That day I cried my eyes out. However, the pain wasn't what it once was. Now I was more angry – angry at myself for not seeing it sooner.

Jason put a hand on my arm. "I'm so sorry to hear this. I knew your ex had cheated, but I didn't know you found out on the same day you heard about Jo. That's coldhearted."

"Yup, so I swore off men." I shrugged. "I'm sure one day I'll change my mind, but for now, I don't think I can trust a man. Not with my heart."

He nodded and took a step back. "I know how you feel. You're the first woman I've really wanted to date since I moved back, too. But you are right. I should let some time pass after grandpop's death before I start anything new with a woman."

"Can we be friends?" I asked. Truly hoping he'd want the same thing.

The light that shone from his eyes when he smiled, sent a warmth through my entire being.

"Yes, I'd like that." He nodded.

He put his hat back on and was about to turn around to leave, when I put my hand on his arm. "Wait a minute. How does a cup of coffee sound? I have something I'd like to show you."

His eyebrows bounced up and down. "Really? Like what?"

I playfully slapped his arm. "Nothing like that. What do you know about the ownership of Jo's estate?"

All joking left his eyes. "What do you mean?"

"Come on, let's get some coffee and take a seat." I led him back to the little coffee corner I'd set up. I motioned for him to sit down and I got to work making us some coffee.

Once we were both seated with steaming mugs of Jo in hand, I pulled the journal out of my bag I'd set at my feet.

Ollie was sitting next to Jason's feet, as she couldn't take her eyes off of him. It seemed female dogs even enjoyed some good eye candy.

I opened up the journal that I had taken to reading in bed the last couple of nights. "This is an old journal of Jo's I found the other day." Ollie barked. I looked down at my little dog who had finally given me her attention. "Okay, Ollie found it." I chuckled. "Anyways, it talks about the land ownership of her family and the Kimballs." I thumbed through until I found the spot I was looking for. "Is this what Homer had been going on about for years?"

Jason took the book and read a few pages. When he stopped, he sighed. Then he ran a ragged hand through the perfectly mussed up hair. Even after running his big hands through his hair, it all fell back in perfect place.

I rolled my eyes. Men and their perfect hair. Why was it that women took hours and hundreds of dollars to get their hair to work just right, but men never had to worry? It wasn't fair. But whoever said life was fair.

"Maisy?" Jason pulled me out of my reverie.

"Yup." I dragged my eyes from his hair to his eyes.

Jason's eyes sparkled and he grinned from ear to ear. He'd caught me checking him out. I felt my cheeks burn with embarrassment.

"These notes make it sound as though the sale was legitimate. Your great-great-uncle? I'm not really sure how you're related to Jameson Barton, but he bought the land fair and square from the Kimball's estate. If these notes are accurate." He closed the book and handed it back to me.

"Hindsight." Jason shook his head.

"Excuse me?" I asked.

"Some of what grandpops went on about is now starting to make sense." He rubbed his face. "This isn't common knowledge yet, and I'm hoping it doesn't make its way onto the gossip scene, but Sam found something else in the autopsy."

I sat back in my chair. "What do you mean?"

Jason stood up and paced around the little sitting area. When he finally sat back down, he took his coffee and finished the rest in one long gulp. "They found drugs in my grandfather's bloodwork."

"Drugs? Like he was on medication? That wouldn't surprise me." I figured the man had Dementia and since I'd seen some commercials for treatment if caught early, I would have expected there would be signs of it in his bloodwork.

Jason shook his head. "No, drugs as in illegal narcotics."

All of the air left my body and fell back against my seat. "You can't be serious."

"Deadly. I'm actually surprised he didn't die from an accidental overdose." Jason kept his gaze on Ollie, who seemed to be hugging his leg. He leaned over and began petting her back.

"What kind of drugs?" I'd heard that this region had an issue with illegal drugs. There was even a large billboard just outside of town stating "One and Done" with a picture of pills and a ghostly image of a young man. It always gave me the creeps when I saw it.

"Fentanyl."

"Like the drugs in the billboard outside of town?" I didn't know much about the drug, except that it was very deadly if not administered properly. Doctors only prescribed it in the hospital.

He nodded. "It seems my grandfather's erratic behavior was from drug abuse, not because he had Dementia. Although he was in the very early stages of it, the doctor said that other than some instability issues or forgetfulness, he didn't have any other symptoms yet. He still spoke just fine, and all of his long-term memories were spot on. It was his short-term memories, like losing keys, that he was dealing with. Normal stuff for people his age."

"So, his running around and cackling, throwing stuff at me and my shop, yelling that Jo got what she deserved, was all from drug abuse?" I shook my head. And to think I'd felt sorry for the man. "Why was he using it?"

Jason cleared his throat.

"Do you need something else to drink?" I asked, realizing that he probably wanted something stronger, like a beer. I wouldn't begrudge him some liquid fortitude right about now, but I didn't have anything like that. My father had been an alcoholic, so I'd never drank. And as far as Jo went, I doubted she drank much, either. Maybe a glass of wine on special occasions, but I couldn't remember her ever having anything more than that.

Jason held his hand up. "No, thank you." He shook his head. "Maybe some water?"

"Of course, be right back." I ran upstairs to get him a cold bottle of water from the mini fridge we kept upstairs full of drinks. As I made my way back down, the word *hindsight* hit me. It was something I'd been dealing with lately, as well. Jeff Minkow, my ex, had shown signs of cheating. I had just chosen to ignore them. Once his infidelity had been flaunted in front of me, the signs flew through my mind, reminding me of earlier fights we'd had. Times when I'd smelled perfume on him. The same perfume his assistant wore. He'd told me it was because they worked closely and spent hours together in the office. I scoffed at the memory. There were a dozen more.

Hindsight. It could be a scary word, but it could also be a saving grace. All of those little things that bugged a person for ages would all of a sudden fall into place and fit the puzzle perfectly. What someone might think is a missing piece, is actually an upside-down piece that was in the wrong place. When turned right side up, and put where it belonged, the puzzle began to take its proper shape and the picture would become clear enough to take all of those other pieces sitting to the side, and place them where they belong. The final picture might not be what we expected, but it was what it was.

How did that play into Jason's story with his grandfather? What had Jason seen, or heard, that he'd just dismissed? Did Homer try to play off his early Dementia diagnosis when the symptoms had really been drug abuse? That was cold.

"Here ya go." I handed him the water bottle. I had questions I wanted to ask but didn't feel it was my place to. If he wanted to talk about it, he would.

Jason took a long drink. "Thanks, Maisy. It does help to talk about this with a friend." He looked up. "Even though Sam used to be my friend, he's still the Sheriff. And it's all different now."

I nodded, knowing exactly what he meant. "It is, isn't it." Did this mean that the tiny romance Jason and I had shared was all different now, too? Would we be able to find a shred of that attraction we once held for each other and learn to help it grow, when we were both ready?

Chapter 17

Wednesday arrived and I thought I was prepared for it, but it turned out I wasn't. Word had gotten around about me taking over the shop and everyone in town, and out of town, came to see what I was doing with the bookstore. Thankfully, Cassidy Beaumont had agreed to work a full shift that day. She got there right before I opened the door.

"Whew, I wasn't sure if I was going to find a parking spot within a mile of the shop today." Cassidy chuckled as she removed her hat, scarf, and jacket. "Did you see the long line of people waiting outside to come in?"

"I did. And I'm shocked. I mean, we did do some social media and the local paper ran a story about us, but this." I shook my head in surprise. "Is so much more than I expected. I hope I have enough coffee and pastries."

Cassidy walked over to the folding table I had set up the night before. Today, it had two large, insulated coffee thermoses, one regular and one decaf, along with about two dozen pastries. "We could cut these treats in half and place an order with Gavin right now. I bet he could have someone deliver more if you wanted it."

I nodded. "I think that's a great idea. No wonder Jo always spoke so highly of you." I grinned when the young college girl began to blush.

She'd been working with me the past few days as much as she could, after classes were done for the day, and she was a hard worker. Even when Joey Mancuso came in to talk Christmas lighting options with me, she still managed to get her work done while chatting with Joey. They were going to make a cute couple, if Joey ever got up the nerve to ask her out.

However, I needed to focus on opening the bookstore to the curious shoppers. And I sent up a quick prayer that God would give me and Cassidy the strength to get through today.

I walked to the door, turned the closed sign to open and put a big smile on my face. The moment I turned the lock and opened the door, the first person in line pushed past me.

"It's about time. Your Aunt always opened early on the day before Thanksgiving. It's one of the best shopping days here in town, you should know this," The elderly woman in a large flowing green skirt, red Santa sweater, and Santa hat said as she stalked toward the table of glass figurines, I'd only just stocked the previous day.

"Welcome, welcome. I'm glad you all could make it today." I looked up at the sky, and while the clouds weren't too ominous, it was going to be a very cold and windy day. The forecast called for a high of forty-two degrees. And if I wasn't mistaken, we were going to get some snow over the holiday weekend. I'd deal with the cold if it meant snow on the ground, and on Siggy. The Saguaro would look so cool with bits of snow all around it and on the arms. I'd just have to be careful to ensure it didn't freeze.

I knew there was a limit to how many people were allowed to be inside at any given time, due to the local fire codes, so I explained to the line of customers that I could only have twenty inside at a time. As someone left, a new shopper could enter.

If the honor system didn't work, I'd have to have Cassidy man the door.

Once that was completed, I walked over to the gruff woman who had been the first through the door. "Good morning, can I help you find anything in particular?"

She waved her hand in my direction without giving me a second look. "No, I know what I want."

I sucked my lips in between my teeth to keep from saying how rude she was, and then I walked over to the coffee and pastry table. "Good morning, everyone, I have fresh coffee and pastries here, please help yourself." I pointed to the items on the table and then noticed I already had one customer at the cash register.

"Hello, is this a gift? Can I gift wrap it for you?" I pointed to the pair of Harry Potter bookends she had put on the counter. Those were one of the items I had ordered specially for the Christmas season.

The middle-aged woman smiled and nodded. "I was hoping you'd hold this here for me while I keep shopping? They're heavy and I didn't want to clunk them around your shop."

"Of course, I understand. What is your name? I'll put a sticky with your name on them so that no one else will pick them up." I had planned on standing behind the counter unless someone needed me, since it was just Cassidy and me. Someone had to run the register. But if someone needed me to show them where an item was located, I would leave my post. And I didn't want anyone else to grab the bookends, I'd only order two sets since they retailed for over two hundred dollars. They were hand carved from oak wood by an artisan in Northern California. If I sold them both today, I'd order more.

She gave me her name and I wrote it on the sticky and attached it to the smooth side that faced the books. Tabitha, the shopper, grinned and walked over to the Teen & YA section. Most likely she was going to buy some Harry Potter books for the person who was going to get the bookends for Christmas. I knew we had at least five complete sets of the series, as well as several copies of each of the other books by the author.

Before I could wonder how many Harry Potter books I might sell today, another woman came up with a basket full of books and a few bookish goodies. She even had one of Aunt Jo's store t-shirts.

"I just love Siggy. I'm so glad Jo put him on a t-shirt. Did you know that your cactus out front is sort of a local hero?" The older woman looked familiar, but I couldn't place her. I'd seen so many people here since I arrived. But her reference to the shop's signature Saguaro Cactus made me think she was part of the local cactus club.

"Mary-Beth, I should have known you'd be here." Verna had stepped into my line of sight, and she grinned at both me and the woman in front of the counter.

"Verna, you know that I always shop here first on the day before Thanksgiving. It's the best shopping day before the Christmas craziness begins." The woman, Mary-Beth, grinned and hugged Verna.

I hadn't seen Verna hug too many people outside of our little group, so Mary-Beth must be a close friend of hers. "Hi Verna, nice of you to stop in today. Did you want to do some shopping?"

Verna tilted her head. "No, dear. Didn't your Aunt Jo ever tell you about today?"

I racked my brain trying to think of the things Aunt Jo used to tell me about the Christmas shopping season, but details seemed to be out of my reach. "I'm sorry, but I don't understand."

Verna put a hand on the counter. "Jade, Ada, Tony, and I always help out during this weekend. Then your aunt would make us all a big dinner next week once the traffic died down a little bit."

"Oh, that's so sweet. Why didn't you guys say anything at dinner last Sunday?" We had talked about a lot of different things, but none of them mentioned joining me today.

Verna shrugged. "I guess we just expected that you'd know about it." She walked around the counter. "I'll handle the cash register; you go out on the floor and help people find what they need."

Mary-Beth picked up her t-shirt. "And be sure to show everyone the t-shirt. Most of the locals will buy one. Have you thought about putting a picture of Siggy on the front of a T-shirt with his Christmas lights on? I know I'd buy another with that image, and your bookstore logo, of course." She grinned.

"I hadn't thought of that. Thank you. I'll call my supplier and see if I can't get an order of those this week." And I would most certainly call them as soon as I had a moment. It was a great idea.

By lunchtime, I had to call the supplier anyway because everyone was buying t-shirts. Some bought several. At this rate I was going to run out before the holiday weekend ended. Thankfully, he was local and had plenty of inventory. He said he'd get me a new supply of T-shirts by Monday, not a lot, but enough to get me through until he could restock. And he loved the idea of the Christmas Saguaro shirt. He suggested I use a red t-shirt for the Christmas cactus image, and I agreed.

It was later in the day when I started to lose steam. We all were starting to lose steam. "Ada and Tony, why don't you two head on home. I'm only open for another three hours." Those two had been here since ten in the morning and barely stopped to eat lunch. Jade joined us after lunch, and Verna left at lunch for a few hours then just came back only fifteen minutes ago. Cassidy was due to leave as her eight hours were up. So I'd still have Jade and Verna helping me for the final three hours.

"Honey, you need to sit down and take a break. I don't think I've seen you off your feet all day." Ada put an arm around me and guided me to one of the overstuffed chairs in the reading corner.

I sat down and sighed. I'd worn my tennis shoes and was very glad for it. My cowgirl boots weren't worn in enough to stand in them all day yet. But my feet still throbbed once I sat down. "Thank you, Ada. I'll only sit for a moment to catch my breath. If you all want, I can order pizza." My stomach rumbled at the thought of cheesy goodness with pepperoni, Canadian bacon, and pineapple.

All heads in the store looked at me and I could see everyone smiling, even the customers. I chuckled. "Sorry, I meant for my workers."

The entire store moaned their displeasure and I thought I might need to consider selling sandwiches, or something that wouldn't leave grease on hands that touched my books and gifts. If I could keep people in my store longer, they might want to buy more books. It worked on me when I went to those big box bookstores that also had nice café's inside. I'd buy lunch and then with a full stomach and a cup of coffee in hand, I'd take my time in the store and spend lots of money.

If only I had more space.

I looked around the store and realized that there wasn't anywhere to put a café inside. I might be able to turn the upstairs into a café, or move books up there, but I'd have to think more about that, after the new year.

"If you want to order the pizza, Tony and I will gladly pick it up for you." Ada looked at her husband, who nodded his approval.

"Yes, I think that's a wonderful idea. I know I'd love a good slice of Western Pie's pepperoni. They make the best pizza in town." Tony licked his lips and his eyes gleamed. Only moments earlier he looked as though he was ready for a nap. Now? He looked as though he was ready to keep working, or rather, to go pick up a large pizza and bring it back for all of us to enjoy.

I licked my lips, envisioning what a slice of pie would taste like in my belly at that moment. "Perfect, what else does everyone like on their pizza?" My aunt's friends told me what they liked and then when Cassidy was about to leave, I stopped her. "Cassidy, if you want you can hang out upstairs and join us for pizza. I can't have you working any later, but I'd be happy to share the dinner with you." She'd worked hard all day long but I also knew that she had homework this weekend. Plus, she was going to work every day except for Thursday, since I was closed for Thanksgiving Day.

"Thank you, but I have plans." She looked down, but not before I caught the pink hue shining on her cheeks.

"Oh, a date? With Joey?" I waggled my brows and grinned. "I approve."

She laughed nervously and twisted a lock of her auburn hair around her finger. Just like I always did when I was nervous. "No, no. Nothing like that. We're just catching a movie after grabbing a quick dinner at Cactus Joe's."

"Ah hah, that sounds like a date to me." I stood up and touched her arm. "You'll have to tell me all about it on Friday."

"Goodnight." Cassidy ignored my teasing and she left.

I placed the order for pizza before Ada and Tony left to pick it up. Then I took the time to run upstairs and bring Ollie down for a quick trip out back so she could do her doggy business.

We had customers non-stop the entire day. When seven o'clock came around, my store was still filled with shoppers. I didn't want to lose the sales, but I was also worn out. And I knew that Jade and Verna had to be as well.

I walked over to the counter where both of them were. "Look, I'll take care of the last of the shoppers, why don't the two of you head home. I'll see you tomorrow for dinner. And thank you so much for today. I would never have made it without your help." I knew that going forward, I'd need to find some more temporary employees to help out. This was too much for a group of septuagenarians and me to handle. Cassidy had classes so she could only work so much until she was out for the Christmas break.

"We're fine. We can help you close up." Jade patted my hand. "But it might help if you turned the sign to closed." She nodded to the door when the sheriff walked in.

I sighed. It was just past closing, but I wasn't going to turn away business from the local sheriff. I smiled and walked to the sign and turned it over. When I turned around, I noticed that Sam had pulled Verna to the side and was speaking with her. Jade looked worried. So, I walked over to the counter where the sheriff looked as though he was grilling my friend.

"Hey, what's going on?" I turned to Sheriff Madrid who had his hand on his service belt. At least he wasn't going for his gun. Then I looked at Verna who was leaning against the wall and looking a little green.

In a voice low enough so that the shoppers couldn't hear, Sheriff Madrid said, "I need to take Verna in for more questioning." He looked back over his shoulder. "Can we leave out the back?"

"What?" I whisper-yelled. I didn't want to catch the attention of the shoppers, either.

"Oh dear." Jade put a hand to her throat and her eyes clouded up with unshed tears.

"Sam, you can't be serious?" Even though he didn't say the word "arrest", it seemed like he was about to arrest Verna Henderson. "What is this about?"

Sam looked down and then back at the crowd still shopping. I wasn't sure if they knew what was going on, as none of them had brought their items to purchase up to the counter yet. However, I did catch a few eyes turn away from me as I gazed at people still in the store. With eight shoppers in play, I needed to get the sheriff out of here, while keeping Verna safe.

"Don't make a scene, let's just walk out back." Sheriff Madrid looked at me. "You might want to call her attorney."

"No way," my lips moved but I couldn't hear the words coming out of my mouth thanks to the rushing sound barreling through my ears. "Verna?"

Jade put a hand on my arm. "Maisy, dear. I'll call her attorney and head over to the jail to be near her. You finish up here and then come and join me." She nodded to the line of customers who all of a sudden appeared on the other side of the counter.

"I'll send them away." I had no patience to ring up customers, my friend needed me. And I needed to be near her.

Jade shook her head. "No, dear. She wouldn't want that. Finish up here and then come to the police station. Besides, there won't be anything for you to do for a while." She looked around. "And maybe bring me a large cup of coffee when you come? Make it fresh?"

I knew she was just trying to keep me busy, but I'd do as she asked. It wasn't until Jade had walked out the back door that I realized someone was calling my name.

"Maisy? Are you alright?" The first lady in line watched me with lines between her eyebrows.

"Yes, yes. I'm fine." I moved to the cash register and began to ring up her order. "That will be two hundred and thirty-one dollars." When I realized how much the order was for, I looked at the items on the counter, and then at all of the women behind her. They all had large loads of items. I wondered if they even knew they had put so many expensive items in their baskets while they eavesdropped on Verna being taken away by the sheriff.

Chapter 18

It took me an hour to close up and set the alarm before I could leave. But I had a full thermos of hot coffee and several paper coffee cups in my bag when I walked into the sheriff's office.

I'd left Ollie in my car. I felt bad, but knew that unless I could run her home quickly, I didn't have any other choice. While it was cold, I had a blanket in the car for emergencies, so I told Ollie to curl up. I also had a doggie water dish on the floorboard and a few treats.

Ada and Tony were already there, too. I was glad I thought to bring extra coffee and cups. I highly doubted the sheriff's station would have good coffee for us. And I knew we were going to need it to stay up until Verna was released.

"What's going on so far?" I asked when I set the thermos down on the seat next to Jade. Then I pulled out the cups as well as a box of sugar and powdered creamer. "Help yourself."

All three of them stood up and sighed. With a collective "Thank you" they each poured themselves a cup of hot coffee. Once we all had our coffee, Jade spoke up. "Verna has her attorney with her, he showed up about twenty minutes ago. But other than that, I don't know anything. The sheriff isn't sharing anything with us."

I sat down with a thunk and sighed. "Do you think they're going to arrest her? I mean she's an old lady. I don't think spending the night in jail is going to be good for her health."

Three sets of eyes glared at me.

"We are not old, just well-seasoned." Jade harrumphed, then took a sip of her hot coffee. "Mmm, Verna would like this coffee right about now. Do you think the sheriff will let her have a cup?"

"Good question. I'll ask." I stood up and poured another cup and fixed it the way I knew Verna liked, two sugars and no creamer. Then I walked over to the desk Sergeant. "Hi, I know Verna is being questioned, but she's old." I lowered my voice on the last two words so as not to upset my friends. "And if the sheriff is going to take much longer, she's going to need some caffeine. Do you think she could have this cup?"

The badge on the skinny man in front of me read – Sargeant Walsh. He looked me over, then picked up the cup. "I'll take it to her." When he turned around and walked down the hallway, I noticed that he sniffed the coffee and then took a sip.

"Hey, that's for Verna. If you want a cup, all you have to do is ask. I have more," I yelled at his back, but the man ignored me.

When he came back to the desk, his hands were empty, so I hoped that meant he gave it to Verna. When I asked him about the coffee he only grunted.

"Small towns." I sighed.

I took my seat and then looked at the re-energized faces of my friends. "What can we do?"

Jade took my hands in hers. "We pray. It's in God's hands now, dear."

She was right.

We all joined hands and each of us took turns praying for Verna, as well as for the police to figure out who really did kill Homer. They needed help from above, and it was obvious.

Sometime after the coffee ran out, a man in a suit I didn't recognize came out to us and headed directly for Tony Hopkins. "Tony, Ada, Jade." He looked at me and put a hand out. "I'm Walker Hopkins, Tony's younger brother."

I shook his hand. "I'm Maisy Bransky. Nice to meet you. But how is Verna? Will they release her now?"

Walker pursed his lips and shook his head. "They aren't arresting her, but they have put her on a forty-eight-hour hold."

"What?" This time I screeched out my disbelief, not caring who heard me.

Walker put his hands up in a gesture to silence me. "Shh. That's not going to help Verna. She knows you are all here and has asked that you go ahead with your Thanksgiving Dinner tomorrow."

"That's the last thing on my mind." I shook my head, not believing what I was hearing.

Ada put a hand on my shoulder. "Maisy, she's right. We need to get together tomorrow." She waggled her brows and then looked to the desk Sergeant, who was watching us closely.

I realized she was trying to signal to me. And I understood – she wanted us to all get together and talk in private about next steps. I nodded. "Of course. Maybe we can even bring Verna a plate of dinner tomorrow." While I wouldn't try to slip in a metal file, I did want to make sure she had a nice meal. Who knew what they served in jail. Knowing this small town like it did, I knew it wouldn't be much better than bread and water. Especially if old Sheriff Anderson had his way.

That man seemed to just hate Verna. Sheriff Madrid was another case. I still hadn't really made up my mind about that man.

The next morning, I got up and headed over to Ada and Tony's house, after I made my dessert. They had said they didn't need me to bring anything, but I offered to bring Aunt Jo's famous Prickly Pear Bundt cake, and they grinned. It would feel as though Aunt Jo was with us when we had dessert later on.

However, I'd totally forgotten that I'd invited Jason to join us for Thanksgiving dinner. When he rang the bell, I looked at Jade and Ada with a question in my eyes. I didn't think they'd invited anyone else for dinner. And when Tony opened the door to Jason, my heart sank.

"Jason, so good of you to join us." I pasted on the best smile I could muster.

The morning had been spent making the big spread so not much talking about Verna, other than to say that Walker called and said Verna was doing fine, but still in lockup. We had decided that we'd talk next steps over the meal, when Walker joined us. But with Jason present, I wasn't sure if we could talk about how to help Verna. He might have thought she did it and he'd want her to rot in jail.

Jason walked in wearing his Sunday best black boots, black jeans, and a burnt sienna cowboy shirt with a bolo tie. I'd noticed that a lot of the cowboys wore bolo ties when the situation called for a more formal look. Almost none of them ever wore an actual tie.

"I like your bolo tie. Is that Russian amber in the center of the slide?" Most of the bolo ties I'd seen men wearing had either a plane silver clasp or a decorative slide that had turquoise in an intricate silver design. But Jason's amber piece matched his shirt quite nicely.

He looked down at his tie and grinned. "Thank you. My grandpops gave this tie to me when I turned eighteen. He said that a gentleman always wore a tie to holiday dinners as well as church." A soft look crossed his face for a moment before he shook his head. "Happy Thanksgiving, everyone. And thank you for inviting me today."

Ada, the consummate hostess, came forward and gave him a hug. Jason handed her a bouquet of fall flowers that included a beautiful sunflower in the middle.

"Oh, Jason. These are so beautiful. How thoughtful. Thank you." She grinned at me and then headed to the kitchen to put them in a vase.

Ollie had to make sure that Jason knew she was there, so she put her front paws on his leg and barked.

Jason smiled down at the dog and scratched her head. "Hey, girl, it's so nice to see you. Happy Thanksgiving."

Ollie, happy that she'd gotten her little bit of loving from one of her favorite men, sauntered over to me and sat down.

Tony put a hand on Jason's shoulder. "Thank you for coming today. It's nice to have another man to help balance out all of these women."

Jason chuckled and the tension that I had felt between my shoulder blades when Jason entered the house began to dissipate. And I felt a real smile replace the fake one I had tried so hard to put on for my guest. "Can I get you something to drink; Iced tea, hot tea, coffee?"

"Coffee would be great, thanks. I didn't get much sleep last night." Jason looked around and his smile left his face. "I don't believe Verna killed my grandpops. I know they didn't get along, but I can't believe it was her."

I put a hand to my heart. "Thank you. I know we all appreciate that. We want to find out who really did it. Maybe after dinner we can all sit down and go over what we know. The sheriff hasn't been very forthcoming with details. At least, not with me."

Jason's nostrils flared. "He hasn't said much to me, either. And we used to be thick as thieves. I don't understand why he isn't telling me much."

"Maybe he just doesn't know much, yet," Tony offered up.

I thought about that for a second and realized he might be right. It had only been a week since the murder, most of the tests they ran probably hadn't even come back yet. "Then why is he holding Verna? And on Thanksgiving, too."

Instead of waiting for after dinner, we all sat around the large kitchen island while Ada and Tony put the finishing touches on our holiday meal, talking about what we knew so far.

Ollie was on her best behavior, which surprised me. I expected her to be in the kitchen begging for any scraps, or sniffling the ground hoping that Ada or Tony would drop something just for her. Instead, she sat next to me, but with an eye on Jason.

Figures, the little girl was in love with the handsome cowboy.

"Ada, do you have a large white board or paper? I'd like to write out what we have so far." I sat next to Jason, at the kitchen island topped by a large slab of granite. On the opposite side of the island was a prep sink and a large butcher block sat on the edge where Tony was cutting up vegetables for the charcuterie tray.

"I know where it is. I'll go grab it." Jade called over her shoulder as she headed back to the den. It only took her a few minutes to push a large whiteboard on wheels into the kitchen.

"It's a good thing this house was built for a large family." I stood up and walked to the board and then pushed it back against the wall of the breakfast nook. The nook was next to the large open-designed kitchen, and I'd be able to write on the board while still talking to everyone, without having to yell across the house.

I wrote down everything I could think of. Then I turned around to meet the curious eyes of everyone in the room. Walker Hopkins had quietly joined us while I was writing out what I knew so far. "Hi, Walker." I waved.

"Happy Thanksgiving, Maisy. I see you've been busy." Walker nodded at my whiteboard.

"Well, it's not nearly enough. Maybe we should start with where everyone was at the estimated time of the murder?" I went back to the board and on the side in small letters I wrote down my name and next to it I wrote Christmas decorating.

Jade walked up and took the marker from me. "I was out looking for Rudolph, he'd run away, and his daddy was really worried."

I remembered seeing Jade running down the street right before I left the bookshop that night, but totally forgot all about it. But, that had been at least two hours before Homer was murdered. "How long did that take?" It wasn't that I thought she had anything to do with the murder, but if she was still out and about, she might have seen someone, or something, about the time of the murder.

Jason raised his hand. "Wait, who's Rudolph? Do we have a missing kid to worry about, as well?"

We all chuckled.

"Oh, that's right. You don't know about Jade's children." I almost put air quotes around the last word, but stopped. I didn't want Jade to think I was making fun of her. And I was beginning to understand how she turned her Gila Monsters into her children. "Rudolph is the youngest member of the little tribe of pets that call Jade's house their own."

Jason clicked his tongue and nodded. "Yes, I'd heard something about you keeping a hoard of Gila Monsters at your house." He looked more closely at Jade. "You aren't worried that they'll bite you?"

Jade's smile reminded me of when I was young and she'd look at me after I'd said something silly. "Jason, they're my babies. They would never hurt me. And besides, they're great at keeping the bugs and rodents away from my garden. Everyone should have Gila Monsters residing in their garden. Nature's pest control."

Somehow, I doubted anyone but Jade would be able to keep Gila Monsters in their garden safely.

"Didn't someone in the news recently die from a Gila Monster bite? I thought I read about that last week in the Westcott Times," Walker stated.

The Westcott Times was more of a local weekly newsletter than a real newspaper. Although, once in a while there was more than the standard recipes, local happenings, and help wanted postings. At times, we were able to get some real news, like a tourist getting bit by wildlife. "I read about that, too. But the tourist was trying to capture a wild Gila Monster out by the old silver mine. And I believe he had a heart condition. The human, not the Gila Monster, which made the venom in the Gila that much more potent."

"Okay, let's get back to the case at hand." Tony put the plate of cut up vegetables and dip on the island counter between everyone. "We know what you and Jade were up to. Ada and I were here, at home, watching the latest mystery on the Family Mystery Network."

Jason looked at everyone around the table. "Why are you all providing your alibi's? None of you are suspects, are you?"

"Ummm." I started then stopped. Why were we all giving our whereabouts? "I guess I started that line of thinking because I had been the Sheriff's number one suspect, until he checked out my airtight alibi."

Jason chuckled. "Yeah, a bunch of nosy bodies watching you from behind their curtains, and some even videotaping it, I'd say you don't have to worry."

When Jason told me he believed in me, it felt as though a ton of bricks had just lifted off of my shoulders. Now, to get Verna such an alibi.

Chapter 19

Jason was right, none of us needed to waste our time on providing our locations around eight the night Homer was poisoned. Which begged the question, "Do we know the exact type of poison used?"

We all looked to Walker, who was representing Verna, so he had to know the details of the case by now. What with the laws surrounding discovery and all of that. I knew there were specific rules that stated law enforcement had to give certain details to the lawyer and the accused, but since Verna wasn't officially charged yet, did they apply in this case?

"I asked the sheriff the same question. He doesn't have the test results back yet. He expects with the holiday weekend that he won't know anything more until Monday." Walker held up his hand to stop all of the questions that bombarded him all at once.

I knew that the sheriff could only hold Verna for forty-eight hours, and Monday was further out than forty-eight hours. Which meant that he could only hold her until Friday night. Unless he was going to charge her with murder.

"Listen, I think the sheriff is using this time to ask Verna more questions and to see if anyone comes forward with more details. Maybe someone saw something that night? Around eight o'clock most businesses were already closed and locked up. So I don't expect there to be many possible witnesses." The attorney shook his head and sighed. "Without more evidence, they won't be able to charge Verna."

"What evidence do they have that makes them think Verna did it?" Jason asked. "Sam refuses to speak to me about the case."

"And for good reason. You're the victim's closest relative. I think the sheriff is worried that you might go after any suspects in retribution." Walker's eyebrows shot up and he tilted his head.

The look that passed between the two men had me wondering what they *weren't* saying. There was some serious non-verbal communication happening at that very moment.

"Okay, I know I'm new here, but," I pointed between Jason and Walker. "There is something going on between you two."

"It's fine." Jason swallowed loudly, then continued, "When I was a Senior in high school, I had a bit of a temper." He ran a hand down his face. "I went off on a few wild rampages when I got upset. So, after graduation I left town and dealt with my anger issues." He turned back to Walker. "I haven't been in any trouble in years. I know how to keep my anger in check now. I promise."

I sat down hard in the chair nearest me. Did this mean anything to the case? Or was Sam just remembering his childhood friend and trying to keep him out of trouble?

Walker got up and refilled his mug of coffee before addressing Jason's statement. "I know, I've checked you out already. I trust that you wouldn't fly off the handle if the sheriff told you anything, but you have to remember, Sam was your friend. He was there with you whenever you acted out after your parents moved away."

"Wait, your parents moved away and left you here? When you were still a kid?" I couldn't believe anyone could do that to their kids. Especially a mother. My mom had sent me back here during the year to stay with Aunt Jo from time to time, but I still *lived* with my mom. And as soon as I was able to care for myself, I didn't come back here that much. I stayed in Florida with my mom while she worked to put food on our table.

Jason's head drooped and he sighed, loudly. "Yeah, my parents never did take to ranch life. But I did. So, when my dad got a job with the railroad over in Denver, they left me here. The plan had been for me to live with grandpops and finish school. Then I'd go off to college and come back here to help him with the ranch."

"But you ended up in New York instead. How did that happen?" I asked.

"Long story, but basically, I followed a girl to the city." Jason shrugged. "Even after we broke up, I stayed since I was making such good money. I figured when grandpops was ready to retire, then I'd come back here and settle down."

"Makes sense." I'd have probably done the same exact thing. Well, maybe not follow a guy to New York, but I would have gone off to college and then tried doing whatever I wanted, instead of coming right back here to a ranch. Although, I supposed that was exactly what I did, just substitute a bookstore for a ranch.

Aunt Jo had always said I should help her with the shop and then one day take over for her, but it was always something we discussed but never got around to planning.

"I think that in time, Sam will see how much you've matured, and he'll trust you with details. I think he needs to remember how much he's grown up, too." Walker grinned.

Tony laughed. "Yes, I remember the two of you running around like little hellions back in the day. He got into almost as much mischief as you did." He pointed to Jason and grinned from ear to ear.

Jason held up his hand and smiled. "Alright, alright. Yes, I was a handful in high school. And so was Sam. But it seems like he's already rewritten his reputation. How long before I get the chance to do so?"

I understood where he was coming from. However, the murder investigation was much more important than his reputation as a youth. And he knew it.

"I suppose, the first thing is to find out who killed my grandpops." Jason's nostrils flared and he stood up abruptly and walked to the whiteboard. "Alright, we know he was murdered using poison in his tuna salad sandwich." He checked off the line I had written on the board. "But we don't know what poison yet."

I stood up and walked up next to him and grabbed another marker. "The only restaurant that serves tuna salad sandwiches is Seven Savory Seas. Is Gavin under suspicion?" I turned to look at Walker and waited for his answer.

"It's not very likely since Sheriff Anderson also ate that same sandwich for dinner that night." Walker Hopkins stood up and walked to the board. He looked over what I'd written so far and nodded. "If I were a betting man, and I'm not, I'd say that someone added the poison to Homer's sandwich after he left the coffee shop that night."

I interrupted him. "Do we know what time Homer was there? And when he left?"

"Yes, Homer walked in just before closing at seven and placed his order. Gavin told Sheriff Madrid that Homer left only a few minutes after seven. Then he finished cleaning and closed up shop before going home. There are cameras from a few stores and the ATM machine on the corner of Barrel Way and Stirrup Alley that show his timing is accurate."

I interrupted Walker again. "What about Homer? Do the cameras show his movement?"

Before we could do anything to clear Verna's name, we needed to know the movements of the victim. Then, we needed to see who was near him that night. The best way to prove it wasn't Verna was to prove who actually did the crime.

Walker nodded. "There is some evidence of Homer on the few cameras we have downtown, but we don't have enough CCTV to get an accurate picture. I wish more businesses would put them up in their storefronts."

I raised my hand. "How expensive is that? I'd be interested in doing it for my bookshop if I could afford it."

Everyone looked at me funny and Jason snickered.

"I think you've got the money in Jo's accounts. But that is something to look at once you get the estate signed over to you from Judge Charles." Walker turned back to the whiteboard and tapped the cap of the marker against his chin.

I wasn't sure what they were all thinking, but I didn't have a lot of money. However, in the grand scheme of things, I probably did have plenty of money to install a small security camera system. But why did they all look at me so funny? And how do they know I have money?

Before I could ask, Walker began explaining Homer's route after he left Seven Savory Seas. "Do you have a map of downtown Westcott? That might make it easier to mark everything out."

Ada jumped up from her chair. "Yes, I do. I know I got one a while back when I visited the information center across from Town Hall." She rummaged through one of the kitchen drawers and then pulled out a folded piece of paper and waved it above her head. "Here it is."

Walker took it from her and opened it up. Then he laid it down on the end of the granite island. "Here," he pointed to Seven Savory Seas, "is where Gavin saw Homer last."

Then he pointed to the corner of Stirrup Alley and Barrel Way. "This ATM caught Homer on its camera holding a brown bag with what is assumed to be the sandwich. In the video, it looked as though Homer hadn't opened the bag yet."

I looked at the map and noticed that Homer had been seen very close to my store. Then I wondered how he got from there to Blind Alley and Prickly Pear Avenue – and how long it took him to get there. "What was the time stamp on the ATM video?"

Walker pointed to me. "Good question." He pulled out a notepad from his coat pocket. "Let's see. Ah ha. Yes. Looks like Homer was seen at seven thirteen on the ATM camera. Then the Antique Mart camera caught him for only a moment, but he was waving his hands around at someone who wasn't on the screen, anywhere near him."

We all sat there quietly contemplating what Walker just said.

"Then how does the sheriff think that it was Verna? If she wasn't seen on camera, why hold her?" I scratched my chin and narrowed my eyes at the map.

Walker moved his finger Northwest of the ATM toward City Hall up on Western Way and Prickly Pear Avenue. It was North of my store and on the other side of Prickly Pear Avenue from my bookshop. City Hall was at most a five-minute walk from my door. "City Hall's CCTV caught Verna moving quickly down Prickly Pear, but they lost her image when she walked by Westcott's Western Museum and History Center on Stirrup Alley."

I looked at the map and wondered if someone else had a small security system that could have caught Verna heading away from Homer. "What time was she seen on the video feed?"

Walker's face softened and he sat down. "That's just it, she was seen at seven eighteen heading toward where Homer's body was discovered."

Jason sucked in a breath. "So, it's possible then?"

I adamantly shook my head. "No, not at all. Just because she was close enough to be in the area, doesn't mean she was near Homer." I pointed to the museum. "That's Stirrup Alley, she could have turned that way and headed home. She does live in that direction and Stirrup Alley would take her to Caballeros Way, then she could turn down Cactus Lane and head home from there. It wouldn't have been difficult for Verna to go that way and never lay eyes on Homer, or his attacker."

Jason slumped in his chair. "So, it wasn't her." He nodded. "I think that's good."

I looked over at Jason and realized that all of the blood had left his face. The way we were talking about Homer and his murder must have been causing him pain. "I'm so sorry, Jason. We shouldn't be so analytical in discussing what happened to your grandfather. I know everyone here never wanted to see him die. No one should go before their time."

I felt like the rudest person ever. When I looked at the faces of my dinner companions, I realized they must have felt the same. I saw pity and sadness on every face. Even Walker felt bad for Jason, and he was defending the woman accused of Homer's murder.

"You know, we should put this all aside and focus on having a wonderful Thanksgiving dinner. I'm sure the sheriff is doing everything he can to find the real killer." While I wasn't sure of that, I knew that everyone there, myself included, needed the assurance that Sheriff Madrid was doing everything he could. And just to get everyone's mind off of the murder I blurted out, "So, do Native Americans celebrate Thanksgiving like we do?"

With the tension so tight, it didn't take much to cut through the thickness. And what I said must have been exactly what we all needed, as the tension seemed to ping and then poof, was gone. Everyone was laughing or chuckling.

"Alright, I think if we all move to the dining room table, I can get the turkey out of the oven." Ada shooed us all away.

In less time than I thought possible, we had all devoured one of the best Thanksgiving meals I could remember having. And when I brought out the Prickly Pear Bundt Cake, Jade teared up and sniffed.

"You know, I thought we'd never have this cake again. I'm so glad Jo taught you how to make it." Jade took a bite of the moist yellow and pink cake before she closed her eyes, slid back in her seat, and moaned.

"Normally, I'd think Jade was overreacting, but I must agree." Tony devoured his slice before I'd even had two bites of my own.

I was going to have to bring this cake to every gathering we had. At least then I'd be sure to make more friends and influence people. Take that, Mr. Carnegie. I bet he'd never thought of using food when writing his novel.

Chapter 20

Friday was Black Friday, which meant that all shops were going to be packed. So, I had left early the night before, right after Thanksgiving dinner. Since Jason was there and he seemed to be having a tough time with us talking about his grandfather's murder, we all decided to wait until he wasn't around. Unfortunately, he didn't leave until I did.

When I hugged Ada goodnight, she whispered, "I'll be at your store first thing in the morning, and we can discuss more at that time."

I knew exactly what she was referring to, so I thanked her for a wonderful meal and said I'd see everyone later.

True to her word, Ada and Tony were both at my shop just before seven in the morning. The local shopkeeper's association had posted that all shops needed to be open from seven in the morning until seven at night all weekend. Normally, we were free to choose our own hours, but with all of the shoppers coming from a variety of places, they had all decided years ago that all shops needed to be open.

Of course, the movie theater still did its own thing. And the restaurants only served their meals during their normal times. A breakfast shop wasn't going to stay open for dinner, and vice versa. But some of the food shops did have extra hours serving what they were best known for, like Seven Savory Seas. They opened up extra early to serve coffee and pastries. Which I was very grateful for. I had put in a standing order for the entire weekend.

When I saw Ada and Tony at the front door of my shop, I opened it up and welcomed them in. I looked around and was surprised to see lines at most of the shops on Cactus Lane. The handmade furniture store next door had at least ten people outside waiting for them to open. I had closer to twenty people waiting, one of them just happened to be Sheriff Oscar Anderson. I was pretty sure he was here in line hoping to get the cactus figurine he bought his wife every year for Christmas.

"Come on in." When they were inside, I closed the door behind them. "Can one of you head over to Seven Savory Seas and pick up my order of coffee and pastries? Every morning through Monday I have an order."

"Don't you have your own coffee maker?" Tony asked.

I walked over to the table I had set up for coffee and treats. "I do, but I thought it would be easier to have Gavin make me a larger carafe to start the day with. And if the line outside is any indication, we're going to have a lot of people this morning and I won't be able to keep up with making fresh coffee."

"Sounds good. I'll head over and get your order." Tony waved and left through the front door.

"Okay, before we open, what happened last night after I left? Did you all discuss Verna's case more? Something I should know about?" I had debated going back to Ada and Tony's house after giving Jason some time to get away from the area, but I knew that I still had things to get ready for Friday morning. In the end, I decided a good night's sleep was the best solution.

And I was grateful when my alarm went off at four-thirty this morning.

Ada looked around. "Is Cassidy here yet?"

"No, she's coming in at ten-thirty today. She'll work until closing." It wasn't that I had planned on needing time to chat with Ada about the murder, it was just that I knew I was going to need help closing, so Cassidy was actually scheduled late for the rest of the weekend.

"All we did was go over all of the details that you already know. The only thing you might not know about is the exact movements of Homer. He was seen heading down Cactus Lane and then he turned left on Prickly Pear. There wasn't another camera that picked him up."

"What about the art gallery? I would have thought they'd have CCTV all around their building." I still hadn't been inside the gallery, but just knowing the little I did about art, they would want to have all angles of the building covered.

Ada shook her head.

Someone knocked on the door. "Isn't it time to open?"

I looked at my watch and slapped my forehead. I put a finger in the air to let the woman at the door know I was coming. But before I did, I turned back to look at Ada. "I need to see if the art gallery has a camera that the sheriff didn't know about. I can't imagine they would let any side of their building go without security cameras."

"Yeah, it's too bad the building next to them is still empty. They most likely would have had a camera, if the fashion designer hadn't moved into the Westcott Western Wear Mall a few months back." Ada moved to the area that housed my restocked glass figurines and smiled while I opened the door.

"Good morning, and welcome to the Saguaro Bookshop. Please let me know if there's anything I can help you with. Coffee and pastry should be here shortly." I motioned for the first twenty to come inside. "Per fire code, I can only have so many in at a time, sorry."

I probably could have gotten more in, but I needed to ensure that Tony could make it back in without any issues. Plus, I didn't want too many people walking around the breakables at one time.

Three of the women made a beeline to the glass items, and they were joined by the old sheriff. I almost laughed when he reverently picked up a piece that was more artwork than trinket. It was also a two-hundred-dollar item. If he gave his wife that, then she must have a fantastic collection of Kiiya Glass.

Kiiya Sanchez was a local Native American woman who was a glass blowing artist. She only sold her pieces in a few places outside of the reservation, and Aunt Jo's store was one of them. Thankfully, she had two crates of pieces available when I called her after Homer destroyed everything I had.

The old sheriff was the first one to bring his items to the counter that morning. And after I rang him up, he left, allowing another shopper in the store.

Tony arrived only moments later with two large boxes of coffee and four boxes of pastries. Not only were my shoppers grateful, but so was I. I could tell it was going to be a three cup coffee kind of day, if not more.

After almost three hours of constant sales, which I was more than grateful for, I had a moment to breathe. "Tony, did you have a chance to speak with Gavin about Homer?"

I had sent Tony there this morning without saying anything, but hoping that he would talk to Gavin about Homer's whereabouts the night of his death.

Tony looked around, and seeing that the four shoppers who were inside the store at the moment were far enough away that they wouldn't hear anything, he moved closer to me. "I did, but my brother was correct. Gavin didn't see Homer again after he left. And since Gavin lives in the opposite direction of where Homer went, he didn't even see anyone who might have been near Homer."

"So, he wasn't able to help Verna?" I scratched the tip of my nose. Someone needed to help Verna, but with the majority of the quarterly sales taking place this weekend, I couldn't shut up the store. But maybe I could ask shoppers if they were near here that night.

While I might not be a trained investigator, I've read my fair share of mystery and cop procedural novels. I knew that I couldn't outright ask people if they had seen Homer that night, or anyone near the corner of Blind Alley and Prickly Pear Avenue. Most people didn't want to be involved in a murder investigation.

I wouldn't want to, either. Except, it was Verna who had become the prime suspect. My Great-Aunt Jo would do everything in her power to help Verna. And since she had died, it was my responsibility to help now.

As soon as one of the customers I'd seen around town was close enough, I spoke to Ada in a voice that I knew would carry. "I can't believe what happened just around the corner the other night, can you?"

Ada's eyes narrowed and her lips parted.

I didn't move my head, but I did move my eyes to the woman near us. She had moved a few steps closer and had her ear facing us while she held a book.

Upside down.

I knew she was listening to us, so I tilted my head just a smidge and gave one nod.

Ada's eyes widened and she grinned. Then wiped the emotion from her face only to replace it with a downturned mouth. "I know, what is this town coming to when a person can't even walk downtown before eight o'clock at night all alone."

"Do you think it was a vagrant? Or one of those drug deals gone bad?" I'd recently read about the drug called Fentanyl, after Jason told me about his grandfather using it, and it had made its way into our little neck of the woods – big time. One teenager had smoked a joint laced with it and died over in Prescott at one of those arts festivals. He wasn't a local, but he was in our area when it happened, so everyone had been worried that it was now easily available here.

Even the high school had put on a special presentation about the dangers of the drug and sent home information with all of the kids for the parents to read. That same week, Archie Simmons had a front-page article about Fentanyl, and the boy who died.

Ada's eyes went so wide, her eyebrows disappeared into her hair-line. She grabbed my hand. "Oh, Maisy, I hadn't thought about that. It could be like that poor boy who died a couple of weeks back in Prescott."

While I had used that avenue as more of a ploy to get the attention of the eavesdropping woman, I hadn't realized that Ada might believe it. I put my hand over hers and lowered my voice, "Ada, I don't think that's what happened."

"But, Maisy, Homer had been acting very strange the past few weeks." Ada's shoulders drooped, and her eyes moved down toward the ground. "Actually, he's not been the same for most of this year. Do you think he had been taking that drug? It could explain a lot of what he was up to."

The eavesdropping woman scurried over to us. "You know, I was wondering the same thing. I was coming out of the pottery studio that night and saw something that had me running to my car."

I turned to the woman. "Really? What did you see?" The pottery studio was on the same block as where Homer had been found. The back of the studio came out onto Blind Alley. While it was closer to Ropin' Way, it was still only one building away from Prickly Pear Avenue.

The woman was wearing a tan and rose-colored denim long coat with a white sherpa collar. Her blond hair was cut to just about her shoulder blades and I could tell she had used a barrel iron to curl most of the length of her hair. It was rather pretty.

I tried such a style once, and swore I'd never try it again. My red hair was too long to hold the curl very long and since it had taken me an hour to get through all of my hair, it wasn't worth it.

"Melinda-Sue, did you see Homer?" Ada put a hand to her chest and sucked in a deep breath.

The woman nodded. "I did. And I saw a tall man wearing dark clothes and a black cowboy hat. I only saw him from the back, but he was arguing with Homer." She shivered. "I ran to my car as quickly as I could and high-tailed it out the other way."

"Did you tell the sheriff?" I asked.

She nodded. "I did, but Sheriff Anderson didn't seem to be interested in what I had to say."

"What about Sheriff Madrid? Did he ever ask you about it?" If only Sheriff Anderson asked her, then did Sheriff Madrid even know Melinda-Sue was a witness?

Melinda-Sue grinned. "You know what? Sheriff Hotty didn't ask me about it. I think I need to head over there after I buy my gifts and sit down with Sam." She winked and walked back to her shopping.

Chapter 21

I shook my head when Melinda-Sue sauntered out of my bookstore. She may not have seen enough of the other person to know who it was, but she was certain it wasn't Verna. That had to mean something, right?

"Lord, please let this be the sort of evidence that Sheriff Madrid will see as pointing to Verna's innocence." After I said my quick prayer, another woman walked up to the counter.

"Did I just hear Melinda-Sue say she was a witness to the murder of Homer?" Wide eyes ogled me as an elderly woman set four books, two glass cactus, and a tote bag down on the counter in front of me.

"I don't think she saw the actual murder, but she did see a man arguing with Homer right before he was killed. Which means it couldn't have been Verna." My goal was to get the entire town talking about how it couldn't have been Verna. Then Sheriff Madrid would have to let her out of jail. I hated the fact that Verna had already spent two nights in jail for a crime she didn't commit.

"If that's so, then why is Verna being held in jail for murder?" The woman narrowed her eyes on me. "She was one of your aunt's best friends, wasn't she?"

I took the items she had set down and began ringing them up. "Yes, Verna is practically family." When I hit the total button, the woman didn't even notice, she just slid her card in the credit card reader and signed the receipt while I bagged her items. "Did you want a store bag, or should I put your items inside your tote bag?"

"Oh, use the tote bag, please." She put her card away. "You know, my neighbor said her son's friend heard that Verna killed Homer because he broke into your store before it was opened. Is that true?"

I shook my head. "No, that's not what happened. Verna didn't kill him, and she wasn't near the scene, either."

"Hmm, maybe it was one of those drug dealers. You know, I've seen some of them skulking around the coffee shop." She shivered. "They give me the creeps." The elderly woman's shoulders hugged her ears, and she picked up the tote bag and turned to leave.

"Thank you for shopping here today, have a Merry Christmas." I waved and smiled as the woman left my shop.

Gossip in this town spread faster than wildfire. I knew that after today, the entire area would know that it wasn't Verna. But the drug connection had me wondering if that was possible. Homer's erratic behavior could stem from drug use. However, it was more likely that he was showing signs of Dementia or Alzheimer's. More and more of the population were contracting that disorder. But, I still couldn't forget what Jason had told me the other day.

Homer had been abusing drugs, but he also was in the very early stages of Dementia. Both of those combined is most likely what caused his erratic behavior. So what killed him? Was it his drug connection?

If so, who was he arguing with?

That was a new question that we needed to add to our whiteboard. Crime novels called it a murder board, but I just couldn't do that. It sounded so...sinister. The sort of thing that might give me nightmares if I wasn't careful.

As it was, I had to listen to an audiobook before falling asleep last night as I had murder on the brain. I had chosen a sweet cowboy romance and was able to fall asleep with a smile on my face.

The rest of the day went by so quickly, I felt as though I had blinked, and it was already dark outside.

Tony and Ada had been there all day long. Jade showed up after lunch, so we had enough hands. Especially since Cassidy had come in and taken over ringing up customers. She was much quicker with the register than I was.

I looked around the store and there were only a few shoppers at the moment, perfect time to take Ollie out for a quick walk and start thinking about dinner.

"Tony and Ada, why don't you two go home? It's already pushing dinner time." I looked at my watch and heard my stomach rumbling. While I had eaten lunch, I hadn't sat down since. "Actually, I was thinking about ordering BBQ from Simone's BBQ, if you want to join us. She makes the best BBQ beef brisket sandwich." I had to wipe the drool coming from the corner of my mouth as I thought about the spicy sauce with hints of hickory, sugar, and a tang that lasts on my tongue. My nostrils flared in anticipation of the delectable meal.

Ada rubbed her hands together. "Ohh, that sounds marvelous. And no dishes. I'm game." She turned to her husband.

Tony's eyes had glazed over, and he rubbed his stomach. "You buy, I fly." He grinned.

"The perfect combination." I pulled out my cell phone and took everyone's orders, then texted them to Tony, and handed him my credit card. Simone's was more of a BBQ stand than an actual restaurant and they didn't use app or Internet ordering software yet. I hoped that she would get inside of an actual storefront soon so she could set up a full-blown restaurant. She'd have the business for it, especially during tourist season.

When Tony returned to the store, I screamed.

There were two other shoppers inside and they jumped at the sound of my voice reverberating off the glass windows. "Sorry." I cringed, then ran to the person who just entered. "Verna? Does this mean that you're off the hook?" I couldn't believe my attempt at swaying publish opinion worked so quickly.

The woman looked haggard, but her eyes were glinting thanks to the overhead lights of my shop. "Not exactly, but I'm free for now. The fuzz couldn't hold me any longer."

I put a hand over my heart and sighed. "I'm so glad to see you. Did they feed you alright in there?" We had sent over some food, but the prison warden rejected our offerings. Basically, Sheriff Anderson said that prisoners couldn't accept outside food. They had strict rules and the food had to come from their vetted suppliers.

I took that to mean they toasted up bread and gave her watered down tea or coffee.

To say that I had zero respect for Sheriff Anderson was an understatement. I think that man needed to retire several years ago. Now, Sheriff Madrid? He seemed like he might be on the ball, but it was too early to tell for sure.

"Well, go on upstairs with Tony and Ada and help yourself to any of the BBQ we have. I bet you're hungry, aren't you?" I was grinning from ear to ear and excited to get upstairs and hear what she had to say, but there were still a few customers in the shop, and I didn't think it was fair to leave it all to Cassidy. Afterall, it was one of the busiest days of the year.

The three headed upstairs before anyone could stop Verna.

"Maisy," Jade bit her lower lip and looked up the stairs. "Would you mind if I popped upstairs for a few minutes? I just want to check in on Verna."

I put a hand on Jade's arm. "Jade, you're a volunteer, you don't have to ask for my permission. In fact, I'd say stay up there as long as you want. Cassidy and I have it covered down here."

Jade looked back and forth between me and the stairs to the break-room. She worried at her bottom lip. "You'll call me if you need any help, right?"

I nodded.

It was another hour before I was able to break away and head upstairs. Word got around quickly about Verna and my store was packed with nosey Nellies wanting to ask about Verna. Thankfully, they all bought something while trying to needle information out of me and Cassidy.

"Cassidy, if more than three or four people come in, call me. I don't want you to have to worry about a crowd. Especially if they're looking for Verna." I looked out the window, but since we were getting close to closing, the streets had begun to empty. I only counted about ten people outside on my block.

"Yes, boss. You go on ahead and have your dinner. I'll clean up down here and get everything ready for tomorrow." Cassidy took the book cart and rolled the few books to go back over toward the non-fiction section.

"Thank you, you're a gem!" I darted upstairs and sank into the chair at the end of the table and noticed that Jade had set a warm plate of food in front of me before I even had a chance to think about eating.

"And don't worry about Ollie. I took her out less than an hour ago and I also fed her dinner."

"Jade, you are such a sweetheart." I sank my teeth into the BBQ beef brisket and rolled my eyes. The tangy sauce dripped down my chin and I reached for a napkin to wipe the sauce off while not stopping my mouth from enjoying the delicious flavors of a Southwestern barbecue.

Verna chuckled as she watched me make my mess. "You know, even after two days in the pokey, I still know how to eat. You look as though you've been on a deserted island without anyone to care if you had manners or not."

I felt my cheeks heat and put the napkin in front of my face while lowering what was left of the sandwich to the plate. "Sorry," I mumbled through a mouth half-full of food. I chowed down as quickly as I could.

As soon as I swallowed my food and cleared my throat with a drink of root beer, I asked, "So, where are we with the case?"

Tony, Ada, Jade, and Verna all looked at each other before looking at me.

"It seems that Sheriff Anderson wants me tried for the crime, but Sheriff Madrid disagreed with him. Especially after learning that a shadowy figure was seen arguing with him right after he picked up his sandwich." Verna said.

"So, Melinda-Sue went over to the police station and told Sam what she saw?" I rubbed my chin before I realized that I still had barbecue sauce all over my hands, and now my face. I stood up and headed over toward the little sink to clean up. "Does this mean he's not going to charge you for the murder?"

I heard a chair squeak against the floorboards behind me. "I think that Sheriff Madrid is going to take a closer look at that intersection and see if anyone else might have a CCTV camera he doesn't know about."

After I turned around and wiped my hands and face with a paper towel, I went back to my chair. "Okay, does anyone here have any more clues? I mean, if Melinda-Sue did see Verna arguing with the killer, do you think she might be in danger?"

Jade slouched back in her chair. "I hadn't thought of that. We need to keep Melinda-Sue's name out of it all."

"I think it might be too late for that." Tony turned the screen of his phone around for all to see. "She posted on the town's Facebook page about her sighting and had asked other people to do the same."

I looked at the post and frowned. "On the one hand, it's a good idea, but on the other, the killer could easily see this and go around killing everyone who might have seen him. Or her." Murder wasn't only a man's vice, women killed as well. And they were the ones who favored poison.

Chapter 22

The weekend flew by, and I about dropped from sheer exhaustion come Monday night. Who knew that Cyber Monday would also be an extremely busy day in the store? Not only did we sell a ton online that day, but people were still coming in droves to buy in the store, or pick-up their orders. One woman came so quickly after placing her order, she must have been across the street eating lunch at Simone's BBQ Pit right before walking through my door and demanding her order.

"Mrs. Costas, thank you for ordering online today, but as you can see, we have been so swamped, that the orders from the past two hours haven't been pulled yet. How about I text you once we have your order ready?" The woman had ordered close to five hundred dollars worth of books. That was a lot of books I'd need to pull from the stacks. And it wouldn't be easy since she ordered from just about every genre.

"I'll wait while you fulfill my order." Mrs. Costas walked to the snack table and poured herself a cup of coffee and took one of the last pastries we had out.

Cassidy raised her eyebrows and shrugged. "Do you want me to pick the order?"

I sighed, knowing that difficult customers really were my job, not my part-time assistant's job. "Thank you, but I've got it."

Once I had her printed order in my hands, I took a book cart and began picking the titles. The first one was *The History and Ownership of Westcott, Arizona.* I glimpsed the inside jacket cover to see what it was about, and just about dropped the book when I found the Barton family name listed as one of the founders of this town.

I mean, I knew that it was my distant relatives that had helped start Westcott, but I didn't realize we had a book that chronicled their endeavors. The next book had me peeking over the top of the bookshelf to see what Mrs. Costas was doing. She was still sitting by the snack trays sipping her tea. But the book – it was weird.

I skimmed the list of the other books and realized that she had purchased books based on my family, Homer's family, and how the town was split between the original settlers, including the family that had at one time run the silver mine.

Each of the books on their own wouldn't have had me batting an eyelash, but all of them together right on the heels of Homer's murder? That raised the fine hairs on my arms. What did she want to know about land ownership? And why? Was she part of the founding families? I really didn't know too much about the history of this town, other than Aunt Jo's family had been here since the beginning and she owned some property. Homer had owned property, but through mismanagement and who knew what vices, he'd had to sell what he had left to his grandson, Jason, to pay the bills.

I continued to pick the books she had ordered and made a mental note to see if we had extra copies of each one. I'd have to wait until after the store closed to see if I had any more copies. Something wasn't quite right with her research, and I wanted to know what she was looking for.

Aunt Jo always said that knowledge was the key to success. And if I wanted to find out what had been going on around here, I'd have to follow the crumbs. I just hoped I didn't end up finding a witch at the end who wanted to cook me alive.

Tuesday morning dawned but all I could see was a blurry blue curtain in front of a bright yellow orb. I blinked my eyes and shook my head to clear the cobwebs. I stayed up way too late last night reading about my family. I still couldn't understand why Great-Aunt Jo didn't tell me about our history.

Well, she had said some, but nothing like what I read in books that had been published by local historians. That list that Mrs. Costas had still rang in my brain. I had copies of all of her books, and I brought them home with me. I was only able to read *The History and Ownership of Westcott, Arizona* before falling asleep with a book on my chest.

At some point in the night, Ollie had jumped into bed with me. Even though I had a very nice doggy bed for her, she still wanted to sleep with me. She must have stayed up late with my reading because she didn't seem to want to get up, either. She burrowed deeper into my covers and then stopped when she was up against my leg.

I put my hand under the covers and scratched her back. "Alright, but don't make a habit of this. I don't need doggy drool all over my sheets."

Speaking of drool... I felt something stiff on my cheek and swiped at it. "Ew, gross." The dried-up drool was now on my fingers. After wiping my fingers clean on my bedspread, I decided it was time to get up. Pulling back the covers, I almost cringed when my bare feet touched the ground. "Brr, I think I have to keep a pair of house shoes next to my bed."

The hardwood flooring of my upstairs bedroom didn't have any area rugs. That was something I was going to need when the cold winter nights hit. We weren't as cold as Prescott, Arizona, but we came close.

I winced as I hobbled over to the chair where I had slung my black robe with cups of coffee embroidered all over along with sayings like "Just one more cup" Or "That's the ticket." Once I was wrapped up, I headed into the walk-in closet and picked out a pair of matching black and red slippers. I sighed before heading downstairs to where a nice, hot pot of Walk The Christmas Plank was waiting for me. I sniffed the aroma of citrus spice, cinnamon, and Christmas before pouring a tall travel mug and adding my sugar and creamer. Then I headed back upstairs to shower and get ready for the day.

Once I was ready for work, I headed back downstairs to get another mug of coffee. As I stood at the coffee maker, I looked down at Ollie who sat by my feet with her tongue lolling to the side.

"Oh, sorry sweetie." I walked over and checked that her doggy door was open, which it was. Then I picked up her dog dish and realized that she'd finished all of her dry food I'd left out the night before. "Am I a bad doggie mommy?" I'd read the bag and was certain that I'd put out the right amount of food for her size. She jumped up on my leg and I reached down to scratch her head. She sat back down and waited for me to fill her food bowls.

At least she still had plenty of water.

When we got to the store, I put Ollie upstairs, where she normally stayed. Once the rush of Christmas shopping was over, I'd be more apt to try letting her hang out in the main part of the shop. But with all of the rush, I felt it was too much for her at the moment. I could just see her running around trying to catch everyone's attention, but getting stepped on instead.

Or causing someone to bump into the table of glass ornaments and figurines.

For a few moments, it was just me in the store and I debated whether or not to call Sheriff Madrid. What I'd read in the book last night had me wondering if there wasn't something more going on. Something akin to a conspiracy. I still had thirty minutes before I was supposed to open the store, so I went back upstairs and grabbed my purse.

Ollie was sitting at the door and chuffed for my attention.

"Hey, sweet girl. Wanna go for a walk?" I leaned down and rubbed her back.

She barked her reply, and I knew she did want to join me. Even though she'd done her business in the back before I brought her inside only fifteen minutes earlier. "Okay, but you have to be on your best behavior." I grabbed the leash and attached it to her collar, then we headed out. On my way out the door, I picked up the book I'd left on the counter. I double-checked the lock on the front door and about jumped when Ollie began barking and growling.

I turned to see who had tried to sneak up on us, and almost laughed. "I see Ollie has learned to not trust you now." I put a hand on my hips and glared at the man who had arrested Verna.

Sheriff Sam Madrid took his sheriff's hat off and held it in his hands. "I was only doing my job."

I shook my head. "Well, I think you might have jumped the gun on that one. Don't you?"

He scratched the stubble on his chin, and I realized it was too early in the morning for him to have stubble, he must have been up all night. Then I took a closer look at the man. His shirt was rumpled, and his pants had a small stain on the left leg.

I decided to give him a reprieve, he was the one I was headed to see, after all. "Why don't you come inside, and I'll make you a strong cup of coffee." I unlocked the door and all three of us stepped inside. I looked out the window before locking the door - to see if I had any early customers, which I did not. The morning was starting to look up

.

Once he had a hot cup of Joe in his hands I sat on the high stool behind the counter after I motioned for him to sit on the regular chair by the treats table. It was such a hit that I planned to keep it up through the new year. I'd even placed a standing order for the rest of the year with Gavin over at the Seven Savory Seas for pastries. The rest of the year I should be able to make enough coffee that I didn't think it would be necessary to also order carafes of coffee from Gavin.

"So, what can I do for you, Sheriff?" I did have questions for him, but thought I should hold off until after whatever it was he came by to ask.

"Gavin sure does know how to make good coffee." Sam Madrid sighed before taking another gulp of the hot coffee. "I needed that, thanks."

I didn't say anything, but I watched him and tilted my head to the right. Was he preparing to grill me for something? Or was he really so tired he couldn't remember what he came by for?

I raised my brows and waited.

"Right." He set his almost empty cup on the table next to him. "What do you know about foxglove?"

"Foxglove?" I wrinkled my nose. "Isn't that a poison that's popular in fiction books as a tool for murd…" I stopped speaking when it hit me. My mouth popped open, and I flustered, not sure what to say next.

"Murder?" He arched a brow and that harried, tired look he had was all gone.

Did he just play me?

"Was that the poison that was used on Homer?" I knew the flower was very pretty, but it wasn't common in this part of the country. Gardeners might plant it, but it didn't grow naturally in Arizona. "It's not a very fast acting poison, is it?"

"Yes, and no." Sam tilted his head back and forth. "While I doubt you would have had time to slowly poison him, others in town might have."

"Oh, so it was a slow poisoning? Something that he continually ate over and over? Or drank?" I wasn't quite sure how that could have happened, but if the levels in his system were low, then it might have been what happened.

"It's also a medicine, digitalis. It's used for treatment of certain cardiac conditions." He paused and looked at me.

"Did Homer have a heart condition?" A niggling in the back of my mind had me shaking my head. I couldn't even think of that other scenario.

"Maisy, I think you know where I'm going with this." He pulled out an official looking form. "Will you sign an order to exhume your aunt's body?"

"What?!" I jumped up so quickly, Ollie barked and ran around in circles. My chair fell back against the wall making a thudding sound. "Please tell me you don't think...No, that can't be."

Sam stood and held the paper out to me. "I'm so sorry, but I think an autopsy should have been performed on Jo Barton."

Chapter 23

Of course, I signed the paperwork. Then the sheriff left, and I downed the rest of the pot of coffee once I called Jade and told her what just happened.

None of Jo's friends were due to come in and help today, but within twenty minutes all four of them were in my store, including Tony's brother, Walker.

"You can't be serious?" Verna, lips pursed, wearing a flowing turquoise skirt, emerald-green blouse, and native American jewelry, stood tall, and glowered at Walker.

I still couldn't believe it. I mean, I did think for one moment that Jo might have been murdered when I first got to town, before Homer was murdered, but that was just me being crazy. Or so I thought. "Why didn't anyone think it was possible?"

I had asked the question two weeks ago, but they all stated that the doctor didn't see anything to make him think she had been murdered. It all looked like a heart attack.

"We did ask, but like when you asked the question, both the doctor and Sheriff Anderson said it wasn't likely." Tony said.

"Not likely doesn't mean not possible." I turned and looked at Walker. "Were you involved in this in any way?"

The attorney shook his head. "No, I was actually out of town when Jo died. I returned right before you arrived. This is all news to me. But I am glad that Sheriff Madrid requested you to sign an order to exhume the body. It's the first step. I'll call the coroner and ask him when it's going to be done and how long before he has any news."

When a knock sounded at the door, we all looked over to see two shoppers. One of the women pointed to her watch, then the door.

"Right, I'm supposed to be open." I sighed and rubbed the back of my neck. "I don't know if I can do this right now." I felt tears pricking my eyes and my nose burned. It felt like I was losing Great-Aunt Jo all over again. "What am I going to tell my mom?"

Verna stood up. "I'll open the store, why don't you head upstairs and wash your face. We can take care of the store for now." She shooed me like a little kid who was getting under her feet.

But, I did as she said. I was in no state to see customers. I didn't understand how they could have it all together enough to wait on shoppers. They were all closer to Jo than I was. How were they keeping it together?

But she was my family.

I walked up the steps and sniffled the entire way to the upstairs bathroom. Once there, I let myself have a good cry. Then I cleaned my face and brushed my hair. Out of the corner of my eye, I noticed a hair scrunchie. Today was definitely a hair up day.

When I made it back downstairs, I realized that I'd not asked the sheriff about what I read in the book the night before, and how Mrs. Costas was looking into land ownership here in town. Was she a murderer? Or did she suspect something fishy going on this entire time?

I had to shelve the thought as the store was crowded when I walked back into the front of the shop. I'd left Ollie upstairs before coming down, and I was glad for it. Too many feet all over would have made the little dog nervous.

Several customers smiled at me and continued to browse through the books and knick-knacks I had on display. I was getting low on the Kiiya Glass, I'd have to call her later in the day and place another order. Some of the people who came in over the past few days came looking specifically for her pieces of hand-blown glass. And while they were here, they ended up buying other items as well. Jo had been smart to carry the Kiiya Glass.

I dove right in and helped customers find what they were looking for while Verna stood at the register ringing up orders. She stayed there until Cassidy came in after class.

"Maisy, rumors are flying around all over town that Jo was murdered! Is that true?" Cassidy took her purse off and put it under the counter as Verna made way for the young woman.

I sighed. It was inevitable that this would happen. I nodded, then shook my head. "Well, we don't know for sure. But the poison used to kill Homer is the type used to cause heart attacks when one wants to murder someone."

Cassidy gasped. "And the sheriff now thinks Jo was murdered, too?"

I pursed my lips. "I don't know. He wanted to exhume Jo's body and have an official autopsy performed. I signed the papers earlier today."

"That's why her grave was just dug up." Cassidy's eyes were wide, and her lips trembled. "Everyone is saying she was murdered."

My nostrils flared. "I wish this town would stop gossiping!" I threw my hands in the air and stormed back into the downstairs supply room, where I kept a desk, chair, and a few items that were too heavy to lug upstairs.

I stared at the back wall, not really thinking. My brain was numb, and I wasn't sure I could take much more. I rubbed my chest, just over my heart and prayed. "Lord, why is this happening to us, to me? Jo was such a good woman. Why would someone want to kill her?" I didn't have anything else to say so I breathed in and out and waited for God to speak to me. Not that He did it very often, but once in a while I could hear His still small voice comforting me.

"Maisy."

I jumped and turned at the same time. "Oh, Jade. You scared me." A chuckle escaped. I knew that voice wasn't God's voice, but for a moment I didn't know it was Jade. Her whisper sounded a bit breathy. Maybe even masculine.

"Come here, dear." Jade held her arms out and I slipped into them as though she was my grandma. I remembered from when I was a kid that Jade had always been a great hugger.

"Thank you, Jade. How are you handling all of this?" Jade had always been the softer of the Fearsome Foursome. Now that the foursome was down to three, I wasn't really sure I should call them the Fearsome Foursome any longer. Although, I usually only called them that to myself, or my mom.

"I don't think I'll be able to process it until the autopsy is complete. Why don't you close up shop today? I think everyone will understand. Most of those inside the store now are only asking questions about the autopsy and sharing tall tales." Jade patted my back and then pulled away to look me in the eyes.

"No, I think I need to work. Cassidy is here now until closing, so she can handle most of the people. I'll just work on reshelving stock." And maybe I would slip out to speak with Sheriff Madrid. He had some explaining to do, and I had a clue to share with him.

After several hours of telling everyone, "No comment," word seemed to get around and nosey people stopped coming in. In fact, it was quiet as a church at the moment. I looked around and realized the only ones left in the store were Cassidy and me. I'd sent Verna, Jade, Ada, and Tony home after lunch. With all of the meals I'd provided them this week, I doubt I'd need to cook them anything. Maybe I'd cover the weekly after church supper at Cactus Joe's this Sunday. They had all been a Godsend, literally. I don't think I could have survived this week without them.

Next year I'll be more prepared for the traffic and hire a few local kids who need some extra Christmas cash.

"Cassidy, if you're alright here alone, I need to head to the Sheriff's station." I picked up my purse from behind the counter, then realized I'd left Ollie upstairs. "First, I need to get Ollie. I bet she needs a walk anyway."

"Sure, no problem, Maisy. Take your time." She smiled at me and picked up a stack of books that I'd put down. They needed to be shelved and I'd forgotten about them.

Once I had Ollie, the book, and my purse, I waved to Cassidy on the way out of the shop. I had been right about Ollie needing to do her business. In front of the parking structure was a small grassy area. She did her job, and I did mine by picking up her mess and throwing it away.

We turned around and headed down Cactus Lane, toward Prickly Pear Avenue. If we turned left, we'd find the spot where Homer was murdered, but we turned right, toward City Hall. The sheriff's station was located inside.

As Ollie and I walked along, I looked at the buildings and tried to see if I could find signs of security cameras. Not everyone had blatant signs these days, so it was possible someone had a camera the cops didn't know about.

When we got to the corner of Prickly Pear Avenue and Stirrup Way, I noticed the custom jewelry showroom, which was open by appointment only, had a sign on their front window stating they had security cameras in use.

The jewelry shop was situated on the corner, so they might have a camera that pointed down Prickly Pear toward Blind Alley, where Homer was found. I looked back behind me and realized that the camera wouldn't have been able to catch the murderer in the act, but it could catch who went down the alley, and back to the main street. If they went that way.

It also probably caught Verna's movements that night, which was why she was released earlier than the full forty-eight hours the sheriff said he'd be holding her for.

Ollie was sniffing a patch of weeds in the gravel and rock space between the sidewalk and the shop. I wasn't paying attention until the sounds coming from her sounded more like she was eating, then sniffing. I pulled on her leash and asked, "What are you eating?"

Of course, she ignored me and pulled harder on the leash.

I balanced my way on the rocks to get a closer look. I wasn't the sort of dog momma who would let her dog eat anything she found on the ground. With Foxglove in food, who knew what Ollie might find.

"Oh, how cute." Instead of food, I found Ollie's tongue moving like crazy over a green and black little lizard. Surprisingly, the little guy seemed to like his canine bath because he wasn't moving, except maybe to get Ollie to scratch his side. I chuckled. "Okay, Ollie. I think the lizard is clean enough."

My dog stopped her lizard washing and turned her head to the side to look at me like I was crazy. Then she turned back, woofed, and trotted off toward the sheriff's station. I knew getting a dog was going to be fun, but I had no idea how much entertainment they provided.

Chapter 24

People were moving all over the sheriff's department. Some in uniform, and some in plain clothes. I couldn't be sure, but it looked like they were scrambling for an inspection.

Or, maybe they were helping the old sheriff move out and the new one into the old sheriff's office? I just hoped they cleaned that room and painted it before anyone else moved into it.

And maybe even disinfected it.

I clanged the bell on the counter, but no one paid me any attention. So I began to hit it over and over until finally someone yelled at me, "Stop that incessant ringing."

I held my hands up and smiled. "I'm here to see Sheriff Madrid."

A large man in a uniform that looked like it was two sizes too small, took the toothpick out of his mouth and placed it behind his ear. "Get in line, lady."

I blinked.

Then I looked around. There wasn't a line.

I looked back at the cop and was about to point out that fact when the Sheriff himself walked out of one office, then stopped short and grinned. "Miss Bransky. What brings you in this time of day?"

"Really?" I glared at him.

Sam Madrid chuckled and waved me back. "Let her through, Charlie. She's Jo Barton's niece."

Charlie coughed. "Right, of course." He opened the small gate that divided the entry room from the open area of what some cops on TV shows referred to as the "bullpen". It was just a large, open space with lots of desks. At the moment, they were empty, but since so many people were moving around, I assumed the desks belonged to all of t hem.

"Excuse the mess, Sheriff Anderson's office is getting renovated, and his stuff is all over the place." Sam led me to a smaller office than what I'd seen when Sheriff Anderson hauled me in almost two weeks earlier.

"No problem." I wanted to ask if he was also getting it disinfected but held my tongue. Just because I didn't like the retiring sheriff, didn't mean that Sheriff Madrid agreed with me.

Sheriff Madrid's office may have been small, but it was neat and well organized. Nothing like what I expected of someone who had just moved in.

"Please," he motioned to a seat in front of his desk.

When I passed a wooden filing cabinet, I ran a hand over the top and was surprised to see zero dust. Not even a speck. Either he had just finished cleaning his office, or this man was the biggest neat freak – ever.

In the desert it was next to impossible to keep dust away. And even worse while renovating a room inside of a large building. Fully expecting to see files on the chairs, I was pleasantly surprised to see both of the chairs free of anything. In fact, when I looked around, I didn't see anything out of place.

There was a picture of Sam in jeans and a snap shirt, with his arm around an older woman who had long hair that went past her waist. Her hair was peppered with a tinge of gray. If it weren't for her gray hair, I would have said she was an older sister to Sam, but I got the feeling this was his mother.

Next to the picture was an award. It seemed Sheriff Sam Madrid had received a distinguished service medal from the local Yavapai-Apache Police Department.

After Sam took his seat, he sat back. "What can I do for you, Maisy?"

Ollie sat obediently at my side, without me even having to tell her. Ever since she met Sam, she'd been putty in his hand. He looked at her, and she seemed to know exactly what he wanted her to do.

The sheriff looked at Ollie and grinned. "Hello, girl. How are you liking it with your new momma? Is she taking good care of you?"

Ollie stayed sitting, but her behind began to wave and she yipped. I could have sworn she answered in the affirmative. Or maybe that was just my newfound telepathic connection with my dog?

Or, better yet, I was going crazy.

"So, this is going to sound weird. But I was coming out this morning to see you when you showed up at my store." I coughed and licked my lips. "You don't have any news do you?"

"About your aunt?" He asked.

I nodded.

"Sorry, nothing yet."

"Of course. I know it's too early." I took a deep breath and took the book out of my bag. "I was reading this last night and have some questions."

Sam put his hand out, and leaned forward. I handed him the book. He read the title, then opened it and scanned a few pages. "Not really the kind of thing one reads unless you need something to help you fall asleep."

"Well, that's just it. I have a customer who ordered this book, along with nine more books yesterday. They all have to do with ownership and land rights here in Westcott. Some are specifically about the founding families." I had skimmed a few pages of each of the other books before digging in to read this book. "On its own, I wouldn't have questioned it. But with all of them together, and right after Homer's death." I sucked in my lower lip and stopped.

"And the possibility of your aunt's murder?" Sam asked.

"Yeah. It has me thinking that Mrs. Costas might know something. I'm not saying she's the murderer, but she might have seen something or heard something?" I shrugged. "She has some questions. People don't go around buying this many books at one time about the founding of a small town without good reason."

"She could just be interested in her new hometown. If I remember correctly, she only moved here a few years ago. After her husband died."

"So, she's not even from here? That makes it seem even stranger, doesn't it?" I would have understood if she was from a founding family, but a newcomer? "Why would she want to know about land holdings and rights? One of the books was all about the silver mine."

Sam's brow arched, and he sat up taller. "She's interested in the old mine outside of town?"

"It seems that way." I held my hands up. "I didn't talk to her about the books, but I think it's worth looking into." I would have questioned her myself, but she was in such a hurry once I had all of her books. And since she paid for them online, there wasn't any reason for her to stick around once I had them bagged.

"I see." Sam looked back down at the book. "Thank you for bringing this to my attention. I'll look into it and see what I can find out." He stood up and looked at the door.

Wow. Really? He was dismissing me so soon? I would have expected him to want a list of all of the books she ordered. I got up and took Ollie's leash and turned to leave.

"Wait up. Do you have a copy of her order?" Sam walked around the desk and leaned down to pet Ollie.

The dog licked his arm and Sam chuckled. "Yes, I love you, too."

I had to look at him to make sure he wasn't talking to me, or someone else on the phone. "Did you just tell my dog you loved her?"

He stood up and I could see the pink beginning to rise on his cheeks. "Of course. I love all dogs. And they love me." He winked.

Chapter 25

Yesterday after giving Sheriff Sam Madrid the list of books Mrs. Costas bought, I went back to the store and worked until closing. It was all I could do to keep from going bat-crazy. There wouldn't be any news about the post-mortem on Great-Aunt Jo for several days. So now, Ollie and I headed into the store for a new day of nosey neighbors asking questions I had no answers to.

Why couldn't real life medical exams be quick like in the movies? Those detectives always had test results in less than twenty-four hours. In the real world, it took up to a week. Or was it because I lived in a small town and all of the samples had to be sent to a lab in Phoenix? That could be why, couldn't it?

I was dreaming and I knew it – literally. I had dreamt overnight about getting the results and discovering that Great-Aunt Jo wasn't killed by foxglove poisoning, it was just her time and she fell asleep peacefully and never woke up.

That would be the best-case scenario.

But when did that ever happen in my life?

I opened the front door and then I heard a noise behind me. Before I had a chance to turn around and investigate, Ollie began to growl.

When I turned around, I realized a man had been standing behind me, waiting for me. "I'm sorry, I won't be open for about another twenty minutes."

"Hi Maisy." A man wearing a turquoise button up shirt, black chinos, and brown loafers walked through the door of my bookstore before I could stop him.

I frowned. "Can I help you?" I recognized the man, but I couldn't quite place him.

Perfectly manicured hands raised, and what looked to be the smile only a Dentist could have created, greeted me and said, "Hi there welcome to the neighborhood I'm your neighbor, Alexander. I own the furniture store next door."

Recognition hit me and I realized I had seen him, and he waved at me a couple of days ago from a distance. "Alexander, yes hello. I've been meaning to come in and see your store. I'm just...well I'm sure you have the same issues I do." I shrugged. "It's been quite busy with the Christmas rush," I chuckled. Something about him made me nervous. Maybe it was the way he just barged into my store.

He chuckled. "Yes, it has been. Business has been very, very good. I think this will be more than enough to get us through till the next Christmas season."

I smiled. Not sure what he was here for. "How can I help you, Alexander?"

"Well, I wanted to know where I should send my next rent check. I was thinking that I might send it early because when we close up for Christmas, I was planning on taking a few days off to spend with my family." A hard glint passed over his eyes, and then he tried to smile, but it didn't seem real.

I had no clue who he paid his rent to. I know I owned this shop outright, thanks to Great-Aunt Jo's smart investing. I didn't know who owned the other shops. "I'm not sure who owns the building. Am I supposed to be paying rent too for something like an HOA or BOA, business owners association, how does that work here?"

Alexander's eyes widened and minuscule wrinkles developed between his eyebrows. "You own the building. In fact, you own the entire block."

"Excuse me?" I couldn't have heard him properly.

"You're Maisy Bransky, Jo Barton's heir, correct?" He asked.

"Yes, that's me." I leaned down and took Ollie's leash off and she went to sniff the man's shoes.

"Then you own this entire block. The businesses that are in this building pay you a monthly lease or rent fee." Alexander frowned down at Ollie and moved his feet away from my dog.

This was news to me. "The attorney said that..." I had to clear my throat before beginning again. "When I spoke with the attorney, he told me there was still some information he had to get straightened out, but all he said was I owned Jo's business, not that I owned the whole block."

I walked us over to the checkout counter and set my purse back behind the counter.

A deep soft chuckle emanated from Alexander's throat. "Well, I don't know what the attorney told you, but Jo's business owns this entire block. If you are now the owner of the business, then you own the entire block, and we all have to pay our rent to you."

"Oh." I knew I had some documents to go through and there was a notebook full of numbers and statements that I just had not had the chance to go through yet. I thought I'd go through them after the first of the year when everything calmed down. "How did you make the November payment?"

"I sent it to your attorney when I heard about Jo. I'm so sorry for your loss. Where are my manners? I should've come in as soon as I saw you and told you what a wonderful woman your Great-Aunt Jo was. And how sorry everyone in town is for her passing."

I looked down and fiddled with the bottom button of my shirt. "Thank you, Alexander. I really appreciate that, but I would say make your payment for December the same way you did in November. I'll call the attorney, Neil Carlton, and ask him what we're going to do. I still don't have full access to everything yet. We're just waiting on the judge to sign off on the paperwork and I think it's going to happen the first week of December due to the holiday and Judge Charles taking some time off to spend with family. The judge said he'd be back the first Monday in December. I don't think there's another judge in the area who can handle probate. My attorney said my case was the first on his docket." I just prayed Neil had it all in hand. It was turning out to be a lot more than I realized.

I owned the entire block? How was I going to handle that?

"I see. OK, yeah, sure I can just go ahead and write the check out like I did before, Siggy Enterprises and send it to the PO Box that we always use." Alexander said.

"Is that PO Box here in Westcott?" If Jo was using a PO Box for certain business transactions, how long since it was last checked? That was just one more item to add to my to-do list.

"Yes, it is. Do you have the keys, or the address, or the box number?" Alexander pulled his phone out of his back pocket.

I never understood why people put their phone in their back pocket. Besides the dangers of sitting on the phone, it was an easy spot to steal from. I never used my back pockets for anything important.

"You know, there was an oddly shaped key in the drawer. I had been meaning to ask Neil Carlton about that key. It must be the key to the PO Box. Can you write the PO box number down? Or text me the address so that I know what box to go and check? I wonder if she's got a lot of mail in there." I rubbed a hand down my face. "Oh dear, it's probably all kinds of bills and maybe even more checks. And who knows how many orders were mailed in. How many units does she rent?"

"I couldn't say how many, but I do know she's one of the largest landholders here within the city limits." He moved over to the treat table and pointed to the coffee maker. "Mind if I make some?"

I froze. I had no clue how much property Jo owned. All of a sudden, things started to get blurry. I heard a rushing sound in my ears, and I think Alexander's lips were moving, but I couldn't be certain. All I knew was that I fell back against the counter, and it held my weight until I could clear my head. I coughed, rubbed my eyes, and looked at the man standing in front of me. "Did you just say that Jo was the largest landholder in town?"

"Yes, as far as I know, she owns multiple businesses or multiple buildings here in town. You know that souvenir shop down the road with a little rooster on the side of the building. She owns that small building. She also owns the movie theater, and I think she owns the land that the Triple K gas station is on, but I can't be completely certain of that one because that's one of those national gas stations. So, she might've sold that to them." He shrugged and began getting the coffee going.

I was grateful that he started the coffee as I needed a large cup, and STAT. It wasn't even nine in the morning and already it was turning into a doozy of a day.

"That's a lot of businesses. I had no idea." Then all of a sudden, the claims Homer had made started to make more sense. He had said she robbed his family of their property. I always thought that he was talking about the ranch. But she didn't own his ranch, not that I know of anyways.

What else does she own…I own… that I don't know about? I needed to start thinking of everything as mine now, but that was tough. Especially since I didn't even know what was mine. That judge needed to get back and let me know what the heck was going on.

I bit my lip and watched Alexander's hands shake as he made himself a cup of coffee. Now that I was paying closer attention to him, he did seem nervous. I decided to play amateur sleuth and see what I could get out of him. "So, Alexander, how long have you lived in Westcott?"

He looked up at me and grinned. The wrinkles between his eyes began to fade and his smile looked genuine, instead of forced, like it had been before. "My family is from here." He held up his hand. "Not long term, like yours. We aren't a founding family, or anything like that. But my grandfather moved here when the silver mine was active."

I sat down behind the counter and listened as he told me about his family and what they had done over the years. "How many still live in the area?"

His smile faded and the sparkle that had been in his eyes died. "I'm the last one. Well, me and my little family. I have a wife and two teenage sons. One is on the local football team, and the other one helps me in my store."

"I'm sorry to hear your parents are no longer with you. That must be tough." I could sympathize, to a point. While my father had left us and I've barely spoken to him since I was a kid, my mom was very much involved with my life, even with me being here in Arizona and her back in Florida. We spoke on the phone several times a week.

"My in-laws are in the San Diego area, and we see them several times a year. That's actually where we want to go after the Christmas rush is over." Alexander stirred more sugar into his coffee.

I needed to know if he knew something about Homer's murder, but I wasn't sure how to ask him. On those cop shows the detective always had a clever way of getting what they wanted out of a perp. I was no detective. "Do you have security cameras in your store?"

He looked up from his coffee and his hand shook, sloshing coffee over the edge. "What?"

"Security cameras. I was thinking about putting some in here. You know, after what happened a couple of weeks ago, I think it might be smart to have cameras all over the place." I took another sip of my hot coffee and peered at him over the rim of my mug.

"You aren't one of those armchair detectives, are you?" He asked.

I almost choked on my coffee. I spluttered and liquid ran down my chin. "What? No." I sighed. "Maybe. You know the sheriff thought Verna killed Homer just because she was in town at the time, and they'd had a tiff earlier in the day. I know she didn't do it. And if we had cameras all over, the Sheriff would have seen Verna going in a different direction from Homer."

"Verna Henderson? Seriously?" He chuckled. "I'd heard the rumors, but thought that they were just that, rumors." He shook his head. "She couldn't have done it." Immediately, he looked down at his cup.

I narrowed my eyes and watched him fidget with the watch on his wrist. It was one of those fancy ones that tied to his cell phone and recorded his steps, heartbeats, and probably even kept track of his whereabouts. "Is the geolocation on your watch very accurate?"

Alexander's head shot up and his eyes widened. "What? Why? I didn't kill Homer."

I was about to say something, when I realized I might be in the presence of a killer. I felt my heartbeat quicken and my mouth went dry. "I didn't say that." I looked down at my wristwatch and wished I'd gotten one of those fancy ones. I'd love to see what my heart was doing at that very moment.

"No, you didn't have to. I can see it on your face." He narrowed his eyes and took a sip of his coffee while eyeballing me.

"That's not what I meant." I sighed and decided I needed to play this off. "I was curious about whether or not those kinds of watches can keep track of a person's movements. Like if Verna had one? Or what about Homer? Everyone is trying to figure out where they both were and at what times that night. The CCTV around town is spotty and there are some pretty big lags in the timelines for where both of them went. If they had watches like yours, I wondered if the sheriff could track them that way. To prove that Verna couldn't have done it, since she wasn't near him when he died."

Alexander visibly relaxed. "Oh, sorry." He scratched his chin. "It's been a trying time, what with a murderer on the loose and the entire town pointing fingers."

I nodded. "I know. I think the only reason the sheriff is looking elsewhere is because a witness stepped forward to say she saw Homer arguing with a man right before he died."

"What? Who?" Again, Alexander's hand shook.

I was starting to seriously wonder if he was the murderer, after all. But why would he kill Homer? It wasn't like anyone had been willing to sell Homer expensive items lately. And if Homer owed money to Alexander, wouldn't Jason step in and help out? "I don't know who the witness was, I just know that's why Verna was let out of jail earlier than expected.

"And that's why you wondered if I had a security camera? You think from my shop I might have been able to get a good view of the murderer?" His shop was on the other side of mine, the side that was closer to Barrel Way.

My shop was closer to the murder scene, but any camera back in the alley might have picked up something. "If you had a camera out back pointed toward Prickly Pear Avenue, your camera might have picked up something important."

He rubbed his chin and relaxed again. Alexander looked off into the distance, almost as if he was trying to visualize what I just suggested. "You know, that might be possible. But I don't have a camera back there, only inside my store."

"I'm going to call a security company and see about putting camera's outside of this building. I think we should at least have that, just in case of a break-in." I highly doubted there would be another murder any time soon. This was the first one in two decades, or more. But theft was a common problem, even in small towns.

Chapter 26

After Alexander left, I called Sheriff Madrid and told him about the strange conversation I had with my shop neighbor. He told me to stop investigating, just like in the books I loved to read. I almost laughed when he said it, but held it back for when we got off the phone.

"Men." I rolled my eyes and Ollie sat at my feet staring at me as though I was the crazy one. "I see the way you tilted your head, little miss boy crazy girl." Did talking to one's own dog constitute a need for counseling? Or did the dog work as a sort of counselor? I preferred the latter.

I bent down and scratched under her chin and her eyes hooded. I knew that she loved it when anyone pet her or scratched her. Then I picked her up. She wasn't very heavy, for a French bulldog. They were usually stalky and firm, which she was, but she was still a puppy. However, she squirmed and jumped down.

So far, Ollie hadn't enjoyed it when I picked her up, ever. Although, she did like to sit next to me on the couch at night. I'd take that as a win.

And she loved jumping up in my bed early in the morning to snuggle in my covers. Most likely because my bed was warm and comfortable.

Thank you heated blanket!

"Okay, let's go upstairs after I take you out once more." Ollie followed me obediently, which had me wondering if she had been given some training before she found herself on the streets, or if she was just that smart.

All day we had shoppers coming in and out, but it wasn't crazy like over the weekend. Which was good. Because I needed to see what all I had to re-order. We'd sold a lot of items I hadn't expected to be so popular, like the Harry Potter bookends. While I knew the glass figurines and ornaments would be popular, I hadn't realized how popular they were. I made a note in my computer calendar to order a lot more next Christmas season.

Today was Cassidy's day off, she had a lot of studying to do for her finals that were just around the corner. So, I was glad for the relatively slow day. When four o'clock came around, I noticed two shoppers entering with raincoats and umbrellas. "Hi, is it raining already?" I'd checked the weather forecast the night before, and it did say we had a chance of rain, but not until later in the evening.

I looked out the window and noticed the sidewalks were wet. I could see it sprinkling, not hard.

An older man smiled at me as he put his umbrella down, then stored it in the umbrella stand I kept by the front door for customers to use on days like today. "Yes, it just started. But the weather service is calling for a severe storm later tonight. You might want to unplug your computers, just in case we get lightning."

"Thanks, I hadn't really paid much attention to the weather today." I pointed to the treats table. "I have hot tea, coffee, and cocoa if you're interested."

The woman with him, his wife I presumed, rubbed her hands together. "Oh, a hot cup of cocoa is perfect on stormy nights. Thank you."

They both walked to the table and prepared their drinks.

"Feel free to browse through the books and gifts. Let me know if I can help you with anything." I had learned as a kid that most shoppers did better on their own. I felt the same way. I hated it when a clerk was anxious for a sale and hovered around me hoping to help me buy more than what I needed...or wanted.

I went back to reviewing sales and making notes for items I wanted to order. Some things I might not restock, since the biggest shopping days were over, but others I would. While we didn't sell out of the glass gingerbread shaped earrings, we did sell a lot. However, I wasn't sure too many more would want to buy them since we were just about to start December. Most people would have already bought what they needed for the season. Or at least, that's what I figured. Since I didn't have room for storing a lot of inventory, I would have to clearance out anything Christmas by the end of December. If I sold out of something, then that might help shoppers to look for something else I still had in stock.

This season would tell me what I might want to stock up on, or order less of, for next year. Since this was my first year running the shop, and it had been quite some time since I spent Christmas here helping Great-Aunt Jo, I figured less was more.

It would be alright if I ran out of things.

One thing I did want to buy more of were the hand carved Nativity scenes I'd already sold out of. And if I had extra, I didn't mind holding on to them until next Christmas. They were exquisitely made and very popular.

I looked up to see where the couple was, and if they needed any help. They had a hand basket with several books, and two of the store t-shirts – the Christmas one with Siggy on front covered in Christmas lights. I grinned, knowing Great-Aunt Jo would be happy with how popular her new t-shirts were this year. All I did was take her original design and add Christmas lights to Siggy, so it was really her design, not mine.

While they continued to shop, I looked up the email for the artisan who made the Nativity sets. I sent her a message stating I wanted to order ten more, if she had them. I'd even sold my display Nativity I had in the front window. I wanted to replace that one right away, if possible.

By the time I was done, the couple were walking up to my register. I looked at what they had and smiled. "I see you found some real gems. Did you find everything you wanted?"

"We did." The woman put a hand on her husband's arm. "Except for one book."

"Oh, what's that?" I asked, knowing I could special order anything they wanted.

The man spoke up, "Do you happen to have any copies of *The History and Ownership of Westcott, Arizona*?"

I felt my eyes widen, then caught myself. I couldn't appear to be shocked by this book title. I held up a finger. "Let me check my inventory." I knew we didn't have any more out on the sales floor, the only copy I had left was at the sheriff's office. "Hmm, it seems like I sold the last copy the other day. I can order more if you want me to." I was already planning on ordering more, but I wasn't going to rush it. If they wanted it quickly, then I would. And I'd tell the sheriff.

The two looked at each other. The woman nodded. "Yes, please."

"This is an interesting book. Is there some sort of land dispute?" With two deaths in the founding families lately, I was beginning to suspect it had something to do with the land. And if that was the case, then Jo was most likely murdered. And Jason and I could be next.

I needed a moment to clear those thoughts as they had me very worried for my life, and Jason's.

The woman's natural smile relaxed, and her face took on a more deceptive façade. Gone were her sparkly eyes, and sweet demeanor. "No, no. Nothing like that. I'm just curious about the area, that's all."

There was more to her curiosity, but I didn't push.

Seemed like a lot of people were curious about the area all of a sudden. I kept that thought to myself, not wanting to let these two know I suspected anything.

Turning my head back to my computer screen, I felt for my cell phone, just to be safe. It was in the pocket of my sweater. I glanced at the computer screen, and then pulled up an order form. "Okay, if you will give me your name and contact information, I'll call you once the book arrives."

"How long before you can get it?" The man asked.

"If you want it on a rush order, it should be here in two days. But, if you aren't in a hurry, I have a large order I'll be placing today, so I can add this to it. And as long as my supplier has more copies, I should have them by the weekend. Will that work?" I looked over at the couple and smiled. It was important to act normal. If I let on that I was suspicious, then they might either run, or attack me.

It wasn't the first time I was grateful that I had a large counter between me and the customers. When Jo set up her store, she prepared for safety. Although, I doubt she ever thought we'd be dealing with a murderer.

Or that she'd be murdered.

Once I had their information, I rang up the sale and put their items in a plastic, reusable, shopping bag with the store's name and logo on the outside. "Thank you, I'll call you as soon as the order arrives. Have a wonderful day."

They waved as they walked out of the door. As soon as they were no longer in sight, I pulled out my phone and dialed Sheriff Sam Madrid, for the second time that day.

"Maisy, I thought I told you to stop playing detective? We have this in hand." The voice on the other end of the call wasn't happy to hear from me.

I wasn't happy to be calling him, either. "Look, sheriff. I didn't go looking into anything. This couple came into my store asking for the same book I loaned you two days ago. I'm calling you to let you know what's going on because I'm *not* investigating anything myself."

Geesh, one would think that I was out walking around asking all sorts of questions to strangers.

Which I wasn't. Even though I wanted to.

I couldn't help it if they fell into my lap today. Okay, so maybe questioning Alexander was a bit too much, but that elderly couple? I didn't do anything with them.

A crackle came through the phone, then a long period of silence.

"Sheriff? You still there?"

"Yes, but I'm not happy with where this is heading."

I had to ask, "Any news on my great-aunt's postmortem?"

This time I heard him sigh. Then he cleared his throat. "I'm heading your way now. I should be there in a few minutes. I have some more questions for you."

He hung up before I could say anything else. Did that mean he had the results? Was she murdered? If she had just died of natural causes, he would have said so, right? I hung up my phone and just about screamed when I heard someone behind me. I hadn't heard the bell on the door ring, so either I wasn't paying attention, or this person was intentionally sneaking up on me.

"Jason?" The breathy voice that came from me didn't sound like me at all. I cleared my throat and put a hand over my chest to calm my beating heart.

He held his hands up in front of him. "I'm sorry, I thought you heard me enter when the bells jangled. I didn't mean to scare you."

I let out a breath I didn't realize I'd been holding. "No, no. It's fine. I'm just jumpy today." I sucked in my lower lip, then released it. "Would you mind keeping an eye on the store for just a second? I want to bring Ollie down. I think today would be a great day for her to be out here and get used to being in the store."

He smiled. "Sure, I love that idea. I think having the dog in the shop with you will be great. You know, if she'd been down here already, you would have known I was here."

That was exactly what I was thinking. Ollie loved to bark and great people. And that bell was something that would catch her attention, even when I missed it. "Exactly. Thanks. Be right back."

It didn't take long for me to run upstairs and grab Ollie. She was already by the door waiting for me, with her leash in her mouth. "Well, I see someone needs to go for a walk."

Ollied turned in a circle and I couldn't help but release the tension I'd been carrying through my shoulders. Everyone should have a dog, or a cat. I bet if more people had pets, the world would be a happier and healthier place. There was nothing like the love and fun a dog provided.

We walked down the stairs together, but before I could step off the last step, she bolted for Jason. Ollie barked and ran around his legs.

Jason grinned, then leaned over and pet Ollie's head. "Hey girl. I think you're such a cute little shopkeeper. Are you going to help your momma sell these books?" He motioned to the shelves next to him that were full of books and bookish gifts, like book lights, stands, and bookmarks.

I walked over to the duo and leaned down to pat Ollie's head. "Good girl." She licked my hand, then went back to loving up on Jason. The girl was nothing, if not smitten with handsome men.

I chuckled, then remembered what Ollie needed. "I need to take Ollie out back for a minute. Would you mind staying for just a few more minutes?" I winced, hoping he'd help. With the rain, I doubted anyone would come inside, but you never knew.

"Sure, I'd be happy to help. In fact, why don't I take Ollie out back to do her business while you watch the shop?"

"You don't mind? If she does big potty, you gotta pick it up. But I do have bags. Then just toss it in the dumpster." I handed him the leash, which had a small holder full of doggy doo-doo bags inside.

"No problem. This is nothing compared to cleaning up after a bull, or all of the cows I have." Jason grinned from ear to ear.

"Better you than me. Cleaning up after a small dog is more than enough." I watched as they walked out back.

Before I could get back to checking inventory, I heard the bell ring, signaling that I had a customer.

Although, it wasn't truly a customer. Instead, it was a handsome man with a deep brown tan and pearly white teeth that almost sparkled when he smiled. Only this time, he wasn't smiling. A grim face met me. "Maisy." He tipped his sheriff's hat and then looked around the store. "Any customers in here?"

It felt like stinging bees were swarming my gut and ears all at the same time. I put a hand to my stomach and shook my head. "No."

"Good. This isn't for the general public. At least, not yet." He ran a hand down his face, then took his hat off and held it in front of him. "We have some test results back."

I saw his lips moving, but was unable to hear anything else as the river rushed through my ears and head. Everything in front of me turned blurry in an instant and I felt as though I needed to sit down.

"Here, let me help you to the chair. I'm sorry. I should have had you sit for this news." The sheriff led me to one of the comfortable and worn leather chairs by the coffee maker. "Are you alright?"

"Coffee," I managed to get out once I sat down.

"Of course." Sam put a pod in the smaller machine and made me a single cup of coffee.

I rested my face in my hands as I began to process what he'd said. "She was murdered, wasn't she? Do you know why?"

"How do you like your coffee?" He asked, sidestepping my question.

"One sugar and two little cups of liquid creamer." I looked up and watched him through blurry eyes. Once he set the cup of coffee in my hands, I took a long sip. "Thank you."

"Of course." He sat in the other chair near me.

But before he could continue, Jason called out, "Ollie did good. You'd be happy." He stopped when he saw me sitting next to the sheriff. "Sam, nice to see you." Jason looked between the two of us and the spot between his eyes crinkled.

I didn't care if the sheriff wanted to keep this a secret, I felt that Jason deserved to know. "They exhumed Jo's body and ran some tests. It seems she was murdered, too."

When Jason dropped Ollie's leash, the dog ran and jumped in my lap.

"Hey, sweetie." I leaned down and hugged her to my chest. There was nothing more comforting than a hug from one's own dog. Ollied licked my face. It was enough to get me to smile.

Jason pulled another chair closer to where Sam and I were sitting, and he plopped down. "Tell me everything."

I noticed the color had drained from his face. He'd probably realized that if Jo had been murdered, it was possible we had a serial killer on our hands.

Chapter 27

The sheriff scowled at me then he sat up straight and looked at both Jason and I before speaking. "This isn't to be shared with anyone else, and I mean it. I don't want this getting all over town and causing a panic. We still don't know what it all means. And there are more tests to be run now that we know about the foxglove."

Jason furrowed his brow. "Jo was killed using foxglove, too? But how?"

"We don't know yet. All we know is that a large amount of foxglove was in Jo's system. The drug is most likely what killed her." Sheriff Madrid looked at me, then up above our heads. "The coroner should have done a proper autopsy when Jo died, not two months later. The body, ah." His voice trailed off and it was evident he did not enjoy this part of his job by the way he squirmed in his seat and refused to make eye contact with me.

"Don't worry, sheriff. I realize the condition Jo's body was in by the time you exhumed her, plus the fact that she had been prepared for burial. It couldn't have been easy to run tests." Just the thought of what they had to do had my stomach roiling. I could never be a pathologist, or doctor of any sort. Shoot, even needles gave me the heebie jeebies.

"If her blood had been drained and replaced with…" Jason put a hand over his mouth and coughed. "How'd they test for foxglove poisoning?"

"A sample of Jo's blood had been stored, but we needed to exhume her body to test her heart. I won't get into the details, but foxglove was discovered in her cardiac tissue. Which means she was poisoned. Unless she ate a salad of foxglove leaves, she was most likely murdered. We are treating it as a suspicious death, for now. Especially since Homer was poisoned the same way." The sheriff pulled out a notepad and pen, again refusing to make eye contact with either Jason, or myself.

"So, you aren't sure she was murdered, but her death wasn't normal, right?" I was confused. If she had foxglove in her system didn't that mean someone did it to her on purpose?

"It's possible that Jo made a salad from leaves in her own garden, or someone else's garden. Those leaves could have been from the foxglove plant. A few years ago, there was a couple who grew their own kale, and in the garden they also had foxglove plants. The husband picked the leaves thinking they were the kale plant, not from the pretty foxglove flower, as it hadn't bloomed yet." Sam turned the page in his notepad and looked at me.

"So, it might have been an accident? Could Homer's death be an accident? Maybe the foxglove leaves made it into the food supply by someone who didn't know what they were doing?" Jason asked.

I nodded. "I've heard of salad kits ending up with certain diseases because of human error. Maybe the foxglove leaves were picked by mistake and were put in a salad kit?"

"Or," Jason held up his index finger. "The supplier to Seven Savory Seas might have included some foxglove leaves in their mixes and Gavin, not knowing it was foxglove, put the leaves on my grandfather's sandwich. Maybe it was just an accident, in both cases?"

I felt the same way, praying it was an accident, and not murder. For both Jo and Homer. While that would still be awful, at least we wouldn't have a serial killer on the loose in tiny Westcott, Arizona.

"If only it were that easy." Sam shook his head. "We didn't find leaves of any sort in Homer's stomach contents."

"Ew." I shivered.

"I can't say if there was anything in Jo's stomach contents since we didn't do an autopsy then. But her myocardial tissue showed a toxic amount in her system. We even found traces of it in her chest muscles. She had been given a large dose of the toxin." He wrote something down in his notebook before looking up at me. "I know you weren't here then, but when was the last time you spoke with her?"

I thought for a moment, then answered, "I'd spoken to her only a few days before she died. We had regular phone calls. She didn't mention anything about feeling bad, just that she wanted my mom and I to come to see her at Christmas." I still felt guilty for choosing to stay home alone while my mom went on a Christmas cruise. I should have committed to coming out to see her. Then she would have known for sure that I loved her.

"Do you happen to know if she grows foxglove in her garden? Or who might grow that plant?" Sam looked back down at his notepad. He scribbled down a few things, but his notepad was turned so that I couldn't see what he was writing.

I thought about the garden for a moment. "I know foxgloves are tall and look like flutes or long thimbles, but I don't think Jo has any in her garden. They'd be dead by now anyways. Aren't they a summer plant?"

Sheriff Madrid looked at me for the first time since he began speaking about Jo. "Yes, how do you know this?"

I shrugged. "Foxglove is a pretty flower, but it's well known in the literature world. I happen to enjoy reading Agatha Christie, J.B. Fletcher - although those were books written after the TV shows, Sir Arthur Conan Doyle, and many more. I like the cozy mystery genre the most. And those tended to use poison quite a bit as the murder weapon. And since foxglove is grown in so many gardens, it's an easy weapon."

The sheriff sat back in his chair and studied me. "Where were you when your aunt died?"

I guffawed. "You've got to be kidding me, right?"

"Well, you did make out quite well with the inheritance. Word is you own most of the town." The sheriff kept his eyes on me and tapped the top of his pen on his notepad.

I jumped to my feet. "I don't like where this is heading. I would have never killed my great-aunt." I put my hands on my hips, leaned closer to the sheriff, and narrowed my eyes. "Besides, I didn't even know Homer well enough to want him dead. And I have a pretty good alibi for that night."

"Doesn't mean you didn't find a way to slip digitalis in his sandwich at some point before you went home that night."

I threw my hands in the air. Then I pointed to the door. "Get out! You had better be doing a better job than this in looking for the real killer." I was livid. If the sheriff continued to look at me for either murder, I was going to have to get an attorney. Maybe even have the Attorney General fire this incompetent buffoon.

Me? Kill Jo? That was the craziest thing ever.

Jason stood up and I noticed his cheeks had turned pink. He averted his gaze when I looked at him. "What? You don't think I did this, do you?"

The emotions I saw on Jason's face told me he wasn't sure what to think, but I couldn't be upset with him. His grandfather had just been murdered, and it was looking like my Great-Aunt Jo, whom most of the town adored, had been murdered as well.

When the sheriff made it to the door, he turned around and looked at me. "Maisy, I don't want to think it was you, but I have to look at all angles. And right now, you're the one who stood to gain the most from Jo's death. I do need to know where you were the day she died."

He was right, and I knew it. Didn't mean I had to like it, but I did need to cooperate. "Whatever. But just so you know, I had no clue what I was inheriting. It should have all gone to my mother, not me. There had been talk over the years of me taking over the bookshop, but nothing else. And before you go thinking it might have been her, think again. Neither of us could have made it here to Arizona and back to Florida without being noticed. Besides, we were both at a charity luncheon that day."

Sheriff Madrid opened his notebook, again. "What's the name of the charity?"

"Pft. Of course, you're going to check up on us. Well," I pulled my phone out of my pocket and opened up the Internet app. I looked up the Florida MS Society and found the page I had seen only a few weeks ago. I turned my phone toward the sheriff. "We were photographed at the event, and they posted a lot of pictures."

Sam took my phone and clicked through the pages. Then he wrote something in his notebook. "Right. Thank you. And I am sorry I had to ask. But I don't think you'd appreciate me skipping people over just because I like them." He arched his brow.

My body deflated and all anger escaped me. I knew he was right, but any hint that I might have killed my beloved Great-Aunt Jo just to get her money was ludicrous. And insulting.

He opened the door and left.

I turned and noticed that Jason was also standing, and he had already put his coat on.

"You don't think I could have done it, do you?" I asked.

Jason sighed and ran a hand down his face. "Maisy, I don't know what to think. This is all so convoluted. The girl I knew as a kid couldn't have killed a fly. And if you really were at that charity event, then you're right, you couldn't have made it back here to kill her before she went to bed."

"And your grandfather?" I was starting to feel that anger coming back again. One part of my heart knew that Jason was still grieving the loss of his grandfather, so the way he was pulling back from me was normal. But there was also the side of me that was hurt he could even consider it possible.

He averted his gaze for a moment, but when he turned his head back toward me, I realized he had made up his mind. Jason stood taller than I'd seen him do since his grandfather had died and he looked me directly in the eyes. "No, I don't think you could have done it. Besides, it sounds like he was seen arguing with a man right before he died. I think that person might be responsible."

I nodded. "Good. Now that we got that out of the way, I need to tell you something I discovered over the past few days." I went on to tell him about the customers who were interested in land ownership of the town and the mine itself. It had to be a clue, although I didn't know what it actually meant.

Chapter 28

Jason sat back down in the chair. "This is getting...I don't know...crazy? The mine? Land rights? My grandfather didn't own anything else. I bought up everything he owned. So why would anyone kill him if it had to do with his land ownership?"

I bit my lip, unsure how much to share, but knowing that I needed a sounding board, I went ahead and shared what I knew.

My great-aunt's friends were all nice and helpful. And not for one second did I think any of them had anything to do with either murder, but this was dangerous. And it seemed Jason and I might be next. Which meant, we needed to be on the same page and look out for each other.

"I found something else last night." I went to the small office on the ground floor. I'd taken the journal home with me the previous night and read the rest of it. And in doing so, found something that made zero sense to me.

When I walked out, Jason was at the coffee table fixing himself a cup. "I hope you don't mind?" He lifted the cup to show what he was making.

I shook my head. "No, please help yourself. That coffee is for everyone who comes through my doors." I smiled, then sat back down in my previously vacated seat. Ollie sat in between my chair and Jason's. At least she hadn't chosen one of us over the other.

Once Jason was settled, I pulled out the journal.

He looked at it and frowned. "You've already shown that to me."

"Yes, and no. When I showed it to you the other day, I hadn't read it all. And in the back, I found some papers." I opened the journal to the back and pulled out the three sheets of paper. While I wasn't completely sure I should be doing this, I had decided that Jason was my friend, and most likely the only other person alive who could understand what it might mean.

"This Last Will and Testament is very different from what I remember the attorney reading after Aunt Jo died." I handed him the paper. "And the signature doesn't seem right, either. Do you know anything about this?" I had meant to pull out the papers the family attorney gave me after the reading of the will, but I was too tired last night. And was running late this morning. But I promised myself that I would look at those papers first thing when I got home later.

Jason took the paper from my hands and began reading it. He took a sip of the coffee and the little lines between his eyes showed up again. Then he just about spluttered his coffee all over the place. I knew where he was in the document. "You've got to be kidding me. I don't believe this." He shook his head.

"It states that you and Homer now own most of the town. The only thing that Aunt Jo supposedly left to me was her house and this business, not even the entire building is mine; according to this version of the will." The signature at the bottom of the last page couldn't be Aunt Jo's unless she'd been coerced into signing it. It was jagged and not very close to the way Jo signed her name. I should know, I'd seen her signature a million times since I took over the bookshop.

"No, that's not possible. Jo would have never done that." He handed me the papers. "This must have been some sort of joke. But it's not funny."

I took the papers. "Do you think it's possible that someone killed Jo to get her property?"

"But you inherited it all." He stated.

"I know, but if this Will would have been accepted, then you and Homer would have inherited it all." I raised a brow.

He held up his hands. "Whoa now. I didn't kill Jo." He shook his head so hard, the longer strands of his hair flew forward and covered his eyes.

Jason's eyes widened, and his pupils dilated. The man was afraid, but of what? I put my hand on his arm. "Jason, I'm not accusing you of anything. I think this is all much bigger than you or I. With several people looking at who owns the land here in town, and this obviously fake will, I think something else is going on. And I think you and I might be in some real danger."

I looked down as I heard Ollie's whimper. She had her front paws on Jason's leg and her eyes had widened as well. I could tell my little dog was worried for Jason. I picked her up and held her to me as I doubted that Jason wanted a dog trying to jump into his lap. Not as he was trying to take in all I had just said.

Jason closed his eyes and his nostrils flared as his breathing came in ragged shots. "Have you shown this to Sam?"

I shook my head, but realized Jason's eyes were still closed. "No, I don't think that's a good idea."

His eyes flew open, and he turned his head in my direction. "What? Why not? Whoever wrote this must be the person who killed Jo and Homer. Sam needs this."

I had originally thought the same thing, but with the way the sheriff behaved earlier when I phoned him about the conversation with Alexander, I had forgotten about it. Not that I was normally forgetful, but manning the store alone had me a bit worried earlier. I shouldn't have been worried, but I was. "To be honest, I did have plans to share this with Sheriff Madrid, but..." I shrugged. "Today got away from me." And I didn't want Sam to read the personal messages in Jo's journal. Towards the end of the book, she began writing about a love affair she once had, and regretted.

Not that the man was married at the time, but she had turned him down when he proposed. From what I could tell, she'd never gotten over him. And that explained why she'd never seriously dated anyone, that I could remember.

The journal was old, but the Will wasn't. It had been dated six months before Jo's death. I sighed, and realized I needed to call Sheriff Sam Madrid, for the third time that day. "You know he's going to suspect you, right?"

"No, I don't think he will. Not really. He'll ask me the same questions he asked you, but then he'll move on to someone else. Can I see that Will again?" He reached out his hand and I gave him the document.

I watched as his eyes scanned the pages. "You know, this makes it look like me and my grandpops could have killed Jo. But I think it was created for just that purpose." He rubbed his chin. "But why did Jo have it? Did she find it somehow? And if so, did she know who wrote it?"

"That's a very good question. I'm going to take pictures before the sheriff confiscates it. And I've got a very good idea who to ask about this." After I took the photos, I called the sheriff. But before he arrived, I sent the pictures to my mom asking her if she knew anything about it.

If Jo spoke to anyone about this, it would have been my mother.

Or, her attorney.

The bells above the door dinged and I jumped. This investigation was getting to me, and I knew it. "Sheriff, that was fast. Where were you? Just across the street, or something?"

"Or something." Sheriff Madrid smirked. He cleared his throat. "What's this about a bogus Will?

I took the pages and handed them to the sheriff.

While he read them, his eyes narrowed, and his lips tightened. "When did you find this?"

"Last night." I didn't want to tell him exactly where I'd found the journal, and I hoped to keep the journal out of his hands, or anyone else's for that matter. Therefore, I was brief and to the point.

The sheriff pinched the bridge of his nose. "Why didn't you say something sooner?"

I scoffed. "Really? When could I have said anything? When you were berating me for sharing what Alexander said? Or when I told you about the people who came in looking for books about local land ownership? Oh, wait." I put a hand on my hip and jutted it out. "That wouldn't have worked, either. Since you told me to keep my nose out of *your* investigation. Or maybe, I should have told you about this when you were accusing me of killing my aunt."

The sheriff closed his eyes and took in a few deep breaths. "You're right. I've not been very approachable today."

"Not approachable?" I scoffed. "Try downright mean. What is going on, Sam?" I thought that by using his first name, like he might still be a friend, he'd be more apt to think of me as his friend, and not a suspect.

But I was wrong.

"Miss Bransky. You do realize that this makes you look even more guilty?" The sheriff held up the papers.

Maybe I should have used his childhood name – Sammy.

I almost laughed. "Not really. If you check the signature, you'll see that it's a fake. And a bad one at that."

Sammy turned his head toward Jason. "And what about you? Did you know anything about this?"

"Whoa, now." Jason put his hands up in a defensive gesture. "I don't need any more land to manage right now. I have my hands full with the ranch."

"Right. And why is it that you've been spending so much time in town lately if your hands are so full?" The brow arch on Sheriff Madrid's face was quite impressive. It went so high; it was almost swallowed up by his hairline.

"This is getting us nowhere." I paced around my store while Ollie watched me from her spot next to Jason. As far as the men went, she'd made her choice. I noticed that when I was arguing with Sam, Ollie had sidled up next to Jason. It probably didn't hurt that Jason had put his hand down and Ollie looked at it, probably hoping to get a treat from him, or a scratch behind her ears. Ever since she moved closer to him, he'd been petting her. Well, except for when Sam practically accused him of being part of the fake Will business.

"I don't know what this counterfeit Will has to do with anything, or who did it. Or even why Jo had it in her office, but I think it might be a clue as to who could have killed her." I glared at the sheriff, waiting for him to agree with me.

"I'll take this back to the station and see if we can find some finger-prints, or something." He looked between Jason and me. "I assume you've both handled this?" He pulled out a plastic bag from one of the many pockets he had on his bullet-proof vest he was wearing.

I hadn't noticed him wearing that before and wondered why he hadn't been, but decided it wasn't any of my business. Maybe the only reason he had it on now was for the plethora of pockets that seemed to hold stuff, like an evidence bag.

"I'll need you both to come and provide fingerprints so we can exclude yours from any possible ones on these sheets."

"Do you have Jo's prints on file?" I knew hers would have to be on them.

Sheriff Madrid nodded.

"Will you let me know what you find out?" I wasn't holding my breath, but this did have a lot to do with me.

"I don't normally share information during an ongoing investiga-tion." Without another word, he turned on his heels and walked out the door.

I tilted my head, and when the door was fully closed, I turned toward Jason. "So, do you think that means he's going to share any info he finds with me?" I grinned, knowing he wouldn't.

"I wouldn't hold your breath." Jason stood up after he gave Ollie one last pet. "I do need to get back to the ranch. Sam was right, I've been neglecting a lot of work lately." He rubbed his chin. "But if you need me, just call and I'll be right here."

I put a hand on Jason's arm. "Thank you, I appreciate that."

"And if you hear anything about the case, will you let me know?" He asked when he had his hand on the door handle.

"Of course. And you, too?" I asked.

He grinned, then walked out the door.

I watched as he crossed the street to his truck.

Then, I noticed the dark clouds in the sky and shivered. "I think we're gonna get a storm tonight, Ollie."

My dog barked her agreement before I went around ensuring that the store was locked up tight. I still had a lot of inventory to shelve before the storm got bad.

Chapter 29

Hours later, the storm raged, and I wished I'd waited to do the restocking.

Ollie barked and ran toward the front door. I followed her and sucked in a breath.

Outside, hail the size of the tip of my pinkie finger was falling like crazy. I prayed Siggy would be alright. That Saguaro was over one hundred and fifty years old. And it was Jo's pride and joy, not to mention the official mascot of the bookshop.

I could hear the plink, plink, plink of the hard balls of compressed snow and rain hitting all over outside. The tinny sound caught my attention, and I turned to see one lone older Cadillac down the street getting pummeled.

Thankfully, I had parked in the parking structure across the street from the store. My car should be fine inside on the second floor. But walking over there was going to have to wait. "Okay, Ollie, I think we're going to have to wait it out here."

She whimpered and ran to the back of the shop.

I followed her, hoping she didn't need to go outside. There wasn't a covering out back that would protect her while she did her business. Or me while I waited with her.

Normally, she scratched at the door if she wanted out, but right now, she was sitting in front of the back door and whimpering.

"Ollie, did you want to go outside? It's not very nice out there right now." I wanted to get her piddle pad trained, but didn't think this was the weather to try it out on. I sighed - heavily. "Alright, we'll go out there, but you need to hurry up. Stick as close to the side of the building as you can."

I put on my jacket and pulled the hood up to cover my head. We headed out back, but Ollie only sniffed around a bit and then ran back inside. I chuckled. "Gonna hold it in, are you?"

Once we were back inside the warmth of my shop, I debated what to do. I'd already restocked everything I needed to. And I had finished reading Aunt Jo's journal. It was time to head home, but that weather sent a chill down my spine. I really didn't like the idea of running across the street in the hail. Although, hail didn't usually last long, maybe I could wait it out?

"Ollie, let's go upstairs and watch some TV while we wait out the storm. How does a food show sound?" My stomach growled its approval.

Ollie chuffed.

We went upstairs.

I turned on the TV and then pulled out the journal. I'd noticed something in the back and wanted to take a closer look. The back of the leather cover had a thick piece of paper glued down, but one edge had come up and there was something underneath it. Slowly, I pulled the back page up and when I had enough space, I was able to get the piece of paper out.

"Huh, looks like Jo had one more scavenger hunt for me." My eyes teared up as I thought back to my childhood and all of the scavenger hunts that my Great-Aunt Jo had created for me and my friends.

This Christmas was about honoring Jo, and her memory. So, I decided that I'd share this with her friends and then maybe on Christmas Day we could all do one final treasure hunt. She loved to put a giant red "X" on the map where she hid the *treasure*.

However, as I looked closer, this didn't look like her usual map. The paper was aged, and the red "X" wasn't nearly as obvious as she usually made them. I showed the paper to Ollie, who sniffed, then chuffed. "Maybe she has changed it up because I'm an adult now? I need a better map if I'm going to believe there's a real treasure."

I was about to fold the map up and put it away, then noticed a date in the bottom corner of the page, 1894. "Well, I'll give her points for authenticity." Then I folded it back up and searched the limited options on the local TV channels. I didn't have cable, only over-the-air television. Once I found what I wanted, I sat back in my chair and Ollie sat on the ground next to my feet.

When the episode of Diners, Drive-Ins, and Dives was over, I turned off the TV and looked outside. "Well, it looks like the hail has changed to rain and it has slowed down enough to be out in it. What do you say we head home?" I looked down at Ollie and I could have sworn she nodded her little head.

Before I could grab all of our stuff, she headed downstairs. I followed carrying two armloads of mostly doggy stuff. "I need to train you to carry your own bag and blankets." Or, maybe I just needed to get more so I didn't have to bring anything back and forth between the store and home.

I was on the second to last step when I heard jiggling.

Ollie growled.

I looked up and noticed someone at my front door.

Ollie ran toward the door and began barking.

The person looked up and all I could see was light shining off their eyes. The person was in a big, black jacket. The kind a lot of people in town wore. I couldn't tell if it was a man or a woman. The person turned tail and ran toward the corner where Simone's BBQ Pit sat, all closed up.

"Hey!" I yelled out, but almost tripped over the bottom step in an effort to dump the stuff in my hands while running toward the front door. The key was still in the door, so I turned the lock and looked outside.

The dark colored Cadillac I'd noticed earlier was heading away from me and heading down Cactus Lane towards the neighborhood where I lived.

I was about to give chase, when I realized that I would never be able to catch up. If they were heading towards my house, I wouldn't get there in time.

For the umpteenth time, I called the sheriff.

"Maisy, I don't have any answers for you." The sheriff preempted me.

"Sam, someone just tried to break-into my shop." I cut him off before he could read me the riot act for asking more questions, which I wasn't trying to do.

"What? Are you safe? Did he get in?" I could hear scraping on the other end of the phone while the sheriff asked me several questions.

"I'm fine. I'm at the shop, but the culprit was in an older Cadillac. Dark colored, but I can't tell you anything more about it. Except, that he was headed toward my neighborhood. Do you think he's going to try and break into my house?" I went through the store, looking to see that everything was still locked, and set the alarm.

Ollie was right on my heels as we practically ran to the car. With the drizzling rain, Ollie didn't seem to mind running. I was confident she wanted out of the rain as much as I did.

"Stay there. I'm heading to your house now. I think we have a patrol car close by, I'll call him and see if he can check your house out." The sheriff hung up before letting me get another word in.

Once we were in the safety of the three-story parking garage, I stopped and put my phone away. "Well, Ollie, do you think we should head back to the store? Or home?"

She barked when I said *home*. I had to agree with her; home sounded like a much better option.

Before I even made it home, I had a message from the alarm company. When I stopped at the stop sign, I looked at my phone and could have hit myself. "Ollie, we gotta go back to the store."

I was about to call the sheriff, when my phone rang. It was the security company. "Your business alarm is going off, the video shows someone breaking in."

"Yeah, I got the notification. Can you call the police? I'm heading to the store now." I'd never owned my own shop, or even had a home alarm, so I had no clue how this worked. Did they call the cops? Or did I?

"Ma'am, I don't recommend you going over there until the police can check it out. We've notified them of an active event." The woman on the other side of the call tried to keep me away, but it was my business, my livelihood. Besides, there were some things in the store that I didn't want anyone to find.

I was just glad that I'd put the journal back in the brick wall after we started to watch Guy Fieri. And I sent up a prayer that the thief wouldn't find it before I got there.

"If you don't mind staying on the phone with me, I'll be careful. How about I drive around the block and see if anyone is still inside?" I didn't have a death wish. Two people had already died for whatever they wanted. But I did hope to catch a glimpse of who it was before they left.

And maybe even stop them from getting anything.

Ollie sat in the passenger seat with her paws up on the side window. She barked when we turned the corner.

"I see it, Ollie." Behind my shop was the Cadillac I'd seen speeding away earlier. "I see a Cadillac behind my shop. I'm gonna get a picture of the plates. Can I text it to you?" I was still on the call with the security company.

"Ma'am, I highly recommend you drive away. It isn't safe for you to be there if someone is still inside your shop." The woman, I think she said her name was Patty, kept trying to get me to leave.

I took the phone away from my ear and snapped several photos of the car. "Can I text you the images? You know, just in case?"

Patty sighed and gave me a web address to use to upload the pictures. "But I would prefer it if you drove away before doing that. Maybe even head to the sheriff's office."

"Uh, oh." I felt the blood drain from my face when I recognized the person coming out of the back of my building.

Alexander stopped before he jumped back in his car. He waved and smiled. "Maisy, isn't this weather crazy?"

"What?" A frantic voice on the phone practically screamed, "are you alright? What's happening?"

"I know the person, it's the owner of the shop next to mine." I paused and squinted as I tried to see where Alexander had come from. "Oh, stink." I slumped in my seat and turned off the motor. "He came out of his own store."

I got out of my car and waved. "Alexander, did you see anyone breaking into my store?"

He tilted his head and furrowed his brows. "What? I can't hear you." He reached up to his head and took out one earbud. "Sorry, I was listening to music. Do you like Def Leppard?"

"Uh, sure. But, someone just broke into my store. Did you see or hear anything?" I looked around to see if anyone else was there, and then I heard sirens screaming as they came toward my store.

Alexander looked around, then back at me. "Did you say someone broke into your store? Did they steal anything?"

I shook my head. "I don't know. It happened less than ten minutes ago. You didn't hear the alarm?" While I was driving back to the store, the alarm company muted the alarm, since we all knew it was an in-progress event.

A sheriff's deputy SUV pulled in behind me, and one drove in from the other end of the alley behind my shop. Sheriff Anderson stepped out of the second vehicle and the words I heard coming from him would have gotten my mouth washed out with soap if I had ever uttered them within Great-Aunt Jo's hearing. "Maisy Bransky. What are you doing here? Didn't the alarm company tell you to stay clear?"

"Hi, Sheriff Anderson. They did, but as you can see, I'm fine." I waved.

The deputy that pulled up behind me called out, "Who's the man in front of you?"

I turned around to see a young deputy that I hadn't met yet. He couldn't have been older than twenty-five, or so. But he was tall, thin, and had blond hair. The young man was rather cute, too. I grinned. "Deputy. That man is my neighbor, Alexander Maple. He runs the furniture store." I pointed to the back door that was so close to mine, that I'd mistaken it for mine when I first drove up.

"Did he break into your store?" The deputy asked.

I looked at Alexander, standing next to the older Cadillac I'd seen earlier, and shook my head. "No, his back door is right next to mine."

"What's going on?" Alexander looked from Sheriff Anderson, to me, and then to the handsome deputy. "Maisy said someone broke into her store?"

Sheriff Anderson walked over to my back door, and with his gloves on, he jiggled the back door handle. "It's locked. I thought someone broke into your store?"

I shrugged. "Maybe they went through the front door?"

"Deputy Jenson, head around to the other side and check it out." Sheriff Anderson ordered. Then he looked at Alexander. "Did you see anything in the last ten minutes?"

Alexander shook his head. "No, sheriff. I had my earbuds in playing loud music." He winced and held up the one earbud he had taken out. "A plane could have flown by and I wouldn't have heard it. When did your alarm go off?"

"I'll ask the questions here." The sheriff gruffed and pulled up his pants. The man needed a new belt. It seemed every time I saw him, he was trying to keep his pants from falling down. "What time did you arrive?"

Alexander looked at the watch on his wrist. "I pulled in here about twenty minutes ago. There wasn't anyone back here."

"That was right after I left through my front door." I bit my lip. If I'd stayed put like Sheriff Madrid told me to, I'd have been in the front of my store when the thief came back. He probably wouldn't have bothered my store if I had stayed here.

The sheriff's radio squelched, and he picked up the microphone on his shoulder. "Sheriff Anderson."

"Sheriff, the front door has been jimmied open, but I don't see anyone here now. The cash register has been thrown to the ground and a few glass trinkets are broken, but I don't see much else disturbed."

I slapped my forehead. "I swear, if I get a hold of this guy..." I decided not to finish my sentence. If something did happen to my thief, then this sheriff would haul me away in handcuffs and probably throw away the key to both my cell and the cuffs. And I doubt he'd look any further, either.

"Glad I already did my shopping." Sheriff Anderson sniggered. Then he cleared his throat. "Alright, let's all go around to the front of the store."

I pulled my keys out to open the back door, but Sheriff Anderson stopped me.

"No, let's walk around and see what we have in the front of the store." He led us around to the front and motioned for us to stop before entering. "Can you see if there is any more damage or something missing?"

I stood up on tippy toes and looked around at what I could. It didn't seem like anything else was touched. The cash register lay on the ground in front of the counter, and to the side were a few glass figurines smashed on the ground. It didn't look like the intruder threw them on the ground, more like when he turned around, his arm swept the table in front of the counter and a few pieces of Kiiya glass were thrown to the ground.

"What is with criminals and destroying the glass figurines and ornaments in my store?" I almost wanted to blame Homer for this, but I knew that wasn't possible.

Deputy Jenson walked out and removed the paper booties he had over his boots. "I don't see any other damage anywhere. But you'll need to go inside and inspect the place."

"Do you want me to wear booties, too?" I asked.

"No, stay out. Let us go inside and process the scene. When we're done, I'll walk you through the building." Sheriff Anderson pulled his cell phone out and dialed someone. "Honey, I'll be home late tonight."

I stepped away when I realized he had called his wife.

"Mr. Maple, I'll need to take your statement. Can you go back inside your store and write down everything you saw or heard since arriving tonight?" Deputy Jenson motioned to the furniture store next door.

His door was closed, and it appeared that only my store had been robbed. All of the rest of the doors I could see looked undisturbed, too.

Once Alexander was back inside his store, I turned to the deputy. "Do you think they targeted me specifically? Or was it just that I was gone, and Alexander was in his shop, so they chose mine?"

Deputy Jenson shook his head. "I really couldn't say. Did you leave any money in your register?"

"No," I shook my head. "I always clean it out each night and then do a drop at the bank or put the cash in my safe that's located in the ground floor office." I winced. "Did you see the safe?"

"I went to the office on the ground floor but didn't see anything out of place. Where is your safe?" The radio on the deputy's shoulder made a sound and he tilted his head to hear.

When the deputy walked away from me, I went right up to the entrance of my shop, being careful not to touch anything or go inside. I took a quick look around, but couldn't see any other damage. The only thing I could think of was that the thief thought I had kept cash in the drawer, which I didn't. No shopkeeper left money out in the open at night.

A few minutes later, Sheriff Madrid showed up and he spoke in hushed tones with Anderson and Jenson. I hoped it didn't mean that someone had made their way inside of my house.

"Sheriff Madrid? Is someone at my house keeping an eye on it?" I didn't keep cash inside the house, either. However, I wasn't sure this was only about cash. I did have some documents back home that a murderer might want to see.

Sam looked at me. "No signs of a break-in at your house, but there is another deputy keeping an eye on the house right now. After we have you search the store, I think you and Ollie should head home."

I'd left Ollie in the car, but could hear her barking her disapproval and I felt like a cad. "I'll go get her while you finish checking out my shop."

I had a sneaking suspicion this wasn't your typical thief looking for some quick cash.

Chapter 30

Several hours later, I sat in front of a blazing fire with Ollie snoring at my feet as I ate the last few bites of my turkey chili. It was warm, filling, and comforting. Exactly what I needed after the past few hours.

Turned out that nothing other than the cash register and the Kiiya glass had been moved. I doubted the intruder had enough time to search past the counter. The sound of the alarm blaring had to have had him doing a quick grab and run.

The sheriffs both thought it was just some kid looking to score some easy cash, but I didn't buy it.

All I knew was that I was very glad I'd put the journal, and the treasure map, back in the hole in the brick wall before I was broken into. I'd decided to leave it there for the night. The last thing I needed was for anyone to see me getting under the desk to retrieve the journal.

It was most likely best to leave the journal inside the wall until this was all taken care of. The journal, and the map, only had sentimental value for me. There wasn't anything in there that someone else would want. However, if someone found it, they'd probably want to take it just to see for themselves if it had anything of value between the pages.

Of course, the Cadillac I saw earlier was Alexander's, not the man who tried to break in while I was there. Sam suspected that the original intruder hid behind the parking structure after I scared him off. And when he saw Ollie and I get into my car, he must have thought it would be safe to go back and see what he could steal.

If only I hadn't left when I did.

And maybe it was something as simple as a kid trying to get a quick buck.

It made sense, but the hairs on my arms stood on end every time I thought about the man at the door. I didn't recognize him, but there was something familiar about his frame. He was tall, but not as tall as the deputy. However, he did seem taller than I was. I got a quick look at the height chart on the door frame and if memory served, the intruder was about six feet tall. Shadows covered the man's face where the hoodie didn't, making it next to impossible to see who it was.

I set my empty bowl on the side table and laid down on my sofa. I stared into the flames and then closed my eyes as I prayed that God would help me to figure out exactly what was happening.

The next thing I knew, Ollie was barking, and I had drool all down my face. I jumped up and realized that I'd fallen asleep on the couch, in front of the fire.

The fire that was no more.

"Ollie, what's going on?" I looked around but couldn't hear or see anything out of the ordinary. The clock on the mantel showed it was just past two in the morning.

The house was cold and dark. Without the blazing fire that lulled me to sleep only a few hours earlier, the only lights were the ones from the outside street lamps. Shadows swayed on the walls, and a shiver went up my spine.

Ollie barked again as I heard something outside. Slowly, I made my way to the kitchen, checking to see if the back door was locked. I knew the front door was because that was how we got inside, and it was instinct to always lock the door behind me. But I couldn't remember if I'd locked the back door after the last time I took Ollie outside to do her business.

Through the windows I could see the tree swaying in the wind. The storm may have been done, but the weather was far from calm. I watched as clouds sped past my house like cars out on Highway 17 as they raced up towards Prescott.

"Well, that explains the shadows, Ollie. Come on, let's get to bed." I motioned for Ollie to join me, but she growled at the back door, just as it opened.

I jumped and screamed at the same time. A tall shadow appeared in the doorway. For a moment, I thought it might be a ghost the way it ambled towards me. I couldn't see anything but darkness surrounding the image.

Then Ollie barked and all of a sudden, I could see the face of the man I knew and trusted. However, Ollie continued to growl. She moved in front of me and barked again, then growled. She was not going to let this intruder get near me. Which was odd, since she loved this guy to pieces.

"Jason? What are you doing?" A ripple of fear went down my back, and I moved toward the counter with the knife block.

"I think you know what I'm doing here, Maisy." He pulled his hoodie down and looked at Ollie. "Knock it off."

"Hey, don't be like that. She's protective of me. And you're coming in here in the middle of the night like some sort of thief..." I shut my mouth and moved faster toward the counter, as I did I felt in my pocket for my cell phone and cursed my unlucky stars.

It must have fallen out on the sofa while I slept.

Everything that had happened over the past few weeks started to make sense. Jason all of a sudden wanting to be around me all of the time, even though his ranch was busy and needed his attention. He kept coming into my shop asking questions, or just hanging around to overhear anything I might say to someone. And I always wondered why during the Thanksgiving Day dinner he didn't want us to share our whereabouts. It had nothing to do with any of us, he didn't want to get caught in a lie about where he was the night Homer was murdered.

Jason was the murderer.

"Why? Why did you kill my aunt?" It didn't seem right, but he had to be the murderer. Why else would he be here in the middle of the night and acting like this? "What were you looking for in my shop earlier?" That I did have some idea about. The bogus Will wasn't the only thing I'd found, but the other document wasn't worth anything. Unless you believed the old wives' tales about the lost treasure in the mine.

Which I didn't.

"You've got the map, don't you." He didn't ask a question, more demanded that I did have it.

I shook my head. "Too many people have lost their lives searching that old gold mine for the lost vein of diamonds. Including the original family who owned it. Every one of them died in the mountain. You know this." When my back hit the counter that held the knives, I almost sighed in relief. My hand went behind my back searching for the only weapon I knew how to use, besides a frying pan upside the man's head.

I'd use the frying pan if I had to, but I didn't want to kill him, only stop him from harming me.

"What I know is that you found it. I know Jo had it, she'd boasted about it once over a few drinks. But she would never tell anyone where it was. And when you found that bogus Will..." Jason scoffed. "I can't believe my foolish grandfather tried that."

I narrowed my eyes. "You know it was your grandfather who wrote that fake Will? What? Were you two in on this together? He created that Will and you killed my aunt?" My hand continued to move behind my back searching for a weapon, while I tried to get a full confession out of the man I had once called "Friend."

He threw his hands in the air. "Of course, not. I would have never hurt your aunt. But everyone knew that she had a heart condition. She'd totally given up her one glass of whiskey right about the time I moved back. Said it wasn't good for her heart."

My aunt wasn't a teetotaler, but she wasn't a big drinker, either. However, she did on occasion have a glass of wine or whiskey. The whiskey was more when she had a sore throat or cold, or so she had told me once.

"So, you took advantage of her condition and gave her an overdose of digitalis? Trying to make it look like her heart gave out?" I couldn't believe what I was hearing. Jason? A murderer? I never would have thought him capable of something so heinous.

"No, I told you. I never would have hurt Jo." He sighed and ran a hand through his hair. "It was my grandfather who did it. But he paid the ultimate price in the end. That fool." He spat the last few words, and I could see veins popping out of his neck.

My hand felt the bottom of the knife block, and my eyes widened. "No." I went limp for just a moment, letting him see the real pain in my eyes. Then I turned around in an effort to keep Jason from seeing what I was up to, and grabbed the chef's knife from the block before quickly twirling around to see that he'd moved too close to me.

"Jason, stop. I don't want to hurt you."

"Then don't." He put his hands on his belt and gave me a saucy smile. "We could do this together. Maisy you and I would make a great team." He motioned between the two of us. "With your map, and my equipment, we could find that diamond vein. I know it's there."

I shook my head. "No, Jason, it's not. You know the rumors were false. And besides, the mine is unstable. That's why most of it was closed off years ago."

"That's where you're wrong. You aren't the only one who has a family journal. My great-great-grandfather was around when the diamonds were found. He wrote about seeing the vein himself. Shoot, he even got a few of them. That's how the Kimballs were able to buy so much land." Jason's eyes were wide and shone in the dim light coming through the kitchen window.

"Then why has nobody seen that vein since then? If it were real, someone would have found it again." I tried to reason, but when someone was so desperate for money, they couldn't be reasoned with.

"Because, the shaft collapsed, and then an extra rough winter set in with lots of rain and flooding, making it next to impossible to dig out the vein again. The journal said the shaft had filled with water and then when they tried to drain it, another tunnel collapsed, killing three of the Montgomery Mine owner's family, including Pascal Montgomery himself. After that, it was closed up for almost a decade, before gold mining started up again, but in a different area." Jason inched a bit closer to me and I moved to the side.

"Jason, did you kill my aunt, or not?" I had to know for sure who did it. I couldn't accept that Homer killed Jo, and Jason killed Homer. It was too far-fetched for it to be real.

He shook his head and rolled his eyes. "I told you, I'd never hurt Jo. It wasn't me, it was Homer who did it. He got mad at her when she called him out about the stupid fake will." He chuckled. "I told the old fool that it wouldn't work and when her attorney found out that my grandpops was trying to get it recorded, both Jo and Neil Carlton, the attorney, got so mad at Homer, they almost had him arrested."

"Are you sure it was Homer who poisoned my aunt?" I was almost afraid to know, but I also had to know who killed Homer. I no longer thought it was a drug deal gone bad. But I couldn't believe Jason would kill the man he had spent most of his life admiring. And for what? A fake treasure map?

For the first time tonight, Jason looked sad. "Yeah, it was him. He bragged about it after she died." He ran a hand down his face. "I thought he was about to tell you what he had done that day you were in the store. You know, the day he died."

I shook my head thinking back to that day. "No, he didn't tell me that. He only said that Jo got what she deserved, and so did I. All that happened to me was vandalism. You saw the damage, and you paid for it."

Jason winced and looked down at the floor. "Yeah, I felt bad about what he'd done. Believe it or not, I really liked your great-aunt. I didn't want her to die. I told Homer we could just search her store or her house for the map, it wouldn't be hard to find."

"But it wasn't, was it?" I knew that they would have never found Jo's hiding place, not in a million years. Shoot, I wouldn't have if it weren't for Ollie finding it first.

Jason shook his head. "When I found out what Homer had done, I went crazy. I knew that if anyone found out, we'd both go down for it. Even though I had nothing to do with her death."

"But, you did want her map?" Insanity must have run in his family, if he did what I think he did. And what he came here to do.

"Yes, of course. Running a ranch isn't cheap these days. I don't know how Homer held on to the place for so long." At some point, I noticed Jason had stopped referring to Homer as his grandfather, or grandpops. Did he feel guilty for something? Or was it a drug deal gone bad that did in Homer? I prayed it was the latter, but feared it was the former.

"I thought you'd made a killing on Wall Street?" I winced the moment I said the word "killing", and knew that was the wrong thing to say at a time like this. I hoped it didn't give him the push he needed to try something.

Ollie continued to bark at Jason, but up to this point, she hadn't done anything.

That was, until he looked me in the eye, and I noticed his blank expression.

Fear rippled throughout my entire being. I still held the knife in front of me, but Jason looked as though he was in another world.

"Jason, you don't have to do this. I know we can figure something out. But that map isn't worth the paper it's printed on." I gulped, praying that somehow, someway, I could get through to the man who seemed as though he wanted to get out of this situation without getting any deeper. "Don't do this." I shook my head.

"Maisy," the guttural voice that came from him sounded otherworldly, almost like he was possessed by someone, or something, else. "It's too late. Without that mine, I've lost everything."

"That's just it, I only have a map. And that map won't do you any good without ownership of the mine. The owners won't let you mine it. Shoot, I bet they'd take the map and try it for themselves." I racked my brain trying to understand who did own it.

"Wait, do you own it?" Earlier, he'd said he bought up all of Homer's property, did that include the mine? Maybe that was why he offered a partnership? But the map was bogus.

"I take it you haven't looked closely at Jo's real Will?" Slowly, Jason shook his head. "You really should have. It might have saved your life. If you won't accept my offer to work together, then I have no choice."

Just as he took one step toward me, Ollie growled like I'd never heard. She sounded like a million dogs, or worse, coyotes, and lunged at Jason's leg. Her teeth sunk into his calf, which broke the freezing glare he'd given me.

When Jason yelled out in pain, he looked down and tried to kick at Ollie, and released a string of curses fit for a sailor. But she moved around his flailing kicks like a boxer in the ring.

"Don't you dare hurt my baby!" I growled and lunged at him with my left fist. Not even realizing what I was doing, other than protecting my little Ollie.

Jason turned back towards me, blocking my attempt at an attack. Then his hands reached out toward my neck. I brought my hands up to try and block his attack, forgetting that I still held a knife in my right hand. I didn't know what I'd done until I felt the knife slide into Jason.

His eyes widened, he looked down at the knife, then at me. "Why?"

I gasped when realization dawned on me. "Jason? Oh, no." My doggy momma instincts kicked in and all I could think of was protecting my little Ollie. It didn't even register that I still held the knife, until it was too late.

I put a hand over my stomach and had to swallow back the bile that had begun to make its way up my esophagus.

"Freeze!" Two male voices yelled out in unison from the kitchen door.

Sheriff Sam Madrid went through the door, gun drawn, and quickly walked in between me and Jason. "Jason, you're under arrest for the murder of Homer Kimball..." he looked back at me, then at the knife in Jason's left shoulder. "And the attempted murder of Maisy Bransky."

Behind the two men, Deputy Jenson was on his radio, calling for a paramedic.

"I'm sorry, Jason. I wish it hadn't come to this. If you'd only told me about your money issues, I would have helped." I leaned back against the kitchen counter, then slid down to the ground, and felt Ollie's warm tongue licking my cheeks.

Chapter 31

The next day, I went into the Sheriff's Station instead of opening my store. I had the treasure map in my purse, along with my great-aunt's journal. Before I walked in, Verna, Jade, Ada, and Tony all stood outside with huge smiles on their faces.

"Oh, Maisy. I'm so glad you're alright," Verna gushed as she made her way toward me, arms outstretched for a hug.

"Dear, I'm so sorry you had to go through that experience," Jade said as she joined the hug.

Ada and Tony stayed quiet, but they, too, joined in the group hug.

I felt tears run down my face, and not for the first time since last night.

In the background, I heard Ollie barking from my car. I'd decided to leave her in the car this morning since I knew the Sheriff's Station was going to be like Grand Central. Sam had already warned me that the vultures were circling.

"Thank you all for coming. I really appreciate it." I wiped my face as I pulled back from the warm embraces of my Great-Aunt Jo's best friends. "I can't believe Homer murdered Jo, and then Jason murdered Homer because his grandfather had gone off the deep end. It makes no sense." Even with the added benefit of hindsight, I still couldn't make hide nor hair of what had happened, and why.

Verna wrapped her arms around her midsection and shivered. Even though it wasn't even in the fifties this morning, the air seemed extra cold, like something else rotten was coming our way. "Honey, murder never makes any sense. Don't try to understand it. Just know that Jo has found justice." She sniffed.

I felt my nose prickling and my eyes watering. I wiped my face and coughed, trying to get rid of the emotions. "You know, I thought I was all done crying for Jo, but I don't think I'm going to be done any time soon."

Jade wrapped an arm around my shoulders. "Sweetheart, if it makes you feel any better, I doubt any of us are finished crying, either. I think this is going to take some time."

Tony coughed, then shuffled his feet. "Have you called your mother?"

I nodded. "Yes, and she wanted to cancel her cruise and come back out here, but I told her not to. I would need her here for the trial, and that might last a long time."

"What do you say we go inside?" Ada nodded toward a photographer who was snapping photos.

I knew it wouldn't be long before a reporter noticed us and headed our way. I wasn't in any mood to talk to them. Besides, they never got their stories straight anyways. I didn't think they knew how to tell the facts, and nothing but the facts anymore.

We walked inside the station just as a buxom bottle-dyed blond tried to race up behind us in her four-inch stiletto heels. When would people learn that in Westcott, you needed cowgirl boots, not fancy heels? Vultures, they were all nothing but bottom dwellers.

"Good, you're here." Sheriff Sam Madrid waved for us to come into his new office.

It seemed over the past week the old sheriff's office had been totally renovated. The new office now had sand-colored paint on the walls, with a deep turquoise, or teal, accent all along the top of the walls. There were Native American works of art hanging on the walls that looked as though they might be worth a pretty penny. In the far corner, behind the sheriff's desk, was a glass case with a ceremonial headdress fit for a chief.

When my eyes rested on the headdress of multi-colored feathers and leather, Sam grinned. "You like it?"

I nodded.

"My grandfather was the chief of my tribe. That was his headdress." He puffed out his chest, then motioned for us to take the seats in front of his desk.

"Does that make you the current chief?" I didn't know much about Native American hierarchy but thought that those kinds of titles were handed down through blood lines.

Sheriff Madrid shook his head. "Not me, my cousin."

I slumped down in my chair and a whispered, "oh" was all I could come up with to say.

"Sheriff," Tony Hopkins started, "are you sure it was Homer who killed Jo? And then Jason who killed Homer?"

Verna followed up with, "Did Jason actually admit to the murder?"

After Sam left my house early in the morning, I called Verna to tell her what happened. She got Jade, Ada, and Tony all up and on a video call. We talked about what happened and decided that I'd keep the store closed for the day, but open tomorrow.

They had offered to come over to my house, but I told them not to, it was too cold, and too late.

While we were talking, I told them everything I could remember. It was Jade who pointed out that Jason hadn't actually come right out and said he murdered Homer.

Sam folded his hands on the desk in front of him. "I'm sorry to say, but he did confess to killing his grandfather, after he found out about..." He cleared his throat. "What happened with Jo." Sam winced when his eyes met mine.

"It's alright, let's just get this over with." I slumped back in my chair and waited for the rest of the story to come out.

"Homer was doing drugs, and I honestly don't know how he lasted as long as he did. Fentanyl isn't something someone can do more than a few times before dying from an overdose. Most of the drugs coming up from Mexico right now are laced with this and killing kids left and right." Sam scratched his head.

"So, Homer was lucky enough to not take too much of the Fentanyl, so who was he arguing with in the alley? Not a drug dealer like most of the town thought?" I remembered that one of my customers had seen him arguing with someone, and then the CCTV cameras had caught Homer on video, but not the person he was arguing with.

"No, it was a drug dealer. Homer owed him a lot of money. It seems that Jason came upon them and heard their argument. He had learned earlier that day about what Homer did to Jo and brought the bottle of digitalis he'd found in Homer's room with him. He told the dealer that he'd pay him once he sold his cattle. The man left, threatening to kill Homer, and Jason, if they didn't pay up." Sam gulped down a glass of water before continuing.

"Are you sure you want the details?" Sam asked.

We all nodded.

"Alright. Jason offered to take Homer home, and took the bag from him. As they walked to Jason's truck, he pulled out the ground up digitalis powder from Homer's room and added the rest of the bottle to the sandwich. When they got inside the truck, Jason gave it to his grandfather and said to eat up, he needed it."

"That's cold-hearted. Even after learning everything Homer did, Jason shouldn't have killed him. He could have turned in his grandfather, and the drug dealer." Tony stood up and paced the small space behind all of the chairs. "Why would he do what he did?" He threw his hands in the air and expelled a lung full of air.

"Because murder never makes sense. In Jason's eyes, Homer was a liability. He had to go. And the only way to save the ranch was to get rid of the man responsible for losing most of the Kimball wealth." The sheriff rustled through a few papers on his desk, then set Jo's map on top of the pile.

"Is it a real treasure map? Or just one of the many maps Aunt Jo used to make for me when I was a kid?" When I visited Jo, she used to make me maps. She called them my treasure maps and they always led to a form of treasure, books. Growing up, I didn't have much money for entertainment, but books were free when borrowed from a library, or given as gifts from a loving aunt who owned her own bookstore.

Jason and I used to search for a different treasure. When we found it, always where "X" marked the spot, a book, or a board game, would be there. Sometimes she even left us puzzles. I always shared my treasure with Jason. And I would have done whatever I could have to help him now, if he'd only come to me.

Sam shook his head. "No, the diamond vein rumor is just that, a rumor. My people have been here for centuries, we'd know if diamonds were in this mountain." He pointed to the large, red X that looked as though it had been put there over a hundred years ago.

The map was old, I knew that much for certain. When I'd first found it, I didn't think too much of it, thinking that Jo had just made it look old. She probably soaked the paper in cold coffee, wrinkled it up, and then left it outside in the elements to give it the old-timey look and feel.

I bit my lower lip, unsure if I should say anything, but it would be public knowledge once Judge Charles finalized the will. I cleared my throat. "Last night, before Sam showed up at my aunt's house, Jason said something. It got me thinking. And since there was no way I was going to get any more sleep last night, I looked it up."

When I paused to get my thoughts in line, Ada asked, "What was that, Maisy?"

"Jason alluded to the fact that I now owned the mine." Again, I paused, waiting to see how everyone reacted.

Tony and Ada shared a look. One I wasn't sure I understood.

Then Verna coughed.

Jade said, "Oh dear." And she looked from Sam to me.

Sam nodded. "Yes, well. I think you do need to check out what it is you own because Jason was right. Yesterday, after we spoke the first time, I reached out to your attorney and he told me a few things. And then after you showed me the fake will, Neil Carlton came clean about the whole thing. I'm sorry I didn't get to your house sooner. But I went out to Jason's ranch first. When he wasn't there, I came back here. Then it hit me that you were in danger, and I grabbed Deputy Jenson, and we went to your house."

"A bit late, I might add." Verna harrumphed and crossed her arms over her chest.

"Oh," Sam chuckled. "Late for Jason, but not too late for Maisy." His eyes sparkled when he looked at me. "You sure know how to handle a knife, Miss Bransky."

I felt the heat rush up my neck and into my cheeks. "Well, I have taken a few self-defense classes." I didn't think to add that I'd also read my fair share of crime novels and knew a lot about how to defend myself. Somehow, I doubted anyone would believe that things I learned reading books would have actually saved my bacon in a real fight.

"However, I've never had to actually use any of my knowledge before last night." I shivered and ran a hand through my hair, then began to flip the ends over and over in my fingers. "I pray I never have to use that knowledge again, but I'm grateful I have it."

Although, it was more dumb luck that the knife hit its mark on Jason, and not the other way around.

"You wouldn't have needed it if the Sheriff here," Verna pointed to Sam, "had done his job in the first place."

Sam held up his hands. "I admit, I should have sent someone over to Maisy's house to help protect her once I realized what Jason was up to. But none of us thought Jason would hurt her," he eyed all of my friends, "did we?"

Jade, Ada, and Tony all looked at their hands, or their feet, but Verna sniffed and glared at Sam. "It's not our job to know that, now is it? Now, if Sheriff What's His Name would have listened to us weeks ago, when we all said that we thought something was fishy with Jo's death, then none of this would have ever happened." She arched a brow, daring Sam to disagree with her.

"I'm not going to argue the point." Sheriff Madrid stood. "Maisy, do you have any more questions for me?"

I took a deep breath and let it out slowly as I tried to think. "I can't think of anything else right now. But if I do, I'll call."

Before I left his office, I turned around. "Oh, one more thing. How is Jason? Physically, I mean. I didn't hurt him too badly, did I?"

"No, not too badly. He may never be able to rope a cow, or shoot baskets, but since he's going away for murder, I don't think that's going to be a problem." Sam closed the door behind us after we all left his office.

Epilogue

Hindsight is a funny thing.

From the moment I saw Jason again in Westcott, I felt a kinship with him. Then, I started to feel a bit unnerved. I thought that was due to the fact that he'd been flirting with me, and I just wasn't ready to date again. But looking back, there were signs that I'd missed, again.

Two weeks later, I was still looking back and seeing what I'd missed. Even with Homer, I should have suspected that he'd killed Jo. Well, I did, but that was for like two seconds. After the way he had acted that last day I saw him alive, that should have been enough to tell me that Homer killed Jo.

"Maisy, Earth to Maisy?" A deep voice that sounded as though she'd just smoked a pack of cigarettes, brought me out of my reverie.

"Verna, sorry. I'm still having trouble accepting some of what happened." I shrugged.

Today was Christmas Eve and the store would be closing soon. Then I'd be headed back to my aunt's house where I was going to make

Jo's famous Prickly Pear Bundt Cake. In the morning, I was sleeping in, and then Ollie and I were headed to Jade's house, where it was Christmas Central. And the lot of us would celebrate Christmas Day together, and share the meal with a local family who needed a little extra help.

Great-Aunt Jo always invited someone to our Christmas Day celebrations, and I felt it was something that we should all continue. Turns out, Jade, Verna, Ada, and Tony all agreed.

"Well, I think I have just the thing to help you." Her smile went from ear to ear and her eyes sparkled right before she turned around.

The sound of the bell above the door jingled and I turned to see the best sight possible, "Mom!" I ran out from behind the counter and wrapped my mother in a huge bearhug. "What are you doing here?"

She pulled back from me, grinning her beautiful smile, and then she wiped a tear away. "Maisy, you really didn't think I'd leave you here for Christmas after everything that happened?"

A man walked in behind her and put his arm around my mom. "Merry Christmas, Maisy. We decided that spending time with you was much more important than cruising around the Caribbean. We can do that any time."

"Charles, thank you so much. I know how much you two wanted to do this cruise with your friends." My mom and I had always celebrated Christmas together, but we'd never made it a big deal. Especially when we weren't in Arizona with Jo.

Jo was the Christmas Queen in our family. But I had a feeling that title was going to move on to someone else.

"I'm so excited you're here! You'll get to see how we celebrate Christmas in Arizona." I hugged my mom's boyfriend. I liked the man, and thought even better of him for being open to coming here instead of the Caribbean.

"Please, tell me you don't have a cactus in the house all decorated like a pine tree?" Charles looked at Siggy outside my window, then back at me.

I was wearing a red Christmas sweater with the Christmas Saguaro Bookshop t-shirt underneath. I'd paired them with jeans and red cowgirl boots. Next year, I hoped to have some sort of Christmas adornment for the boots. Maybe a jeweled Christmas Saguaro Cactus to match my necklace and earrings. "Maybe." I winked at him.

Later that night, after mom helped me to finish the cake for the Christmas dinner, all three of us sat around the kitchen table finishing off the Cactus Cream Pie I'd picked up from Cactus Joe's on the way home. "This pie is almost as good as Great-Aunt Jo's Bundt cake."

Charles slipped his fork with the last bite from his plate into his mouth and sighed. "I have heard so much about Aunt Jo's Bundt cake, I can't wait to try it. Are you sure we can't have a sliver of it tonight? Or better yet, as our Christmas breakfast?"

I chuckled. "You sound like me when I was a kid and spent a few Christmases here with Jo. No, tomorrow we'll be having green eggs, red chocolate chip pancakes, and lots of hot coffee once I'm up and running."

"Green eggs?" Charles' face looked as though it might turn green any moment. He put a hand over his stomach. "Oh, I think I ate too much."

Mom and I both laughed.

"Don't worry, honey. The shells are green, but the inside of the eggs are exactly the same as what you'd find in the grocery store." Mom turned to me. "Does Verna still raise the Ameraucana chickens? I'd have thought she'd be tired of shocking everyone with her green eggs by now."

I chuckled. "Yes, she still has them, but she did add Black Copper Marans to her hen house. Those turn out purple and mauve eggs. That took some getting used to, though." I shook my head. "It's funny what we expect something to taste like solely based on color. All of the eggs taste the same to me, some might have a stronger flavor, but still the same. However, when I first tried the purple eggs, I thought I wouldn't like them. Turns out I do."

"Is that what makes the Bundt cake pink? The purple eggs?" Charles asked.

"Nope, that's a Barton/Bransky family secret." I winked. "The inside of the colorful eggs are still yellow and clear, just like the white eggs you buy in the grocery store." I had really enjoyed being able to eat eggs from hens that were raised locally, on an organic diet. That wasn't something we could easily get in Florida.

The idea of going all organic really intrigued me. And now I had the means to afford it, thanks to Great-Aunt Jo and how she managed the property her relatives had left her. I prayed that I would be just as good of a steward of the land as she was.

Once the dishes were all cleaned, and the kitchen put back together, Mom, Charles, and I sat in the living room with a nice fire and glasses of hot apple cider.

"You know, I think this is going to be the best Christmas I've had since our last one here with Great-Aunt Jo. What do you think, Mom?" I took a sip of the hot, spicy drink while I watched the flames dance around the fireplace.

My entire being felt warm and safe, for the first time in weeks. Probably, since I'd moved here.

"I have to agree, Maisy. And that brings up something I've been meaning to ask you. How would you feel if I came out here and joined you for Christmas every year?" She had put her mug down on the coffee table in front of her and turned in her seat to get a better look at me. "Now that you own the bookstore, I know you can't get away to visit me for Christmas."

"Mom, I think that will be the best Christmas present ever. But you should know, I'm going to celebrate like Great-Aunt Jo always did. I'll decorate her house, store, and sing Christmas carols all month long." Since I'd decided to celebrate like my great-aunt always did, I'd felt closer to her, and even closer to God when I was in church.

Last week's live Nativity really hit me hard, and I knew that I wanted to grow closer to God, and read His Word on a daily basis. Even though Christmas today was really quite worldly, I knew I could still honor Jesus in my heart, and in a variety of ways, like keeping the extra chair open for anyone who needed it. Or donating my time at the local soup kitchen.

In fact, I'd already signed up to help with providing Easter meals to those in the area who needed a little extra help.

And everything I did, I did in Jo Barton's name. It was her money, after all, that made this possible.

When we walked into Jade's house, I grinned. Standing in front of the ten-foot-tall Christmas tree that was way too tall for a house this size, was our newest sheriff.

"Sam, Merry Christmas. But why the uniform?" I pointed to his tan and green uniform. "I guess, the green could be seen as sorta Christmassy." I tilted my head and checked him out from head to boot. Not really, since it was more of a desert green than a bright Christmas green. But he was rockin' it.

Not that I was the least bit interested in men these days. Nope, I'm gonna stay single forever like my Great-Aunt Jo. She had the right of it.

"Merry Christmas, Maisy. I'm working today and can only stay for a short while; I need to be out on patrol soon." Sheriff Sam Madrid took a drink of something from a coffee mug, most likely coffee.

"I'm surprised you're working today. Being the sheriff, doesn't that mean you can pick and choose your holidays?" I set down a large box that held Christmas presents, and Sam came over to help me unload them.

"Only a few of us in the station are single, so I thought I'd work and let the deputies who have families take the day off. It's always pretty quiet around here on Christmas Day, so..." He shrugged.

"That's very nice of you. I wish I had a boss like that." I grinned, knowing I was now my own boss. And nothing beats the feeling of working for oneself.

Everyone in the room chuckled, then mom walked over. She smiled and introduced herself and Charles to Sam.

I walked to the drinks table and poured myself a cup of hot spiced apple cider. Then I leaned against the wall and watched everyone who meant something to me in this small town in a little Southwestern state. As I sipped, I realized that Jo was right to live here and never leave. The people who were her family, have become my family. When once I thought I had next to no family left, I now realized that I had an entire town full of family and future friends.

Small town living might be a bit trying at times, especially when they all seemed to know exactly what everyone else was doing, but it was also comforting to know you could walk down the street and see friends everywhere you turned.

I never enjoyed Christmas in Florida like I do in Arizona. I think moving forward, I'm going to honor Christmas like Aunt Jo would. And in doing so, I'll keep her memory close to my heart.

Jade had invited a local single woman who was doing her best to raise five little kids on her own. When the kids opened their presents, I understood how the Grinch's heart grew that one Christmas. There was nothing like seeing the excitement on a child's face when they opened up a gift. Especially a gift they never thought they could have.

I looked up to heaven and thanked God that He put me here. "But Lord, please tell Great-Aunt Jo I miss her."

Instead of the tears that I'd been fighting since I first learned of Jo's death, I felt peace and comfort, as though I was exactly where I belonged.

The End

Author's Notes

F amily means the world to me. It's more than just DNA and blood, it's the people who choose to be a part of your world, your life, for better or worse. The latest term is "found family" and I have some great memories with found family, as well as with actual blood relatives. This series does have blood ties as well as the family that is chosen. I plan on writing more about found family and how tight-knit that small circle can be.

Do you have a ride-or-die friend? That's your found family. Is there someone you choose to spend your holidays with? Or, someone you may not see in person a lot, but when you do it's like coming home? Those are found family members. Cherish them and let them know how much you love them.

Grandparents are an absolute gem! My grandmother died over ten years ago, before I started writing, but I know she's up in Heaven cheering me on every time I get in front of my computer and write. She loved to read mysteries, and I know she'd love the quirkiness of the Fearsome Foursome in this story. They'd most likely be her ride-or-die friends, or found family. As I wrote about Great-Aunt Jo, I kept thinking about my grandma and how much I missed her. I don't have any regrets with the time I spent with her, thankfully. When she started getting sick, I moved back to So Cal so I could spend more time with her, and I'm so glad I did. She ended up living for quite a while after I moved back, and even with hindsight, I know that I wouldn't change that decision for anything. So, if you still have your grandma around, be sure to spend time with her and listen to her stories. That will stick with you for the rest of your life.

Hindsight can be very powerful, and when you look back on your life I pray that you don't have any large regrets. While Maisy is a fictional character, she did regret not spending more time with her Great-Aunt Jo, who was basically a grandmother to her.

I hope you keep reading this series, I have a lot of fun things planned for Maisy and her friends. And for those on my newsletter, I'll be sharing tidbits in my newsletter before the books come out. I'll also be sharing some special short stories in my newsletter before they are published. So, if that is the sort of thing you like, then check out the next page where you can join my newsletter and get a free book, or two, from me.

I pray that God will bless you in all your endeavors and make it possible for you to find the time to spend with your family, whether it's a found family or blood ties family. All family time is precious, and time moves too quickly to miss out.

Also, for those who are curious about some of the recipes in this story, I've included the Cactus Cream Pie recipe! So keep reading...

And yes, the Poor College Student Burrito is real! I can't tell you how many times I ate that for lunch and dinner. It's filling and very cheap to make. The food goes a long way, especially when you can now get a rotisserie chicken from Sam's or Costco for under $5! That wasn't an option for me when I was in college, but it is now, and I do make those burritos still. LOL

Cactus Cream Pie Recipe

This is basically a variation of a coconut cream pie. If you have a favorite family coconut cream pie recipe, then you can just modify it by adding in 3 tablespoons of Nopal powder. Then do everything as you would your regular pie. However, for those who don't have a recipe on hand, here is how I made my Cactus Cream Pie, it's also dairy-free since I have a dairy allergy. If you don't have an allergy to dairy, then you don't need the more expensive dairy-free ingredients. Feel free to substitute them for the regular half and half as well as a regular frozen topping like Cool Whip or Ready Whip canned topping.

<u>Ingredients:</u>

1 Cup Sweetened coconut flakes

3 cups dairy-free half-and-half

¾ Cup white sugar

½ Cup flour

2 large eggs

¼ teaspoon of salt

1 teaspoon of pure vanilla extract

3 Tablespoons Nopal powder (Prickly Pear powder)

1 9-inch graham cracker pie crust (chocolate or regular. You can also use a regular pie shell if you prefer.)

1 cannister of coconut milk Reddi Whip topping (Or any dairy alternative) (be sure to follow instructions on the can if use an alt topping).

<u>Directions:</u>

Preheat oven to 350 degree F. Spread coconut flakes on a large baking sheet.

Once oven is preheated, place the baking sheet in the oven for about 5-10 minutes, stirring occasionally. The goal is to get them lightly toasted, or golden brown.

In a medium saucepan, combine half & half, sugar, flour, eggs, and salt. Over a low heat, bring it to a boil while constantly stirring. Once the mixture thickens and coast your spoon nicely, then it should be ready. This takes about 15 minutes, but keep watching and stirring to make sure.

Remove the pan from the stove and stir in ¾ Cup of the toasted coconut, 1 teaspoon vanilla extract, and 3 Tablespoons Nopal powder.

Pour your custard mixture into your prepared pie crust. Place in refrigerator for at least 6 hours, preferably overnight.

Put the other ¼ Cup of toasted coconut into a zippered baggie and save for garnish.

When you are ready to serve the pie, that is when you want to top the pie with your whipped topping. If using the can of alternative whipped topping, be sure to read the instructions, some require you to run it under warm water first. Then begin on the inside of the pie, and in a circular motion, cover the pie with the topping. Top with the reserved toasted coconut.

Contact Me

For those of you who love social media, here are the various ways to follow or contact me:

BookBub: https://www.bookbub.com/authors/jenna-hendricks
TikTok: https://www.tiktok.com/@jennacleanauthor
Instagram: https://www.instagram.com/j.l.hendricks/
Twitter: https://twitter.com/TinkFan25
Facebook: https://www.facebook.com/JLHendricksAuthor
Website: https://jennahendricks.com

www.ingramcontent.com/pod-product-compliance
Lightning Source LLC
Chambersburg PA
CBHW061652190726
48289CB00006B/1838